,

About the Author

Tariq Mehmood is a writer, film director and campaigner. In 2001 he co-directed *Injustice*, an award-winning documentary which examined the thousand plus deaths that have occurred in police custody in Britain over the last 30 years. His first novel, *Hand on the Sun*, was published by Penguin in 1983. He also writes in Pothowari, his mother tongue, and is a founder member of the Pothowari-Pahari Language Movement. He was an editor of *Chitka*, the first magazine to use Pothowari-Pahari, and is the author of the first ever children's books to be published in that language, *Syana Gidr* and *Nas Gidrah Nas* (Paraala Publishing, 2002). This is his second novel.

while there is light

tariq mehmood

First published in Great Britain in 2003 by Comma Press
www.commapress.co.uk
Distributed by Carcanet Press
www.carcanet.co.uk

A CIP catalogue record of this book is available from the British Library

ISBN 1 85754 729 2
The publisher gratefully acknowledges assistance from Arts Council England
North West, and the Regional Arts Lottery Programme.

Set in Monotype Baskerville by XL Publishing Services, Tiverton
Printed and bound in England by SRP Ltd, Exeter

To my mother and my daughter, Naseem,
to whom I couldn't say farewell

Context

In the summer of 1981, Britain was caught in a wave of urban rebellion. Riots tore at the hearts of inner city communities, from Toxteth to Brixton, Moss Side to Handsworth, Leicester to Leeds. It was also a time of heightened racism – instances of alleged police brutality towards the African-Caribbean and Asian communities had been reported against a backdrop of xenophobic rhetoric from the government. Indeed in April, Brixton police had introduced a stop and search policy, named 'Operation Swamp' after Margaret Thatcher's famous assertion a few years before that Britain 'might be rather swamped by people of a different culture… and people are going to react and be rather hostile.'

In Bradford, following minor disturbances in the city centre on July 11 1981, 12 Asian youths, mostly members of an Afro-Asian youth organisation called The United Black Youth League, were arrested and charged with conspiracy. Petrol bombs had been found with the police claiming they were intended to be used unilaterally. The youths maintained they were only ever a precautionary measure should self-defence was called for.

The case became known as The Bradford Twelve. A country-wide campaign, with international support, was mobilised to defend the youths. The legal team consisted of solicitors Ruth Bundy and Gareth Peirce and the barristers included Mike Mansfield, Paddy O'Conner, Helena Kennedy (now Baroness), Ed Reese and Lord Gifford. The writer Tariq Mehmood was one of the central defendants in the case. He conducted his own defence during a nine-week trial at Leeds Crown Court. All defendants were eventually acquitted and the trial established a legal precedence for the principal of collective, community self-defence, with many of the lawyers involved – not least Gareth Peirce – going on to play key roles in other historic false arrest cases like The Guildford Four and The Birmingham Six.

This novel is not a political or legal history of that case. It is rather a fictionalised account of the events leading up to such an event, the personal journey of an individual caught up in it. All characters are entirely fictional and any resemblance to persons alive or dead is purely coincidental.

I

10 November 1982,
HMP Armley, Leeds

Mother, I am now in jail, in this bitch of a country called England. I may never see you again...

Anger, like a restless ghost lashes around inside my head. I want to shred this letter and feed it to the winds. But the ghost, like a lost, motherless child, clutching at a longing, stops me. Its tears drop out of my eyes. The letter lives on, imprisoned in my jacket pocket, waiting for its moment.

Each time I try to post the letter, I end up re-reading the first line:

Mother, I am now in jail, in this bitch of a country called England. I may never see you again...

I wrote this wretched letter on remand at Armley Jail in Leeds. I'm not quite sure why I wrote it, for I didn't care much for mother. Perhaps I was trying to keep my sanity in the cockroach infested cells of that groaning redbrick jail, or maybe, I just wanted to hurt mother for sending me to this callous land.

I have been out on bail for over a year now. The trial will start in two months time.

I am drunk again. I have once more broken the curfew. I should have been indoors after 7 o'clock. I stagger through another misty Bradford night. The sweaty cannabis-filled Mayflower nightclub is closed now. Thudding reggae songs still rage in my mind, drowning out incomprehensible thoughts. Two monstrous eyes zoom out of the darkness. A blue car, with screeching tyres comes towards me. I steady myself for the arrest. A jeering skinhead leans out of the car and hurls a garbled obscenity at me. Letting out a drunken jubilant laugh, I stick two fingers up into the night. The insult misses me and melts into the last song I had danced to in the Mayflower: *Money in my pocket, but I just can't find no love.*

'I got no bleedin' money, and who the fuck wants love?' I hiss out against the song. It fights back, going round and round in my head. It wins. I sing out loud while my hand searches my pockets for the onion, my nightly companion. In the vain hope of disguising the smell of beer and fooling my uncle, to whose house I must return, I bite the onion. My taste buds died some time during the night. I light a cigarette and chew through the onion, spitting out the skin. Thick fog is swirling around the base of a flickering street lamp. It is directly opposite my bedroom. It has for as long as I can remember been here, flickering. The fog encircles the lamp, slowly rising. The lamp crackles. Sparks fly out and fall into the fog below. I wait for it to short circuit again. It stops flickering and starts beaming down uninterrupted light. The fog climbs down the lamp, slithers along the pavement, curls around a red letterbox, slides under the wheels of passing cars, sinking down over a rusty grill at the road side.

I stumble across the road, checking for the police. It is quiet. The letterbox blocks my way. During the night, new graffiti, in silver white spray have been added to its flaky red skin. The world starts spinning round. My mouth is burning from eating the onion. I take deep breaths, trying to chase away the fire. The letterbox seems to be smiling. I bend towards it and shout, 'Fuck it!' I pull the letter out of my pocket and lob it at the letterbox. It misses and falls to the ground. 'You won't get away that easily, you bastard.' I retrieve the letter and shove it into the letterbox mumbling, 'Get a load of this, Ammajee.'

As soon as it is out of my hand a heavy emptiness engulfs me. A cursing friend, who has lived in my pocket, is no more.

I tiptoe up the stairs to my bedroom. No one is awake. They never are when I come home. Closing my bedroom window, I look out onto the street below. In the distance, there is the unmistakable, unintelligible laughter of drunks. I close my eyes. Images of the lamp flash in my mind. I search for a familiar voice amidst the drunken laughter. The lamp metamorphoses into shapes with golden borders. Inside these borders, trapped human figures dance to the beats of a Reggae song. The thumping music gets louder and louder, bashing against the sides of my skull. I collapse.

A throbbing pain pounds in my head. I have slept face down on the floor. Forcing myself up I try to cover my eyes against the sharp rays of sun streaming in through the window. I hear my uncle's heavy breathing. The floor shakes as he stomps up the stairs. A moment later, there are three painful knocks on the door. I nervously open.

'Well, Saleem,' Uncle Shafqat begins, 'how much more time do you need?' Without waiting for my answer, he turns around and starts walking down the stairs. Waving his right hand above his head, he says, 'I don't care about your decisions any more.'

Before coming to Bradford my uncle had been a strong man with a heavy voice. That was a long time ago. Now his voice, like his body, shakes to its own rhythm, sucked dry, prematurely aged. I am a terrible disappointment to him. But I didn't really care for what I had come to believe were his old, ignorant ways. He had convinced my mother that by the time he finished with my education, I would turn out to be a doctor. As I grew older, the only interest in medicine I seemed to display was needing regular attention. As he realised I was unlikely to become a doctor, he asked me to become a pilot. I, of course, agreed. I had for that matter never objected to becoming a doctor. What he didn't really understand was that my school was not interested in educating us and we therefore showed scant regard for it. After finishing school, I ended up leaving home and all but became a bum. If ever our paths crossed then my uncle would say,

'Get a job. Any job or you will forever wander the streets like a stray dog.' He would usually qualify this with, 'And you'd probably be happy to be taken to a homeless dogs' hotel in this godforsaken country.'

He is a proud man, my uncle. Proud of the fact that he had only once been in debt and that was when he had first come to England. He had repaid that debt many times over. Though the monetary side of the debt had been long since cleared, he still felt obliged to some Choudry saab whose name I had heard a thousand times but could never remember.

Walking down the stairs I hear Uncle Shafqat shouting, 'I don't know what he's decided.' My aunt groans as my uncle continues, 'I tell you, if you want to destroy a family, then don't kill them. Simply bring their son to England and those poor bastards will die of their own greed.'

'Karma allayow, what has he decided?' my aunt asks nervously.

'Who is he to decide?' my uncle replies. 'When he can't even get rid of the smell of onions from his own breath.'

I tiptoe towards the front door. I have to sign on at the police station. I am about to turn the latch, my aunt raises her voice, 'Why do you have to bring onions into such a serious issue as this?'

I freeze in my footsteps at the prospect of my uncle having unravelled my secret. For all his legendary shrewdness and bygone strengths, he was a simple man who took everything at face value. But there was that chance that on this occasion he had thought a little deeper. He had put up his house as security for my bail. The bail conditions stipulated that I had to surrender my British passport, sign on at the police station daily, stay in my uncle's house, remain under curfew between 7pm and 7am and not to go one mile near a public meeting or a demonstration. When I had walked out of the court on bail he had said, 'Respect my honour. If you run away, I will lose all I have.' Before letting me back into his house he made me promise never to let alcohol touch my lips again. I, of course, agreed.

'That sister fucker is always eating onions,' Uncle Shafqat says. 'You tell me, who would want someone like him?'

I grab my coat and rush out the front door and sign on at the police station. The hangover slowly withers away as what is left of the day slips by in the familiar haunts. Hunger and lack of money finally force me to return home early. To my relief, there is no one there. My aunt as usual has left my breakfast paratha, as well as chapattis for lunch neatly wrapped in a cloth on the side of her clinically clean table. I bolt down both my meals, and go to bed early for a change.

When I get into the bedroom, a neatly packed suitcase is sitting on the bed. On the suitcase there is my Pakistani passport, an air ticket, some money and a small handwritten note. The note is written in English by my uncle. It says, *Your mother is sickening for you. Go now and see her. You may never meet her if you lose your case. Your return flight is in six weeks. Come back.'*

The flight is for the next day. I had resolved never to go back to Pakistan. Let alone now. I contemplate my options. If I am arrested trying to leave the country, I will surely go to jail and take all my friends with me. Uncle would never have bought me a ticket unless there is something wrong with Mother. Maybe he is just trying to help me. My friends will feel betrayed. But they will be fine once I'm back. *If* I get out and come back that is. A thrill of excitement runs through me as I hold the ticket in my hand. 'What the hell, it's only a few weeks.' A faded image of my mother flickers through my mind.

Edging my shoulder bag forward with my feet, I jostle my way back to where I think my place is in the queue. It is a long nervous line, full of anxious faces. It curls and heaves around numerous vexed airport employees and melts into a number of check-in counters. Two armed police officers eye me suspiciously. I turn my head away from them, holding my breath. The police officers walk past, scanning other passengers.

I stand in the queue for an hour or so, my heart pounding in my chest. A number of people casually walk up to me, look me in the face with pleading eyes, but seeing the sorry sight of my suitcase, they retreat silently.

Our part of the terminal is buzzing under waves of anxiety. Just about everyone is dressed in their best, giving the place the air of a colourful mela. I look around fearfully, hoping not to be recognised.

The head shaking from side to side in front of me could pass for a mop, I think to myself, were it turned upside down. I would have recognised the owner of the mop earlier as Mohammed Iqbal Sarwar, alias Gino, son of Choudry Karamat Ali of Glodwick, Oldham, were it not for the fact that today, that distinctive, rarely combed head of hair shakes out over a brand new jacket. He is close to me but doesn't see me. He towers over the fragile frame of his mother who is giving him her final advice,

'... and give my salaam to Aunt Khatija and make sure you go to everyone's house as soon as you get there. This year has seen many deaths and you must go and say your fatia in each house, and make sure you raise your hands and move your lips when you do this.' She rubs Gino's fat face gently with her hands as she speaks. She wipes her eyes with the corner of her white dupatta, and continues: '... and you can choose whoever you wish, and I'll be happy. It would make my heart fill with joy if you were to choose Najma. She's such a good girl and no one has ever said anything bad about her and she is a beautiful girl and she has just passed her BA as well and how many girls in our biradari have got that much education, do you know? She's the first one. Of course there was, what's her name...'

Gino's mother sees me. She glares at me. She had often

told me that I was the one who had led her son astray. Gino shakes my hand but avoids eye contact, and blushes. A tense smile flickers across my face.

In the 30 years or so of his life, Gino had been many things at many times. During hippie days, his hair was longer than the women in his family. Then he was known as 'Babe Gino'. When the punks turned up, he chopped his hair and put purple streaks in what was left of it. He donned split trousers and wore T-shirts with numerous zips and a safety pin through his nose. He became 'Gino the Kid'. Somewhere during this time, he became a Rastafarian and started calling himself 'Jah Gino'. At one time he tried to join a gang of Hell's Angels but failed on some ritual or other. Shortly after this, he gave up all his vices, started going to the mosque, praying five times a day. During the holy month of Ramzaan, he kept all 30 fasts. But for some reason, which none of his friends ever understood, on the last fast, he turned up in a pub where he broke his fast with some dates and a pint of bitter. I was taken aback by the news that he was off to get married. He often swore that he would never marry and zealously disowned the very institution of arranged marriage (apart from his sister's).

Gino turns his back on me. He moves away a little and drops a large polythene bag stuffed with letters.

'I told you a hundred times I didn't want to carry this lot with me,' Gino protests in his thin voice as he bends down to pick up the letters. 'Why can't they post them? I feel like an ass carrying all this.'

'You don't have to behave like one,' his mother reprimands adjusting her dupatta. 'These messages will get to their destinations tomorrow and who knows when post would get there and just think of all those people who will pray for you. Besides, it's what everyone has to do.'

People turn towards some raised voices. A group of about 20 men are following someone. An unintelligible slogan buzzes around the airport. It is followed by a thunderous roar of

'Zindabad'. I conclude that it had to be a Pakistani politician. They always come and go like this.

Two police officers that were following the followers clutch their guns even tighter as another roar of 'Zindabad, Zindabad,' goes up.

Straining my ears I try to fathom the name of the politician. The followers stop moving, as though to a command. They split into two halves and then regroup behind a tall saintly figure of a man who walks straight towards me. I recognise him. He is no politician. A dainty voice of one of his followers leads another chant, 'Pir Sultan Sheikh of Dok Chaklala-jee!'

'Zindabad, Zindabad,' the followers reply. With his heavily scented flowing white robes, his Holiness darts past me and disappears into the toilets. A few of his followers go inside, while the main body stands outside, sheepishly silent. His Holiness was well known, but less for his miracles. He had recently come out of prison where he had been serving time for sexually molesting young boys. Whilst he is inside the toilets, I rush back towards my place in the queue as I suspect pir saab will try to get to the front and I'd be damned if I let him do this. The pir comes out caressing his white beard and, along with his followers, walks towards the first class check-in counter.

It is close to departure time. A mother cries while combing the hair of her irate teenage son, who chews gum, nodding mechanically. Some passengers are flushed with joy at the chance of going back home. Others like the mother are torn between two worlds. Hordes of children are running amok. A few young men wearing their baseball caps backwards idle around. Some of these wear trousers which are ridiculously too large for them. One family stands close to each other. Silent. They all have sleepless bloodshot eyes. Some are crying. A halo of grief hangs over their heads. There is a gap between this group and the rest of us. Everyone knows why they are going back.

I am being carried away with thoughts of death when I hear a young woman laughing. I quickly turn around and come face to face with her. She smiles at me, winks and deliberately brushes herself against me as she follows a short fat bearded man and goes past me. The beard is blissfully unaware of anything. I rush towards the check-in counter next to the one she has gone to. I look over to her. She smiles back at me again. It is my turn to check-in. A couple of lads on another counter are arguing with the check-in clerk. 'Stop thinking like a thief,' I think encouraging myself, 'be a lout.'

I place my suitcase on the conveyor belt and to my surprise the check-in clerk lets it go through.

'Any hand luggage?' the clerk asks, his eyes transfixed onto the computer screen. He is a thin blonde man who has prematurely lost hair from the middle of his oblong head.

'Only this little bag, mate,' pointing to my shoulder. I smile falsely, pretending that the bag is weightless.

'Smoking or non smoking?' the clerk asks.

'Yo, mate!' I grin mischievously. The clerk throws a bored look up at me. Nodding towards the woman I continue, 'Can you try to give me a seat next to that young lady over there, please?'

The clerk scratches his chin and emphasising his words asks, '*Smoking or non-smoking?*'

'I don't care,' I plead, 'just put us together.'

'Now how do you expect me to do that?' the clerk says coldly, 'I don't have any control over all those other counters...'

'Can't you just go over,' I interrupt him and nodding towards the counter next to me, 'to that counter and find out which seat she's on and give me one next to her?' The clerk continues with his job. 'Go on, mate, *please!*' I lean closer to the clerk and plead once again, 'I'll give yer a fiver.'

'What the bloody 'ell do you think this is, eh?' the clerk says raising his voice and taking off his round glasses. The belt of my shoulder bag snaps under pressure and to the relief of my backbone the bag falls to the floor with a loud bang. The clerk looks at the bag with disbelief and above the noise of the Public Address system, on which a woman's voice is trying hard to pronounce a name, the clerk ridicules, 'You're not in Pakistan yet, you know.'

'All right, all right,' I try to calm the man, 'I'll give you a tenner.'

'Make it 15,' he demands quietly in a matter-of-fact manner, placing his glasses back on his nose, 'but I can't promise.'

I grudgingly count out three five-pound notes. He walks over to the next counter and whispers something into the ears of the clerk at that counter. She points to the screen. He nods and heads back towards me.

'No can do, mate,' he smirks.

'What do you mean "No can do"?' I implore.

'All seats near her are gone.'

'Fuck it,' I beckon for my money with my right hand. The balding clerk stares back at me blankly and asks, 'Smoking or non-smoking?'

'Smoking, and by a window, but don't put me next to anyone with a beard. I might as well drown me sorrows away.'

I let out a sigh of relief when I get inside the aircraft and shove past passengers who are struggling to stuff their overweight hand luggage into overhead lockers. I find my seat, place a plastic bag full of duty free beer on it and somehow manage to stuff my shoulder bag into a locker. I slump, and pray to the Almighty to spare me from a bearded fellow traveller.

I cannot relax. The aeroplane slowly fills. Both seats next to me remain empty. I begin to enjoy the prospect of travelling the next eight hours, stretching out across all the three seats. An old lady shows me her boarding pass and asks in Pothowari, 'My son, is this my seat?'

Filled with horror at the prospect of sharing my space with her, I gape at her, but a part of me feels affection towards the old dear, and I almost answer back in Pothowari, but end up saying in English, 'I'm sorry madam, I don't speak your language.'

'You mother fucking son of a wild ass,' the old lady curses. A wry smile flashes across her round bespectacled face, 'Can't speak your own tongue. Living with English, you've become one of them as well, eh!'

A smiling hostess strolls towards us and with an air of officiousness she says condescendingly to the old lady in Urdu, 'Please, madam, take your seat and fasten your safety belt.'

'My daughter, talk straight to me.' The old lady grabs the hostess by the arm as she tries to squeeze past her, shows her the boarding pass and asks, 'Where do I sit?'

Pointing to the aisle seat, the hostess says, 'This is your place.' She calmly squeezes past the old lady, weaving through other passengers who are in different stages of flight readiness.

As soon as she sits down, the old lady falls into a deep sleep. Her face is slightly swollen, like the faces of those who are forced to take a lot of disagreeable medicines, though it still retains a toughness born out of hard times. She looks as if she must have been a handsome woman in her youth. I begin to have second thoughts about drinking on the flight. I try to think rationally. Was drink really that important that I should allow it to upset this lady? But didn't *I* have any rights? If the plane takes off with me in it, then I will drink my heart's fill. The old lady starts to snore loudly. Breathing heavily through her nose she releases the air through her mouth. Her lips flap. She lets out a whistling sound that seems to come from somewhere deep inside her. By the time she gains consciousness I have downed two cans of beer.

The old lady takes her coat off and starts muttering something to herself. At first I think she is praying but then realise that she is humming a song my mother used to hum to me. I feel ashamed of myself. The aircraft shakes violently. The captain announces we are passing through heavy air turbulence.

'You son of a donkey.' The old lady points a finger at me and shouts, 'Because of your drinking this plane may fall down.'

From this moment onwards, whenever the plane enters into turbulence or performs some alteration to its height or direction which isn't to the old lady's liking, she lets a barrage of poetic obscenities loose at me.

'And when I come back I don't want to see your pig face sitting there making my air impure,' she swears getting up to go to the toilet.

'Still here, you son of a squint-eyed camel?' she curses when she comes back.

I close my eyes and remain in this position, trying not to irritate her any further. Just before sitting down she sniggers, 'You must have been conceived by a pig – you've drunk so much you've fainted.'

When she can find no other reason to swear at me, she curses me for the fact that I don't understand her. I fight hard to avoid laughing.

Perhaps she ran out of swear words or maybe she just got bored, but she asks a stewardess to find her another seat. It's only after she has gone that I realise that half the journey is over. I'm well away from England. Now I just have to get through Islamabad airport without getting arrested. By which time, as I have now failed to sign on, the police would have gone to my uncle's. But if I come back, he won't lose his house. I am extremely tired and look forward to sleeping. But the stewardess, who has escorted the old lady away, brings a bulky man back with her. At first his face is hidden behind the hostess, but soon it reveals itself. It is the beard, whose daughter had cost me fifteen pounds.

As soon as the beard gets close enough, he takes my hand, and whilst holding it firmly in his own rough hands, introduces himself as Arif. He gives me a cigarette and takes one for himself. After offering me a light he lights his own, inhales deeply and says,

'You know son, these PIA are complete scoundrels.' Exhaling a long wavy line of smoke he continues, '...and their grandfathers and *their* grandfathers were thieves as well.'

'Why's that then, uncle?' I ask, hoping that he will give a quick answer with which I could agree and avoid any further discussion. The thief inside me nervously studies his face to see if he has read my thoughts and the diplomat outside continuously nods his head politely. A thick curly beard covers most of his face. He has hair right under his eyes and his round nose had recently been shaved. The roots of his beard betray wiry grey shoots. The thief sniggers with the thought, 'We're all trying to hide something,' and of course the diplomat continues with his diplomacy. Unkempt dark hair creeps out from under a well-worn Afghan cap which sits uncomfortably on Arif's head. Notwithstanding the bushy beard, he has a tough face into which a pair of piercing black eyes are sunk.

'PIA never invest – they are always trying to make more money out of old things.'

'How's that then, uncle?' I ask, exaggerating a yawn which I hope he notices. The thief has retired.

'Well, you take this aeroplane,' he waves his hand around the cabin. 'It is the same one on which I travelled to Britain in 1962.'

I perk up, 'That was before I was born and this plane is only a few years old.'

Arif places a cigarette in his clenched fist and inhales through the top of his hand. He coughs violently. Getting his breath back, he clears his throat and continues, 'But nowadays you can make anything look young. They've simply painted this chackra and that's why you think it's new,' he pauses, takes another deep swig and once again starts coughing.

'Uncle, why don't you stop smoking?'

Arif clears phlegm from his throat. 'It has done me no harm,' he replies. 'As I was saying, I can prove that this is the same aeroplane I first came to England on.'

'How's that then, uncle?'

'Take off your shoes, son,' he insists. 'Go on. Take them off and also your socks.'

I do as he suggests.

'Do you feel the cold air on your feet?' he asks.

'Yes.'

'Well, that aeroplane that I first came to England on, it had a hole in it as well.'

'But, uncle,' I protest, 'we're above air and there are no holes in this aeroplane. If there were we would all get sucked out and that cold air which you feel is...'

'If we're above air, then how are we breathing?' he interrupts, laughing to himself. Then suddenly, tensing in ponderous silence, his sharp eyes age and he lets out a deep sigh and says, 'You know, son, I've done many things in my time which were bad. I've had drink, oh yes, oh yes. I've had a drink in my time. But I never strayed from my faith and never lost respect for my parents – may Allah grant them a place in heaven. Not like kids today. And you know, it's all right if you've got sons, but me, well, Almighty has blessed me with so many daughters that he's broken my back. Well, I wouldn't have had so many if I had listened to my pocket and not to people's advice, "You must get a son," they said, "even if you have to pull him out of a well." I've done all the pulling I can. My line's broken now. Anyway, I can't keep track of my daughters any more, and ever since my eldest one, Nasma, I am travelling with, she grew up... you must have noticed us, we were standing next to you in Heathrow?'

'No, no, I'm sorry, uncle, I didn't,' I lie. 'I was lost in so many of my own thoughts, you know how it is?'

'Yes, yes. It's flying. It brings everything out. Anyway, as I was saying, I am forever getting wrong numbers called on my telephone. I'm not stupid, but of course my girls think I am. It's not their fault you know, it's all these boys. They are mostly badmashes hd haramis, they are.' Looking me straight in the eyes he asks, 'You're young but you seem like a nice boy. What do you think?'

'Well, jee,' I reply hesitantly, 'you are quite right, uncle-jee. Mostly they have just one thing on their minds and they have no respect for sisters and mothers.'

'Are you married, son?' Arif asks eyeing me up and down.

'Yes, uncle,' I lie again.

'I knew you would be. You look a decent sort. Your parents must be proud to have a son like you. What work do you do?'

'I've just finished university.' I don't want to disappoint Arif.

'Well, never mind. At least you're not a bum, and you'll get a nice job because you're educated.' Arif offers me another cigarette, which I refuse. He lights his and continues, 'I can see you're a decent man... me, I've done everything. Nowadays I drive a taxi. I'm too old to do anything else.' Turning to look me in the face he asks 'You're too young to have driven a mini-cab – aren't you?'

'Oh, I have over Christmas, uncle.'

'That's a good time, gorays go mad, don't they?' He laughs. I laugh with him as he continues, 'When I drive a cab, I feel like a road sweeper.'

'How's that then, uncle?' I smile warmly at Arif.

'Well, *you* know these bloody Angraiz.' Arif locks his eyes with mine. He waits for me to nod my head in confirmation before continuing, 'I pick 'em up and drop 'em off at pubs. I pick rubbish up from pubs and drop them off at our hotels. They eat there and then I drop them off at home. I can never make any sense of what they're saying. They nearly always talk rubbish. Drunken rubbish, they talk. Last week I picked a couple up from their house, husband and wife, well at least I think they were, but who knows. Shameless they were.'

Arif inhales deeply and pauses. The tip of his cigarette glows. He continues, 'I dropped them off at a pub. Then later I ended up picking them up again and then I dropped them off at a club. It was a bad night, it was. Raining and windy it was. Then till

3am I got no other job, well apart from a small one, and I spent more on petrol doing that one. When I got this other job I never dreamt I would end up picking them up again. In fact, I had completely forgotten about them. When they got into my car I recognised them, but they didn't recognise me. Anyway, as soon as they got into my car, they started arguing. I don't let people smoke in my car, but I didn't stop them because they were arguing so much. I don't know why, but his wife, she was a young woman, she just took her clothes off. Just like that. She just took off everything. I could see her in my mirror. And you know, how dirty these people are, well I mean they don't shave do they and I adjusted my mirror so that I wouldn't see her and put my foot down. I was close to their house and got there quickly.'

He looks over his shoulder and lowers his voice. It is only just audible over the noise of the aircraft, 'When I stopped outside their door, her husband just got out and left his wife and went inside. I was really embarrassed as you can well imagine. Without turning around I asked her, "Please pay my fare and please go home madam."'

'What did she do?' I ask.

'At first nothing. She just sat there for a second or two and then she started crying. Just like that she did and said, "I'm not leaving until that bastard comes back and apologises to me". I got out, knocked on their door and called her husband and asked him to pay me five quid and take his wife out of my car. He came charging out shouting, "I don't want nowt t'do with that whore – you can keep her". As I say you've got to be careful with drunks you know. I shook my head and said, "I don't want her – I just want my fare, mate." He put his hands on his knees, bent over and started laughing like a mad man and when he raised his head his eyes were full of tears. He shouted across to his wife, "Did yer hear that, you dirty little slut – even he don't think you' re worth our bleedin taxi fare..." Now when she heard her husband say this, she just became hysterical and started kicking my car seats. I didn't know what to do so I called Base for help. Well, you know some of our lads never turn up when you need them. I mean when some gorays attack you, most of us will help each other but some think only of themselves and they never turn up. Well, as soon as a driver came, he radioed Base and before you knew it, they were all there. In fact, I'm sure there were some from other bases as well, you know. By then of course, she had fallen asleep...' He stops mid sentence.

'And what happened then?'

'You can imagine what they said about me and my beard.'

'No, I mean what happened to her?'

'Oh her,' Arif sighs, adjusts his seat and falls asleep before finishing what he was about to say.

A little boy's tired cry keeps me awake. It is a pitiful cry, one that wants freedom from this environment. The child begins to holler. Arif starts snoring. It's time for a stroll I decide and push myself out of my chair. The child is wriggling about in his mother's lap. She sits in tired resignation, holding on to one of his legs, staring blankly at the large screen in front.

After nudging myself past Arif I look up and down the aircraft. Most passengers are asleep. A few have buried their heads under their blankets. Some like me are wandering about stretching their legs. Here and there a few reading lights beam down on their hosts. A group of men have collected at the rear of the aircraft. As I am mulling over which direction I should go, two young lads sitting in the central aisle start play fighting.

'E'll do it – I tell yer, e'll do it,' one of the lads says to his friend excitedly in a broad Bradford accent.

'Shut yer bleedin trap will yer,' the second lad replies.

'Ah know he will. I've seen it before, haint I?

They were referring to *The Saint*, a film which PIA was showing. It was an old Simon Templar movie which I had seen. I remembered *The Saint*. He is a James Bond type of a hero, a super detective, but one distinctive feature about his films is the beginning of the credits and the ending where The Saint is given a white circle over his head, like an angel. Now all The Saint had to do was to turn up somewhere and women, often scantily dressed, who were of course very beautiful, would chuck themselves at him. The scene the boys were getting excited over involved The Saint edging a woman towards a bed. He had just made quick work of most of the baddies and only the main villain remained somewhere, trying to blow up the world. The Saint and the woman are on a boat, which is swaying gently up and down on soft waves. The Saint walks over towards the window and looks out at some seagulls flying above the clear blue water. He draws the curtain, while embracing the woman, slowly unzipping her dress. They are about to kiss.

'The bastards, they've bloody cut it.' The lads stand up, stare at each other in disbelief and shout in unison. They look towards me and then at other passengers for support. PIA censors had of course crudely cut the passionate part of the film. Realising their mistake the boys lower their heads and sit down giggling.

The Saint is now chasing the final villain. An irate man rushes past me, cursing, 'This is supposed to be PK786. They don't have a prayer mat. And there are people drinking sharab. And staff can't tell me which way Mecca is and they call this...' The man's voice fades into the buzzing roar of the aircraft.

I turn and pace down the aisle towards the group of men congregating at the back aircraft. There are three of them now. After greeting them with a loud 'Salaam' I offer them a round of cigarettes. They all decline. They are standing close together in solemn silence. One of the men has deep, bloodshot eyes. He is a tall, dark skinned, middle-aged man, with a large nose and short curly hair. He has black rings under his unblinking eyes. After standing silently for a moment I ask him in Pothowari, 'Is all well, brother?'

Without moving his head he turns his tired eyes towards me. A large tear trembles out of one of them. Looking away from me, he clears his throat and retorts, 'What happens to pardesis has happened to me.'

A chill runs down my back. I could easily have been in his shoes.

'I had only been back in England for two days when I heard,' the man says after accepting a lit cigarette from one of the other passengers. 'My cousin told me. He told me that Almighty had taken my mother. Why did He do that...' The man stops to blow his nose. Tears gush down his cheeks. He continues, 'When I was in Pakistan I took her to hospital myself. She wasn't that ill, you know. She needed a simple little operation. It wouldn't have killed her if she hadn't had it. I took her to Mangla Hospital. I thought I would give her the best treatment. She got yarkaan from there, from hospital. We then took her to PIMS, a big hospital in Islamabad. They said she would be all right. I took her home. I had to come back to England, to this sister fucking place and when I landed, my wife told me to phone home. When I phoned my cousin, he told me she had gone.'

'It is Allah's will,' someone says.

'But what did Allah have against my mother?' He asks looking each of us in the eyes. His own have dried, they are redder now. He raises his hands questioningly. Smoke from a lit cigarette creates an apparition in the air. He continues in a crackling voice. 'She had never harmed anyone in her life and she wasn't even sixty yet.' The man looks on the floor, searching for something, and then quietly disappears into the belly of the aircraft.

The three of us who remain behind stand in deep thoughtful silence for a few moments after the bereaved man has gone. I don't really understand why the death of a complete stranger should so upset me. Leaning over to the window I raise the blinds and stare out onto the world below. Night is just beginning to lose her battle. The skyline is puffed up with soft clouds through which we roar onwards.

Our journey is nearing its end. I block out thoughts about the police raiding my uncle's house, my friends', who must be wondering what has happened to me. Instead, I imagine myself sitting in our white 1969 Toyota Corolla being driven up the GT Road. My mother in the back all flushed with happiness and father proudly driving and cursing kamikaze Pakistani drivers. She was very fat, my mother. I knew deep down that this was due to depression. I was her festering wound. But I blamed her for bringing it on herself in the first place. It is only now, after seeing the big man crying, that my feelings towards her soften. I think back to my last trip to Pakistan, over five years ago. Like now, it had been during the summer. One hot night, along with a throng of other lads from my village, I had gone to Jhelum to see a film. Jhelum is a few hours' bus ride from Banyala and we returned that night at around 3am. Everyone was fast asleep. Our rattling old pedestal fan brushed waves of air across my family as it turned from side to side. A marriage party of crickets and other creatures of the night seemed to be having a mela. The whole yard was thick with an intoxicating scent of the flowers of raat ni rani – the princess of the night. Silver moonlight had lit everything up. Had it not been for the fact that I was scared of waking everyone up, I would have stared on at this dream-like image of my family. I stealthily scaled the wall of our yard and jumped down. Our dog had rushed at me and was growling. It was a small dog, one that didn't quite fill one with terror. But it was a noisy beast and I was worried lest it wake the whole house up. Just then I heard my mother. She had been asleep at the far end of a long line of people. Her voice was cut by the wind of the pedestal fan.

'It is late, son and you must be hungry,' she said.

'I'm all right. Go back to sleep,' I snapped, nudging past an enormous air cooler. The ceiling fan was spinning at full power. Droplets of water, spraying out of the cooler had deliciously chilled the room. Holding up my arms I felt every hair on my body come to life as the spray of water from the cooler hit me. Before I had had much time to settle down my mother came into the room. She was carrying a tray.

'You mustn't stay out so late,' she said putting the light on.

The fluorescent lights flickered a few times and then buzzed into life engulfing the room in an oppressive illumination. An array of insects attracted by the light came rushing into the room. Every now and again some hapless creature would end its life by hitting the fan above with a loud crack. Putting the tray on a small table next to my bed, Mother said, 'This is not England. It is not safe to be out so late and you must have walked all that way from GT Road and there are so many snakes in our jungle at this time of year.'

I began to get angry with her interference in my life. I had lived for so long on my own that I found it difficult to adjust to family life and resented being told what I could do or should do. Even though I was hungry I didn't want her to tell me to eat.

'Take this out of here,' I shouted, knocking the tray off the table, 'and leave me alone.'

My mother gritted her teeth, collected the pieces of the broken plate, cleaned up the mess I had just made and quietly left. I was so upset that I found it impossible to go to sleep. I lit a cigarette and stared at the insects hovering around the lights. I was stubbing out the cigarette when my mother came back with another tray of food. She smiled and said, 'I know you are hungry but you need to control that temper of yours.'

My eyes stung as I noticed lights flickering on the veranda. The whole family was now awake. A shadow floated across the floor. My younger brother sleepily came and stood silently by the door.

'Don't get motherly now,' I cried.

Mother's smile disappeared and she froze in her tracks. My brother, Karim came forward and stood close to her. I said, 'Parents give their children so much, what did you give me eh?'

She squatted on the floor next to me holding onto the tray with shaking hands. Karim placed his right hand on top of her head and looked confusedly back at me. I knew I was hurting her, but I wanted to cause her more pain. Sitting up I said: 'They said you were mad and that is why they took me, eh.' My uncle's face flashed through my mind. I had gone to England as a young child who had been adopted by him. Over the years he had convinced me that my mother had gone insane.

'We were very poor, son,' Mother said clasping her mouth with her hand, 'and no one asked me. They just did it. Your grandfather and father decided. They said it was for the best.'

'You're lying,' I said. 'Why didn't you stop them?'

'Allahjee!' My mother cried aloud. 'Why don't you just end my life, son? If that will make you happy, then my life would be worth it. Just don't kill me with your questions.'

'Instead of just sitting there,' I shouted towards her pointing an accusing finger, 'just tell me what you gave me, eh.'

'I gave you this.' My mother replied ripping open her kameez. My younger brother rushed towards me and punched me in the chest crying. A bird screamed in the jungle beyond the house.

I don't know how long I've stared out the aircraft window but now the clouds below are bathed in a white glow. The image of my brother dissolves into the clouds. Though I'm flushed with shame at my cruelty towards her, I still have a nagging sense of self-righteousness.

'Well, brothers,' a heavy voice asks in a Lahori accent, 'one journey is nearly over.' The owner of the voice is a small round man with a childish smile. An ugly scar runs down his light skinned face. He is sitting on the stewardess' seat facing the rear of the aircraft.

'Inshahallah,' agrees the other. He is an old man, perhaps in his seventies.

I nod politely.

'This PIA is a strange airline,' the Lahori states matter-of-factly, 'Look at that.' Pointing towards an air steward he continues, 'I mean, all other airlines have good-looking young women to serve you. Just look what PIA have bestowed upon us.' He goes silent. I try to work out what he is going on about. The steward at the centre of our attention is serving breakfast. He is a huge man, with a long bushy beard and a large bulging belly, not dissimilar to Arif's. The steward plonks trays of food in front of passengers. Lahori says, 'I bet he is safarshi.'

'What's that?' I ask naively. I have not heard of this particular religious sect.

'Someone up there gave him this job.'

'We all have our beliefs, brother,' I reply.

'Yes. Yes.' Lahori laughs. 'I mean he is a sirkari. I can even tell you what he did before he got this job.'

'What's that then?' I smile handing out a round of cigarettes.

'He was definitely a fauji. Look at him. He thinks he's lobbing hand grenades and not food.' We all let out a hearty laugh. The steward is now quite close to us. The Lahori shouts across to him jovially, 'Brotherjee. Is all well?' The steward looks towards us emotionlessly and continues with his chores.

'And you, brother,' Lahori asks me, 'is it happiness or sorrow that brings you back home?'

I hesitate before answering, 'Oh, that depends what is fated for me – she could turn out to be anything.'

'You are a good-looking young man,' Lahori chuckles. 'Besides, it wouldn't make any difference even if you were the ugliest of God's creations, I mean even if you were squint-eyed, with one leg and had a scar bigger than mine, it wouldn't matter. You are still bound to find a beautiful bride.'

'Why's that then?' I ask.

'You're a Valaiti, my boy,' Lahori says flicking his ash into a cup which we've been using as a makeshift ashtray. Lahori takes one last drag from his cigarette and throws it into the cup. It hisses out of existence.

'You watch me words, son,' the old man sniggers in a broad Leeds accent, 'they all become witches after marriage...'

'Oh babajee!' Lahori interrupts, looking first at the old man and then at me, 'you've just said what needed to be said, when they are brides, they all look very beautiful, but God knows what happens when they become wives.'

'I think I'll just remain as I am,' I say in English.

'Aye, it'll be loads cheaper an' all,' the Yorkshire man adds.

'Babajee and you younger brother, yaar, just talk Punjabi. I've talked so much English that my mouth has become all cocked.'

We smoke and chat about nothing in particular. Sunlight begins to flood into the aircraft from many windows. Closing the shutter nearest to him, the old man says in Pothowari, 'Closer we get to Islamabad, worse I feel…'

'What are you doing, baba?' Lahori interrupts closing his eyes as though in a trance. A melancholic smile imprints itself on his lips. His scar twitches and he says, 'Don't spoil my mood now. I am in Lahore walking by university canal through a tunnel of trees. It hasn't rained for a month and every green leaf of every tree is crying under so much weight of brown dust. I can feel cool gusts of it glazing my body. I hold my hands up and I wait. Brown muddy water flows faster and faster. My soul wants to leave my body and dance. A raindrop dances above me and drops down. Another drops. Mother earth sighs and I breathe her soil-scented breath. Then it comes down like a river. And it comes until everything is cleansed. Trees shake their arms and leaves change into clothes of every shade of God's green. Now you tell me,' he says opening his eyes, 'Lahore is Lahore, is it not?' The scar pushes the smile off his face.

'Yes. Yes. Lahore is Lahore,' the old man replies, 'but my heart is beating faster.'

'Why is that?' I ask.

Lahori groans.

'Islamabad shouldn't be called an airport but a thief port,' the old man says. 'I have never been back home, and I have been home a lot, without being insulted. They treat us Mirpuriay like they would their own goats and cows.'

'What do they do, uncle?' I ask alarmed.

'If it was in their power,' the old man says, 'they would take our skin off. Passport officers and custom officers have their dalay, you know. These touts look for vulnerable passengers. I mean, when they see someone like me, especially with a young girl, then they will come up and try to frighten me. "You have a jowan daughter with you, uncle," they will say, "It is not good for daughters to stand around in this manner. I will sort everything out for thirty pounds." Some people get really frightened and just pay up. And when you get through and manage to pick up your luggage, touts are eavesdropping on your conversation. They identify Mirpuris and then tell Customs, who you can bet will then stop us only...'

'Oh chacha, leave this talk,' the Lahori says smiling broadly, 'they have no mothers or fathers.'

'And you brother,' I ask Lahori, 'how long are you coming home for?'

'How long am I coming home for?' His smile disappears and his face tightens. The scar looks as though it has come alive. After sitting in contemplative silence, Lahori says, 'I can never go back to England. They rejected my asylum.'

'How long were you in England for?' the old man asks.

'Five years.'

'That's not bad,' the old man says lightheartedly, 'you must have saved up a little bit.'

'Mine was no false case babajee,' Lahori says raising his head up towards the old man. 'God had been very benevolent to me in Pakistan and I did not go to England to seek money. I told them only truth. Now I don't know how long I will live.' Pointing from his face to his stomach he says, 'This scar goes all the way down. It will never heal.'

My ears pop as the aircraft descends. I look out of the

window. We are swimming inside the clouds.

'How did you get this scar, uncle?' I ask turning away from the clouds.

'They came in broad daylight. There were hundreds of them. I knew Imam Azharuddin, he was leading them. I knew many others. They were all chanting. I could see them from my window. It was as though they were all drunk. No, it was more than that, it was like they were possessed. They went straight for our mosque. It was a beautiful mosque. They burnt it down. They burnt everything in it as well. It is a miracle that people inside managed to get out. Then they went through all our houses. They took anything that was valuable and burnt everything else. My brothers and I refused to leave. There were five of us brothers. They hacked my brothers to death and left me for dead as well. When I came round I was inside a police station. I was lying on top of my brothers' corpses. When I got up, a policeman ran out screaming. He thought my corpse had come alive. I heard an officer swearing at him go back and attend to me. I saw this officer when I came fully round. He refused to let me go until he was given a lot of money. I don't know how I made it to hospital. Maybe it would have been better for me to be buried along with my brothers.'

'When did this happen?' I ask.

'Six years, two months and three weeks today.'

'Why?'

'I am an Ahamedi.'

'I don't know what an Ahmedi is, uncle.' I apologise.

'Does it matter how one follows God?' the old man says in a voice charged with emotion. 'It is those Maulvis. They cause so much mischief. We should hang them from their beards.'

'You don't know how true that is, chachajee,' Lahori says rubbing his hand across his moustache. 'My brothers may today have been alive if they hadn't gone there...'

'Where's that, uncle?'

'You Valaiti goat wouldn't know even if I told you,' the Lahori replies.

'What happened then, my son?' the old man asks.

'It was because of Suliman, my doctor brother. He was always worried about everybody else. He used to say that this mohallah didn't have any doctor. Suliman was not bothered about money but he was an excellent doctor, he was. He used to work in a big hospital in Lahore, but they threw him out. Jamaat ghoondas were everywhere. But he was not one to get depressed. He always said no doctor should be without patients. He needed to heal more than his patients needed healing. Anyway he had hardly opened his shop when people started flocking to him. This upset Imam Azharuddin.'

'Why should a doctor upset an Imam?' I ask innocently.

'Well you see, Imam Azharuddin used to treat people with his taveezes. He would give a taveez for anything. Appendix, typhoid, anything anyone could catch, he had a spell for it and for only five rupees. My brother used to give a proper prescription and accepted whatever anyone could afford. Nothing if they had no money. He never asked for money though. Of course Azharuddin lost a lot of customers, especially as now people started getting better. Imam Azharuddin was always threatening my brother, but Suliman ignored him and continued on with his work. Slowly he managed to build a nice house. By and by we all moved in close to each other. There were already a few Ahmadis but they didn't get on with Suliman. They blamed him for creating so many problems. Then six years two months and three weeks ago, all hell engulfed us. Imam Azharuddin was having his afternoon nap. Someone went up to him and showed him a page from the Holy Quran. It was slightly burnt. Azharuddin immediately turned on his mosque's speakers and started saying that Ahmadis were burning our Quran. I've told you everything else.'

'What happened to the women and children?' the old man asks.

'I do my best to support them. We are now in Almighty's hands.'

'Didn't Home Office believe your story?' I ask.

'I wouldn't be with you if they did,' Lahori says letting out a false laugh. 'They came for me one morning and didn't even give me enough time to pack. I don't even have presents for my children. Just one little bag with a few clothes is all I could manage.'

'English are clever bastards you know,' the old man says breaking an icy silence. The aeroplane shakes as we pass through air turbulence. Steadying himself with his thin long arms he continues, 'If one person makes a mistake, they punish everybody.' He pauses, lights a cigarette and inhales deeply. He is an unusually tall man. Short silver hair thinly covers his head. His eyes are deeply sunk into a freckled face. He opens a shutter, leans over and continues, 'And me, I will not stay a day longer in England than when I get my pension.'

'You've been in England too long babajee,' I joke. 'Like them, you hiding your age as well, eh.'

'Oh it's true I should have had a pension a long time ago,' the old man says clearing his throat. 'I am not an educated man and when I first came to England everyone said I was too old to go and that they were looking for young men. In those days I was so healthy that I could have fooled anyone. I could eat a whole goat on my own without burping! Anyway, I put down my age less than it was. I thought I would be able to work longer that way.' He continues nostalgically, 'When you're young, you think you will never grow old. I can still see my mother standing by an old parrot kikker and I can still hear those parrots making a racket. It was a tree under whose shade I had played and grown up and had watched my mother get old. A long time ago, when I had shown her my passport and told her how I was now 'officially' much younger, she had laughed and cried and said, "A mother's son is always her baby and her baby can do no wrong..."'

'How much did you increase your age by?' I ask, trying to

lighten the atmosphere, trying to block my mother coming into my thoughts.

'Oh, I don't know – fifteen years.' The old man snorts, 'I know I should have done it other way round. Now I'm just hoping to get my pension before I die.'

'You don't look like someone who is about to drop dead, chachajee,' the Lahori throws his head back, chuckling.

'I've got a plan for that as well,' the old man giggles. 'I'll get my own back on England – but I've got to get my pension first.'

'What plans 'ave you got then?' I ask.

'Well,' the old man says lowering his voice, 'I've always used my thumb print. I can't sign my name you see. Well, when I die I'll tell my grandchildren to chop my thumbs off and keep stamping my pension book. How will anyone ever find out?'

'Where will they keep your thumbs, uncle?' I ask.

'In a freezer of course.'

'And what happens when there's a blackout?' Lahori asks.

'Well, there wouldn't be if you Pakistanis didn't take all our electricity.'

'Yaar baba,' Lahori says, 'leave politics out, will you?'

'We'll get a generator.'

We are smiling when the 'fasten seat belt' signs light up. We exchange addresses and after bidding farewell to each other, return to our seats. Arif is still fast asleep. The mother is now wrestling with her other children. The baby has fallen asleep. I manage to get back into my own seat without disturbing Arif. After fastening my safety belt, I lift the shutter. A ray of brilliant white light cuts into the aircraft. We are below a thin line of broken clouds, which pepper a crystal blue sky. Below us runs a rugged brown landscape on which a dark snake-like scar wriggles. It might be a long river or perhaps a road. I cannot tell. The aircraft turns. My ears pop again. My thoughts start riding on the words of the old man: 'a mother's son is always her baby and her baby can do no wrong.' They pierce through memories I'd buried deep in the stowage of my head. I start thinking again about the night I knocked food out of her hands. That night, when everyone had finally gone back to their beds, mother had returned to my room. Sitting by the side of my bed, she'd quietly stroked my hair and told me a story about a mother and her son. I can almost hear her voice. I can feel her breath on the back of my neck. I can hear her words and see her sitting there under the noisy fan into which the insects had finally stopped committing suicide, preoccupied rather with the rays of daylight breaking through. The cockerels heralded a new dawn as my mother told me the story of a son who had fallen in love with a woman. She was a beautiful woman who wanted him to prove his love for her. And he was so madly in love he was willing to do anything. She asked him to bring his mother's heart for her. The lover, intoxicated with passion, had rushed home, slaughtered his mother and ripped out her heart. Carrying the heart, he ran frantically back to his beloved. He was so maddened with love that he scrambled carelessly through thorns and bushes. On the way to his beloved he tripped over a boulder and fell heavily to the ground. 'Bis-mil-lah,' his mother's voice had cried out of the heart. 'Be careful, son. Watch where you are going, you may hurt yourself.' Mother continued to talk whilst I faked sleep. She must have known that I was only pretending to be asleep, for she continued to tell me what she would do on my wedding day. She was tired of celebrating other people's happiness and wanted to celebrate her own. She would sing all night and all the girls would tease me as they led the groom through the village streets. There would be singing every night. The tthol would play and she would dance the sammi. There would be fireworks and this would be the biggest wedding Banyala had ever seen.

I don't know how long she sat beside me, but when I woke up she was coming towards me with a cup of tea. I had only woken up because of a power cut that had forced all the machinery to suddenly stop. I had tossed and turned, sleepily praying for the electricity to come back. The wretched flies which seemed to have prior knowledge of power cuts, had chased me out of the bed.

In the five years since that day I have never talked to my mother. Let alone apologised. I had not even written her a letter and the letters I wrote to my father contained greetings and messages for everyone else but her. The Yorkshireman had stirred the motherless child inside me and I now longed to be with her. I imagine apologising to her. I will get to her before the letter I had just posted. I will tell her about my case. I will promise her that, should I get acquitted, I will return on the next flight to her and get married to a woman of her pleasing.

We land at Islamabad airport on a bright flaming morning. The hot air tickles my face as I walk apprehensively towards the arrivals' lounge.

Dazed by the sudden change in environment, I edgily follow people walking towards the immigration counter. I am called over to the Health Desk. A small dark-skinned man with a ridiculously large moustache sits behind the counter. I give him a card which had been distributed on the aeroplane. 'Be cool son,' I say to myself, 'it's just a health counter.' The clerk jots something onto my health card, scribbles into a worn out old register and without looking up at me demands in Urdu, 'Five pounds.'

'What for?' I protest in Pothowari.

'Fee,' he replies looking up at me with his beady eyes, shaking his head incredulously.

'But what for?'

'Does it matter?' he retorts in Pothowari.

'Does it matter!?' I exclaim.

'It's only five pounds,' he says looking me straight in the eye without flinching.

'Only five pounds!' I huff.

The clerk scribbles something somewhere, stamps

something and waves me on. I hear Arif's voice, 'One must not get angry with these chaps,' he laughs offering me a cigarette.

'He was asking me for five quid for nothing,' I protest walking with him towards the immigration queue.

'Don't let it worry you, son.'

'But it's not right. It's corruption.' I begin to speak louder and louder as I get further away from the Health counter.

'No, no, no, no,' Arif giggles, tapping my shoulder in a fatherly way. 'You pay lots of money for nowt in England. Just think of it as VAT and you won't feel so bad about it.' His daughter stands close to him looking nervously around.

Armed soldiers stand behind the immigration officer. Irate passengers are pushing their passports towards him. He mechanically stamps these. I hold out mine. He grabs it. Looks at my face for a moment and stamps.

I clench my fist triumphantly. After fending off numerous over-eager porters, I manage to fight my way to a broken old trolley when I notice the old lady, who had sworn her heart out at me, struggling with one of her suitcases. I walk up to help her and say in Pothowari, 'God be with you, ma-jee.'

'Bah gum, you little bastard,' she replies in a Bradford accent, 'I knew you understood every word I said.'

I am trying to digest what she has just said when she disappears behind a couple of bored policemen, guarding the exit.

I don't recognise this chaotic world. All the faces seem to merge into moustaches and shouts and smiles and announcements. Whilst looking for my mother, I fight off an array of moneychangers, porters, taxi drivers and beggars. I am beginning to become paranoid at the possibility of my parents not being there to receive me. Perhaps they had not been informed about my flight. Just then, the sight of my cousin fills me with happiness. I rush towards him and embrace him tightly. His body shakes. Pulling away from him, I notice a piece of cloth across his forehead. His hair is unkempt. His eyes are bloodshot. He looks at me with apologetic eyes, which suddenly fill with tears. 'Is all well, cousin?' I ask. He doesn't reply.

'Where is Father?' I ask.

'At home,' my cousin replies with broken words that blot out all the noises of the airport and imprint themselves in the air.

I ask fearfully in a low voice, 'Where is my mother?'

My cousin embraces me, shaking gently.

II

A dry scream explodes in my mouth. I throw my head skywards and yell an inhuman groan, 'What have I done?'

I try to free myself from Cousin Hamza's embrace. He tightens his arms, shaking silently. Could there not have been a mistake? No names have been mentioned. Perhaps I have misunderstood.

'The funeral has taken place,' Hamza whispers, 'but she is waiting in her grave for your goodbye.'

'Why didn't they wait for me?' I scream.

My eyes remain tearless.

Someone passes me a bottle of water. It slips through my hands and falls to the ground. A moment later the bottle is handed to me again, this time it is open. The passengers who I met on the aeroplane may have said something to me, or perhaps I just imagine this happening in that sun bleached car park of the airport. I don't remember walking here but I must have, for I stand next to my father's car. Everything seems to have been drained of colour in the fierce dry heat. Looking at some happily reunited family, my stomach tightens. How could I have written those things? How could I have posted that letter which I knew was going to cause her so much pain? The car chassis burns my hand. Torments judder through me with the heat. And I was going to ask her to find me a wife! And she died waiting for me to decide. I had gone to earn money, and yet I had hardly sent her any and even then had resented sending the little I had. What were my years in England worth now?

Apart from cousin Hamza, three others get into the car. Although I know all of them, they shook hands with me earlier, I didn't recognise them then, but now I can put names to their faces. Hamza manoeuvres the car out of the chaos of the airport car park. A bedraggled beggar child appears from somewhere and walks perilously close to the rear of the car begging, 'Hik pound.' Before long many beggars surround our car. Bypassing other returnees they seem to be targeting me. A young woman with a small child attached to her hip, pushes through the throng. She pleads, 'I am a mother. I have no one to look after me. No one to help me bring this child up. In God's name, brother, give me a pound.' I am about to do exactly that when Hamza throws well practised obscenities at her. Flashing a stubborn glance at him, she opens the car door and touches my chin. Pointing to her child she asks, 'What is a pound to you, my pardesi brother, eh?'

I have a small amount of Pakistani currency and hand her a ten rupee note. She throws it back at me saying, 'This is useless. Give me English note.'

I take out a five pound note. Before I hand it over Hamza slams the brakes and gets out enraged. The throng steps back, but the woman stands her ground. She calmly grabs the ten rupee note, tuts, and retreats saying to my cousin, 'And what difference would it have made to you?'

A number of cars behind us start honking their horns. Getting into the driver's seat Cousin Hamza curses them under his breath.

Waves of heat rise from the cracked tarmac of the car park. The air burns as it slashes my face. Traffic roars on the main road outside the airport. The inside of the car is like an oven. I am drenched in sweat and choking under wave after wave of grief laden pangs. I am desperate to get home. My eyelids twitch uncontrollably.

I don't want to make this journey. I didn't want to turn down the hill that leads off from the GT Road which snakes down the jungle in which mother often walked, carrying a huge bundle of grass on top of her head. I will be able to see the village as soon as our car crosses the old railway bridge that sticks out in between two red-brown hills. It is by the pohai, just past where I used to watch older boys from our village hunting wild pigeons. This is the very bridge where my mother often walked. Just past the bridge the road winds down into the shining waters of the kas, with its silver-grey sand, where I spent my childhood. And then I will be able to see the outline of our ancestral graveyard. There to the left of me, as our car pulled out of the stream, runs a path that leads to the village where my mother lived. I will be able to see houses clearly now and my house. Oh, right now that house will be full of people. Some crying. Others idling around on whatever space they can find. And then, when I have travelled a few yards further down the hill, I will see the graveyard. A graveyard I had believed was only for my ancestors. Never had I thought of finding my mother there.

A traffic policeman flags us down as we turn out of the airport car park. The policeman casually strolls up towards us. He looks pale, ghost-like, walking through a halo of exhaust fumes from a passing bus. When he comes closer I see he is a dark man with a thick black moustache. His duty shirt is too small for him.

'What does this dog want?' I hiss indignantly.

'Shh,' Hamza replies under his breath, 'let me handle this.'

'Why didn't you stop?' the policeman asks.

'I didn't see you,' Hamza replies.

'You taxi drivers are always blind?'

'It's my uncle's car.'

'It's always *chacha-mama's* car.' The policeman sneers dismissively with his greedy eyes fixed on Hamza. 'Let me see your papers.'

'We're in a hurry.' Hamza says handing him a bundle of papers, wrapped in a dirty old cloth.

'Everyone is always in a hurry,' the policeman says, inspecting the outside cover of what must have been a logbook.

'We've had a bereavement,' Hamza says.

The policeman bends down, stealing a glance at us in the car. Straightening up, he hands the papers back to my cousin and says, 'A funeral must not be delayed.'

As our car pulls away from the policeman I ask Hamza, 'When did she die?'

'About twelve o'clock last night.'

I was flying somewhere over Europe at that time, I think. Drinking. How could I have done this when she was dying? Why did I not once telephone when I'd been repeatedly told she was ill? Let alone telephoning, how could I have not written to her in five years, apart from the letter which will now arrive after I get there. 'You selfish bastard,' I curse myself, 'you could at least have given her a day of peace.' I used to ridicule my parents in the presence of bemused friends. 'I was just donated to this white man's hell,' I used to laugh, 'to earn pounds and to post pounds.' The lad who went to Valait was not *me*. I was born again in England, a Paki at first, and an Asian later on, then a Black with pride and finally as a rebel who sought a different world, one where no one who would have to go through what he had.

'How long had she been ill?' I ask, half-pretending I didn't know.

'Two years,' Hamza reminds me softly. 'But she only had the operation a month ago.'

'Why didn't someone tell me?'

Everyone keeps quiet. My thoughts rush back to England, I hadn't even bothered to open the last letter from my father. I had reckoned he would only be asking for money and I didn't have any to spare. It's probably still lying somewhere unopened. Punching the seat in front of me I ask, 'Why didn't someone tell me it was so serious?'

'She was all right when she came out of the hospital...' Hamza replies.

'When did she go to the hospital?'

'Three weeks ago,' Hamza says. 'She had kidney stones and they said it was just a routine operation. She was perfectly all right when she came out. You know, Khala....'

I stop listening, curses rage in my head. Why didn't I know?

'It is Allah's will,' whispers Hassan who was sitting quietly next to me, placing his rough bony hands on my clenched fist.

'Why blame Allah for what surely I have done?' I look Hassan in the eyes. Behind him, the road whizzes by. New, plush buildings now stand where I had last seen trees. These abruptly end as we come towards Islamabad Highway. Here we would turn right. My thoughts run way ahead of our car, on to the end of the highway, turning left onto the hustle and bustle of the GT Road.

Helping me out of my leather jacket Hassan curses a fly, which has trapped itself inside our car. Though all the windows are open, the hapless creature buzzes blindly around trying to escape.

Saber and Shahid, the twins, join Hassan in trying to rid us of the fly. Saber sits in the front passenger seat and Shahid in the back with us, next to Hassan.

'This fly's life will end at my hands,' Saber says rolling a newspaper.

It is a fat fly with a colourful nose. Saber waits patiently as the fly drones across to the front windscreen. It bumps about in front of Hamza. Saber leans across, striking the screen with the newspaper. Hamza swerves the car, narrowly missing a bus, which is trying to overtake us.

'Have some fear of God, yaar,' Hamza protests steadying the car.

'Allah owns our life,' Saber says with a smile. The fly escapes death, it is in front of him, tempting fate. Stabbing the fly with the end of the newspaper, he says confidently, 'There. It is done.' As soon as Saber lifts the newspaper off the screen the fly burst into life and flies over his head to the back of the car. 'It seems that Almighty has blessed this creature with more life than we can take.' Saber says.

Saber has changed little in the five years since I last saw him. Even as a boy, he was deeply religious, and now, to the everlasting pride of his father, has performed two Hajs. Of course the fact that he was working in Saudi Arabia at the time was unimportant in his father's reckoning.

'What has Allah got to do with your inability to rid us of this pest?' Shahid retorts. He is the only self-confessed atheist in the whole of our extended family.

'It was written and so it happened and...'

'Nothing is written,' the atheist interrupts lighting three cigarettes at the same time. Passing one to each of us, apart from Saber, he continues, 'Problem with our country is people like you, false Hajis with wild bushes instead of beards, waiting for Allah to answer your prayers.'

Letting smoke out of his nostrils Shahid asks, 'Just tell me one person whose prayer has ever been answered.'

'Maybe you should pray first and then ask this question,' Saber replies covering his face against the cigarette smoke.

'Just leave your fighting for once,' Hassan protests, flicking his half-smoked cigarette out of the car. It bounces off the road and disappears under a passing tractor heading noisily in the other direction.

Our car comes to a stop at some traffic lights. Apart from the fly, everyone inside is silent. The simmering argument between the twins has deflected my pain. Now the horror is back. A succession of disjointed thoughts flashes through me: my father standing in our courtyard. Bloodshot eyes. How would I greet him?

How could I look him in the eyes? My sister, Shabnam pulling her ruffled hair. What would I say to her? What happened to me in England that caused me to inflict so much pain? My brother, Karim leaning against a wall – I've made him motherless too. Women wailing. The hill blossoming in multicoloured flowers my mother used to hate. How could I see them again? The graveyard – my first stop – my mother's open grave, basking in the sun. My mother waiting for her Valaiti first born, waiting for a farewell, which he didn't deserve. And I would see her inside it, inside a freshly dug brown hole. And then what will I do? Tear off my western clothes?

I have forgotten where I am, or whether I am awake or asleep. The sun sparkles through the leaves of a distant tali tree. I am brought out of my dream by the honking of horns. Hamza isn't moving even though the traffic lights are green. Looking across at the lights through my blurred vision, I realise his problem. All the lights at the crossroads are green. Cousin Hamza cautiously drives forward. And just as we turn right onto the Islamabad Highway another traffic policeman flags us down. Hamza curses, parking behind a line of other vehicles. Around us, all manner of motorised monsters go deafeningly to and fro. Brand new trucks, adorned like brides, in an orgy of colours, tassels dangling off their sides, mirrors tiled into smiling pictures of women, parandahs dangling off side mirrors and black ribbons blowing in the wind. Some of the trucks, overloaded with wheat, along with buffaloes and cars slowly head north to Peshawar, perhaps to Afghanistan and beyond. Old bangers chug along, fighting for space with buses, vans, cars, scooters, cyclists, animals and pedestrians.

'What now?' I ask.

'Chourbazaari,' Hamza replies.

A policeman strolls towards us.

'This is Pakistan,' Saber says. 'Mulk-e-Khudhadad.'

'You were stationary in a green signal,' a tall, emaciated policeman says to Hamza.

'Sorry, sir,' Hamza replies. 'All painchoud lights were green.'

'Ahm,' the policeman nods folding his arms across his chest.

'Mother fuckers weren't working,' I bang on the window.

Hassan grips my arm tightly in disapproval.

'You could see traffic on other side of road wasn't moving. Any driver would know his signal must therefore have changed as well,' the policeman says judiciously.

I get out of the car shouting, 'My mother is waiting for me in her grave and what are you doing to us?'

A passing lorry leaves a trial of smoke after it. It drowns me. Saber and Hassan push me back, coughing, into the car. Ignoring us, the policeman calmly eyes the documents. His moustache twitches. His dark eyes glint. 'Where is your radio licence?' he asks Hamza.

'We don't have a radio,' Hamza replies.

'What is this aerial for then?'

'It's just for show.'

Turning away towards a group of police officers, with a slow movement of his index finger, the policeman orders Hamza to follow him.

'How much did you pay him?' I ask Hamza when he returns.

'One hundred rupees.'

'It would have been ten rupees if you had said nothing,' Shahid adds.

'How much is a radio licence?' I ask as Hamza drives past the checkpoint.

'Twenty rupees.'

'Why isn't there a licence?' I ask.

'Ask your father,' Hamza replies.

We travel the next few miles in solemn silence, punctuated only by the fly and the roar of passing vehicles. Although the fly continues to buzz as before, I no longer find its presence irritating or offensive. I begin enjoying the erratic melody of this stranger in our midst; its song echoing sorrows I cannot articulate.

'There,' Shahid says proudly grabbing the fly off the back windscreen with a sudden movement of his hand. 'Every creature has a right to life,' he adds releasing the fly out of the window. For a moment it flashes like a dark ghost caught against a white background, and then it is washed away in the back draught of a speeding car travelling in the opposite direction.

We slow down as we approach a bridge that runs across the ancient river Sawaan. The river has long since dried out and now acts only as a tributary for rain waters that flood past our ancestral kas and flow into to the river Jhelum. Tali trees, to our left, are sprinkled around in different shapes and sizes and on our right new housing colonies are springing up past thick, wild vegetation. Ever since I can remember I have had a fascination with the tali. Perhaps it was due to its cool shade, or maybe its small leaves which, to my mother's irritation, I used to love collecting as a child. Waves of nostalgia ride out of the talis. I remember now how much I loved these trees with their leaves bent down with the weight of dust, shortly before a monsoon rainfall. And I loved them then just after the rain had stopped, especially when they used to shake water off themselves, like mother's favourite goat used to do after standing in the rain. Unlike the talis, the goat forever seemed to be sad. In those days the talis stood tall and proud, like a big chesty wrestler. Now, beyond the trees, on Sawaan's furthest bank, small dots glow in the sunlight bouncing off streams of water. Soon those dots reveal themselves to be buffaloes. As we get closer I see people throwing water over their animals. Some of the dots turn out to be trucks, which, like the buffaloes, are also being cleaned.

'Toba!' Hamza mutters as our car comes to a complete stop. 'Allahjee, forgive us.'

In front of us, just past a lorry loaded with rocks, stands

the mangled wreck of a car. It had gone head first into a blue and white Peshawar bound bus that was on the wrong side of the road. The front of the car has completely caved into the bus. The interior of the car is covered in shattered glass and twisted metal. A naked plastic Barbie doll lies upside down inside the wreckage. Flies swarm around a dark brown stain on the road next to the car.

'How could anyone have survived this?' Hamza says.

No one replies.

All the traffic going past the scene of the accident slows down. It always happens like this, Hamza tells me later, some drivers slow down out of curiosity, fearing the same fate. But hardly have we crossed the bridge when the furious rush of the road begins again.

Further on, parts of the road are so badly damaged we have to slow to a crawl again. A cracked ridge runs along the sunken road. Every now and again, all manner of vehicles manically drive at each other on those parts of the road that are still flat. Somehow they miss colliding head on. I had never thought anything could happen which could make me cry more than a few passing tears. People I grew up with in England rarely cried and if they did, it was usually in private. I want to holler but there is no moisture in my desolation.

I lean back and catch a reflection of my eyes in a small mirror stuck to the ceiling of the car. The eyes are accusing. A tear clings to them as if refusing to fall, upwards. Sitting up again, I stare into the thick, dust-covered vegetation floating past the window.

'For God's sake, cousin,' I wail, turning forward. 'What are you doing, yaar?'

A car is coming towards us, overtaking a long line of crawling lorries. The car is indicating left. But there is no opening in between the lorries.

'He wants to live as well,' Hamza says calmly, maintaining his speed.

The oncoming car swerves, missing us by millimetres and somehow manages to squeeze in between two lorries.

'This is God's special land,' Shahid laughs as Hamza dodges another oncoming car.

'Don't worry, Saleem,' Hamza says, we're nearly on GT Road and we'll be flying soon.'

The Grand Trunk Road isn't anything like I remember. When I last travelled it, it was more like the one we've just come off, a gigantic bazaar, one without end, not the speeding organised chaos of this.

Our car starts to shake violently. We slow down to a crawl, close to a new Shell petrol station. Its large board advertising petrol and diesel is overshadowed by an assortment of rundown hut shops, hotels, meandering cows, buffaloes, donkeys, goats, dogs and young children, playing in the sunlight carelessly close to lanes of hectic traffic. An old woman pops out from behind a bush. She walks straight across the road. A speeding Lahore-bound van honks its horns as it narrowly misses the old woman. Unperturbed she descends into a dip, which separates the two carriageways of the Grand Trunk road and continues to cross to the other side. Our car picks up speed again. I lean back watching the old woman. A puddle of water shines off the road behind us like an oasis in a desert mirage. She is standing in the middle of the water, traffic whizzing past her on both sides. Perhaps like me she doesn't fully understand how the old road has changed. She becomes a small dot and dissolves into the mirage.

About a mile or so past the old woman our car makes a loud flapping noise.

'What's happened?' I ask.

'Nothing. Nothing,' Hamza replies. 'Just a puncture.' Getting out of the car Hamza says, 'Shahid, get some stones.'

After placing small boulders in front of the front tyres, Hamza quickly jacks the car.

'How can we make it home on this spare tyre?' I protest gaping at the spare tyre. It is completely bald. The other tyres are not much better than the spare.

'Pakistanis can fix anything,' Hamza replies.

The sun pierces my head. A surge of anger rushes through me. Could they not have hired a decent car to take me home at a time like this, I think.

The GT Road is littered with tyre repair shops. There is one near every hotel and petrol station and many more in between. They are hard to miss. They advertise their existence by placing a few old tyres on the side of the road. When we pass the first I shout, 'There's one.'

'Just relax,' Hamza says. 'We will stop soon and have a cup of tea whilst we wait.'

'I don't want any tea-shee,' I protest, 'just get me home.'

Hamza ignores me, lights a cigarette and continues driving past numerous tyre shops. I hold back an angry volcano that rumbles and hisses deep inside of me. The volcano is about to erupt as we pass the Mankiyala Stupa and Hamza decides to pull over. A ghostly chill engulfs me for a moment and then, just as quickly, dissolves into the hot air brushing my dry face. The last time I left for England, my father had stopped at the same hotel. Mother had been with us.

'See that stupa, Saleem,' Mother had said, sitting on a metal chair under the shade of a large banyan tree. The tree was still there and so were the chairs. Like a child telling a long-held secret, Mother pointed to the earthen mound, saying, 'It is thousands of years old. It was built by Buddhist people before this land was blessed by Islam. And nowadays it is the shape we build barns in for storing hay for the animals. In those days when these stupas were built, in their centre, there used to be a pot of gold which lay hidden for a thousand years without anyone disturbing it. But you English stole it and took it to England. It is probably imprisoned in some museum of yours.'

Maybe I should have gone to jail. And stayed there, safe, preserved. Frozen by that chill Bradford air that wrapped itself around me the morning they raided my bedroom.

I'd gone to bed late the night before and, as usual I'd drunk far more then I should have. In the parched clamour of hangover the first thing I thought was someone had stolen my duvet. At first I just curled up more. Impatient voices chimed with a wild discord of arbitrary thoughts.

'Come on, sunshine. Up you get,' one of them said a little louder than the others. I'd barely opened my eyes when a strong, leathery hand grabbed me by the arm and yanked me off the bed.

Police officers around my bed were filling bags with my belongings, tying them up and labelling them. The wardrobe was being emptied. One officer was closely inspecting my overburdened ashtray; another rummaged through piles of dirty clothes; a third was going through the assorted books and magazines stacked up around my bed. Someone knocked against the unshaded light bulb, sending shadows swaying across the room.

'My name is Detective Inspector Handley,' a tall, wiry plainclothes officer said matter-of-factly. He was standing on my trousers.

'You must have got bored chasing prostitutes on Lumb Lane,' I yawned.

'Now, lets make it easier for everybody, Saleem. I know you know why we're here,' Detective Inspector Handley said firmly. A shadow crossed his small face. He had a pointed chin that protruded from a deeply etched face.

'No, I don't know what you're doing in here,' I groaned back. 'And where's your warrant?'

DI Handley smiled and shook his head. Two plainclothes officers stood silently staring at me. A uniformed officer walked in, whispered something into DI Handley's ears, who nodded and the uniformed officer disappeared. Handley stepped off my trousers and kicked them towards me with a shining black boot.

'Watch me bleedin' crease.'

'Cut the crap,' the man with the heavy Bradford accent ordered, throwing a faded black T-shirt towards me. He was a stocky man, slightly shorter than the inspector, packed like a wrestler.

'You don't have t'play the 'ard one with me, you know,' I said in the broadest Yorkshire accent I could manage, putting my head through the neck of the T-shirt.

'You will go to the police station with Detective Sergeant Gower,' Handley commanded pointing to the burly Bradfordian.

I didn't flinch.

Detective Sergeant Gower grabbed my arm and hissed, 'Move.'

Using all my body weight I managed to stop from being pushed out of my bedroom.

'Gently,' the inspector ordered Gower.

DS Gower immediately loosened his grip.

It was around six o'clock in the morning. Traffic was only just beginning to sprinkle onto the roads. I used to live on my own in a two bedroom flat in Maningham. I wondered if anyone knew what was going on inside my flat. But it was too early for any of my friends. A constant stream of policemen, some in uniform and others in plain clothes walked in and out of my bedroom. Most of my clothes and books had been thrown into bags, labelled and taken away. Two plainclothes men, who had been in the room when I woke up, quietly observed the operation.

A few uniformed officers along side of DS Gower pushed me out of the bedroom. At the door I stumbled but managed to steady myself. I heard something crashing in the small bedroom opposite mine. Sajad was screaming. I had forgotten he was staying with me that night.

'What are you doing to him?' I shouted.

'Move!' Gower thundered. I could feel his breath on the back of my neck. It stank of stale beer and cigarettes.

Sajad screamed again.

'You OK, Saj?' I turned round and shouted.

A tall, uniformed policeman, who had been standing a few feet in front of me, clenched his fist and rushed towards me. My body tensed. He brought his first towards my face and stopped just short and whispered, 'You won't get another chance.'

'I am not going anywhere till I see me mate.' I had already concluded that they were under orders not to give me a hiding, at least not in my flat.

'No one is harming him,' Gower said.

'I want to see him.'

'Open the door,' DS Gower shouted towards the officer guarding the small bedroom.

Sajad was standing on the bed covering his groin with a small pillow. A policeman was pulling the pillow. Sajad nodded towards me and said, 'I am not getting dressed in front of these bastards.'

'Give the lad a bit of respect,' Detective Sergeant Gower ordered and pushed me along the corridor towards the front of the flat.

'He only came to stay with me last night.'

The night before, Sajad had turned up at my flat around 8pm, carrying an army issue rucksack on his back.

'I've left home,' he had said as soon as I opened the large, freshly painted front door. His big green eyes flashed with excitement, 'And I am never going back.'

We walked quietly up the large winding staircase. I showed Sajad the spare bedroom. He emptied his rucksack. It was full of books about weapons and soldiers. We sat around in front of my old black and white television in the living room and watched grainy figures prancing around.

'Yaar, any chah-sha? And I am starving as well,' Sajad asked.

'Go make yourself a cup. And one suger for me,' I waved towards the kitchen. 'There's some bread and eggs in the cupboard.'

Sajad didn't move for a while and sat there quietly smoking. Offering me a cigarette he said, 'I've never made chah, or eggs.'

'Boil the fucking water. Put a tea bag into some boiling water, add some milk and sugar and what have you got?'

Sajad sat in embarrassed silence for a short while before going off into the kitchen, the entrance to which was behind the sofa. I heard him fidgeting around, opening and closing drawers and banging pots and pans. A short while later he burst into the living room shouting, 'It fucking blew up.'

'What did?'

'The machoud fucking kettle,' Sajad said.

'Perhaps I should just have done it for the plonker,' I thought, walking to the kitchen. The kettle was still steaming. A liquid resembling tea was flowing over the sides. Sajad had put milk, sugar, water and eggs into the kettle.

My flat was a regular port of call for an assortment of runaways. There were those who didn't wish to get married; married ones who didn't wish to be married anymore; those that would do anything to get married and those who'd had too much to drink and were scared of facing their parents. I had come to resent the lot of them. It was not so much that I had to sit for hours and listen to them ranting and raving about the intricacies of their family politics. I not only acted as an unpaid social worker, an emotional cushion, but they also cost me money and as a general rule they never did their share of work. I'd lost track of the number of occasions I'd told the runaways, 'There's no mum here, clean your own crap.' I had some basic rules, which had evolved over years of dealing with runaways. No girlfriends; they had to open the door if their wives or parents came; no family bust-ups in my flat and the most important one was to get them to make sure they did their own cooking and cleaning. But none of these worked.

Another shove from Detective Sergeant Gower.

'I need a piss,' I said.

Gower nodded.

Two policemen were examining the bathroom. One of them had ripped off the side panelling and was shining a powerful torchlight around the back of it. He looked up at me and then stood up and walked out of the bathroom. I tried to shut the door but a uniformed officer kept it ajar by sticking his foot in the way. The back panelling of the bathroom was made of small-mirrored tiles. I could see the officer staring at me through the opening in the door. They're after your arse and you let them stick the boot in, I cursed.

The flush in the toilet was temperamental at the best of times. The only sure way was to lift the lid of the cistern, dip a hand into the water and pull the plug. I was about to do this when the policeman at the door charged in at me shouting, 'Oh no you don't.'

'It's the only way to flush it,' I said, zipping myself.

The policeman pushed me aside and started to search inside the tank. After a few seconds he shook his head at DS Gower, who'd materialised from somewhere.

'Get your shoes on,' Gower snapped, nodding towards the living room.

'Are you arresting me?'

'Get your fucking shoes on…' Gower repeated, pulling me into the front room.

Most of my walls were decorated with posters and pictures. Many had been ripped off or torn. A picture of Leila Khalid, a serene smile on her face, with a bullet in the ring on her marriage finger had been slashed with a sharp instrument. A police officer was taking a picture of a poster of Malcolm X, carrying a gun in one hand and with his other holding a curtain back, through which he looked out onto the world outside. Another picture of a mother separated from her children with the words 'Bring Anwar's children home', was being trampled under the feet of officers. The posters represented a little piece of something that made some sense in someone's life.

The living room was a large square-shaped box with two enormous windows overlooking a busy connecting main road. An officer was tuning the old black and white television with a twisted metal coat hanger for an aerial. The well worn red-brown carpet had been rolled up. Some officers were prising up floorboards. Two uniformed officers came out of the kitchen smiling triumphantly. They were carrying bin liners, full of empty milk bottles.

'What the fuck were you intending to do with these?' Gower asked.

'Chuck 'em out,' I laughed

'There are 121, sir,' a young blond-haired officer, holding one of the bin liners, said to Gower.

'You've got some explaining to do, me lad,' Gower said kicking my shoes towards me.

'Getting rid of empties,' I said putting my shoes on, 'is not *my* job in this flat. My job is to make sure there is milk here and me flatmate is supposed to return the bottles. He's a lazy twat as you can see.'

'Explain this to the judge,' Gower said pushing me out of the front room.

There were two doors in front of me and I was determined not to go through them unless I was formally arrested and forced to do so. Steadying myself I pressed onto the floorboards and asked, 'Is there a crime called keeping empties?'

A couple of heavies walked towards me.

'You can either walk down the stairs quietly or go down with the aid of my boot,' Gower explained.

I flattened my back against the wall.

'You're going to the station,' Gower boomed.

'Like fuck I am,' I protested trying to push off the advancing heavies. 'Not till you tell me why.'

The other officers in the room stopped to look at me with amusement. The two heavies grabbed my arms and quickly twisted them behind my back.

'You've nowt on me,' I protested as the heavies forced me out of the room.

I was frogmarched down the stairs and whisked out of the front door. Dawn was just passing. A few misty shadows clung stubbornly to the ground. There was hardly any traffic on the roads. A postman, steam billowing from his mouth, dropped letters into people's houses. A few neighbours – strangers – stared at me. A group of elderly workers, by the corner of the traffic lights, waited for their lift to work. I had always seen them there. But the pavement felt like the beginning of a road I'd not been on before. I was shoved into the back seat of an unmarked car. Police vehicles, with beacons flashing had blocked both sides of the road. Numerous police cars, with their beacons flashing were parked up and down the road. A helicopter hovered above. Moments later we were racing towards the city centre, with two police outriders in front and a police van behind. The helicopter tracked our journey to the station. I felt alone, and thought of Mother, just as I had when I first arrived. I closed my eyes, and as always, saw her crying as she dressed me for the first time in western clothes.

I lie in the sad shade of the banyan tree on the chairs in the mechanic's yard surrounded by stacks of tyres in varying stages of decay. A gentle wind ruffles the leaves of the banyan tree making its long, dangling roots tremble. The tree's shade stretches over our car, spreading to the dry jagged lips of the road. Just beyond the shade lies the splattered carcass of a dog. Vultures dodge speeding traffic to peck on its flesh. Passers-by cover their noses. A large, white goat nervously eyes the vultures, steps ghost-like out of the sunshine and strolls into the shade straight towards me. Another cool wind kisses my cheeks. I close my eyes as an unwanted smile latches itself to my lips. Perhaps this is the chair my mother sat in, on my last visit. Perhaps this is the same goat, I wonder, wiping the smirk off my lips, that on that last occasion, had stolen a cake from under her nose.

'You are surely owned by bastards!' Mother cursed the goat as it darted away with her cake. Father, Karim and I had roared with laughter watching her leaping over the chair after it. Like a fat kukkar she had flapped after it, followed it through the bush and disappeared into the thick green foliage of ripening maize field behind.

We were still laughing when she came back. Her kameez was ripped and her dupatta was covered in thorns.

'Her owners must be childless,' Mother had cursed. 'They must have been conceived by pigs!'

'You have torn a two hundred rupee suit for a two rupee cake!' Father said, wiping tears from his face.

I open my eyes. The goat is gone. Mother isn't there. A vulture with the dog's intestines dangling from its beak is warding off zealous colleagues. Brown film has formed in the cup of tea that someone must have been placed in front of me whilst I'd had my eyes closed. A few tealeaves are stuck to the sides of the cup. A dead fly is floating in the tea. Shahid, who has been standing silently close by, grabs my arm and stops me tipping the tea onto the ground. Taking the cup out of my hand he dips his finger into it, collects the fly in the film of tea clinging to his finger. 'This is a Pakistani lachi,' he jokes, pretending to lick his finger. 'It improves taste.'

'Pour it away, yaar,' I groan. 'Who knows it may have sat on shit or something.'

'We can't be frightened of little flies,' Shahid replies downing the tea in a couple of gulps.

'How much longer will this take?' I ask, waving across towards Hamza who is giving instructions to a young boy.

Shahid stares blankly at the remains of the dog. Kicking an empty can, I stroll towards Hamza.

Hamza is engrossed in a passionate discussion with the puncture repair boy. The boy is standing in a naked patch of sunlight in between the shade of the banyan tree and that of the veranda of a tin-roofed hotel. He is thorny bodied, ten- or twelve-years-old. He has sharp, nervous eyes and a small, round, grease-stained face. A tattered, over-sized oily vest hangs loosely over his body. He stands barefoot in the sun quietly shaking his shaven head.

'Nothing I can do on price, elder brother,' the repair boy says firmly. 'Masterjee is not here and I am only his student and I have to do what he says and there is nothing else I can do...'

'What's going on?' I interrupt.

'Just keep quiet, Saleem,' Hassan grunts. Along with Saber he is sitting on a bed inside the tyre repair shop, under a ceiling fan.

The boy steels a searching glance at me. Turning to Hamza he points to a dusty old tyre inner tube and says, 'I can give you a genuine English tube, or I can repair your tyre, and that is a lot more than Masterjee would have me do. But as he is not here I will do this much for you.'

Walking out of the shade I shout at Hamza in English, 'Just pay him and let's go.' The sun stabs into my scalp. Hamza doesn't understand English. Switching into Pothowari, 'Yaar. Let's pay him what he wants.'

The puncture repair boy snatches another sly glance at me. He lowers his head and starts making patterns in the oil stained ground with his foot.

'Just repair this puncture,' Hamza orders the boy. Turning to me he says, 'And this is not England.'

'I just want to get home,' I nod meekly. 'Money doesn't matter.'

The boy hesitates for a few moments and then goes into the shop and comes back out with two thick four-inch square pieces of metal. He strolls over to the hotel's tandoor, nods at the tandoorchi, a thin, sweat-drenched man who keeps leaning in and out of the tandoor, slapping uncooked rotis onto the sides and pulling out crispy brown puffed ones. Inbetween these actions, the tandoorchi manages to take a few drags from a cigarette. After each drag he places the cigerette back in between his toes. Through a ventilation hole, the repair boy places the metal pieces deep inside the tandoor.

The smell of fresh rotis coming out of the tandoor makes hunger dance in my stomach. 'Why is he not fixing our puncture?' I ask Hamza.

'He is,' Hamza replies. 'Electricity is down.'

'Let's buy a new tube and go.'

'Look, yaar,' Hamza replies calmly, 'what's happened has happened. Be a strong man.'

What is a strong man supposed to do, I wonder? They must think I'm a wimp. But I don't care for their thoughts. My mother is waiting for me and here they are haggling over a few pennies.

The puncture boy expertly takes out the old tube from the tyre, fills it with air from a large pressurised tank and dips it into a tub of black water. After locating the hole from the bubbles he wipes the area around it, marks it with chalk and flings it onto the ground. He picks up a pair of tongs and goes to the tandoor. He returns a few moments later, holding the red-hot pieces of metal with the tongs. He dips the metal plates into the tub of water. They sizzle. Plumes of steam float up into the shade. The boy pulls the plates out of the water and waits for the steam to evaporate. He spits on them a few times. His spit bounces into oblivion. He waits for a few moments, then places a rubber patch on the hole of the tube and presses the metal plates on top of the patch. After checking the puncture has been repaired, he places the tube back inside the tyre and begins bashing the tyre with a large hammer until it settles around the rim of the wheel. Driving the air into the tyre, the boy constantly moves the rim to ensure that the tyre fits neatly. He replaces the repaired tyre onto the car when an argument between him and Hamza suddenly flares up, with Hamza protesting over the quality of the new valve the boy has added.

'I can guarantee you it's genuine Valaiti, elder brother,' the boy says, 'and that is why it is three rupees more.'

'Look son,' Hamza says, 'I was driving a car when you were still drinking your mother's milk and this valve is as Valaiti as my arse.'

The tyre boy descends into thoughtful silence, shakes his head and takes the money from Hamza. 'I'm glad it's you and not unclejee who owns this car. He would have got me to fix his tyre and just sworn at me and gone on his way. Just as he always does.'

By the time we leave, the vultures have finished with the dog and the leftovers have all been driven flat into the road.

A large earth digger with the letters NLC inscribed into its sides, claws into the brown innards of a hill as we approach Gujarkhan. Sitting under constantly rising waves of dust, rows of thin men in red turbans are working alongside all manner of large road-laying machines. Some of the men are squatting, shaded only by the dust clouds. They smash rocks with large metal hammers. Metal bashing against rock punctuates the noise of the machines. Some of the men wear flip-flops, whilst others steady the rocks with the cracked souls of their bare feet. Sparks and rock splinters shoot up, hanging over them like flies over a fresh wound. A cigar smoking babu wearing a white colonial hat over his T-shirt and trousers is hovering over freshly flattened earth that's being sprayed with water. In the distance, the rooftops of Gujarkhan sparkle. Our car jerks violently and then the engine cuts out.

'What now?' I throw up my arms in disbelief.

'It's overheating,' Hamza replies.

I sit in silence as we freewheel down the hill into Gujarkhan, slowing down as the road flattens. A throng of people, buses, cars, tangas, and trolleys explode into view. Whilst I sit silently the others discuss the intricate details of some card game or other which they'd all played at the airport waiting for me to arrive. There is a dispute over who owes whom money. Our car comes to a complete standstill. Sounds of the city hover over us like the roar of an aeroplane.

'Let's just get a taxi,' I plead.

Hamza ignores me and gets out of the car.

'I can guarantee this car will make it,' Hamza says confidently opening the bonnet. The other three follow him out and stare inquisitively over his shoulders. Shutting the bonnet with a loud bang Hamza says, 'This car could make it to England and back, with Uncle Shafqat driving it!'

England and back. To that cold, clinical land where people talk of change but never do, and back. To a land where sons never return, and back. To a country of forgetfulness, and back. What have I done with my life?

Hamza pours water into the radiator. A jet of furious steam shoots out of it, narrowly missing his face. He waits a few moments and then puts more water into it. The car stops steaming. Hamza gets back into the car, turns on the heating and we set off again. We sit silently as our car edges through the chaos of Gujarkhan. We slide through a traffic jam of whispers, picking up speed along the GT Road. The closer we get to Banyala village the more familiar the surroundings become. There is only one major bridge left before we turn off for the final leg.

The Tarakki Bridge, like large swathes of the GT Road, is under construction. Once again we become stuck in a chaos of angry vehicles, blanketed by a cloud of dust and exhaust fumes. Only one lane of the bridge is open and everyone wants to cross it at the same time. Some army VIPs are being led towards the bridge. A helicopter hovers noisily above us. Every few yards soldiers wearing handkerchiefs across their faces stand to attention. Countless horns roar intermittently, creating a maddening dim. Beggars, water and newspaper vendors run from one vehicle to the next. A few bearded men pray under the flimsy shade of a dying tree.

A few lathi and machine gun-toting policeman finally manage to clear a path for the dignitaries. Wailing sirens compete with the horns. The VIP cavalcade races past us. The helicopter moves on. Frustrated engines, turning over till now, begin to rev louder, waiting for the last of the VIP escorts to pass. Everyone makes a mad dash for the bridge. Somehow we manage to get through.

The road curves up in a sharp incline. This place had once been called Pohai, the turn. We begin our ascent up its snake-like curve, behind a monster of an overloaded truck, crawling up the hill. What had been so important in my life to have stopped me even sending a message? It should be me lying in that grave, not her. I shiver at the memory of the letterbox outside my uncle's house in England. How could I have been drunk? How could I have cursed her even as I posted the thing. That cursed letter, which would arrive after me. What will I do with it now? Someone is laughing, a macabre laughter deep in some dark crevice of my head. I want to race inside and go back in time. Just once. To sit with her, even for a moment and to beg her for forgiveness. Even if it is to hear a 'No' from her mouth. Just one moment is all I ask of you, Almighty. What is one moment to you? What difference would it make to you? But the laughter mocks me.

My stomach tightens with a burning, groping pain, one reaching upwards for a way out, but all exits are blocked. I gasp and swallowing the pain is strangely sweet this time. I want to be rid of it and yet I need it to linger, to burn and consume me in all its fury. I spit out of the window.

We are close to the highest point on the road. Soon I'll see my village and beyond it the outline of the hills, stretching high above our ancestral graveyard. I close my eyes, but they spring back open. The momentary darkness is splattered by the all-embracing sunshine. There's the village, far away, across the twinkling waters of the kas. The minaret of the mosque winks in the sunlight. Everything seems to move in slow motion. When we reach the summit, I shut my eyes, dreading the sight of the graveyard. I hold my eyes shut. My childhood returns. It was from this point on the hill that we used to catch buses before a road was built through the village. And below the hill, in the small gorges, covered in all shades of green, sprouting out from the red-brown earth was the place I used to come with my mother when she came to cut grass for our black and white cow. I could see the young boy that was me, sitting in the shade of a wild tali tree, stabbing ants with a small stick as mother made small piles of grass, her kameez sticking to her sweaty back. Her dupatta tied to the back of her head.

'And don't you go poking your little fingers in any holes,' she used to say. 'A snake might sting you. And then what will I do?'

It was a mystery to me how she could see me with her back turned towards me, just when I was about to poke my fingers into an interesting hole. I was never scared in the jungle even when mother was out of sight. For I knew she could move faster than any monster lurking out there, and no one was stronger than her. I feared not the charaels, who could change from a goat to a woman and then to some other beast, always trying to entice naughty children towards them, so that they could devour them up in one fell swoop. Nor was I scared of any other creature of the jungle for I knew that mother would always see them, no matter which bush or tree they tried to hide under. Sometimes when I became bored, waiting for mother, I would collect small bundles of dry sticks and pile them up into larger ones, just like she used to do, before putting them all together into an enormous, demon sized bundle. She would always tell me off for doing this. On these occasions she would say,

'You could have been pricked by a thorn. And this grass is so sharp it could cut right through your little hand. And then what would I do?'

But there were times in the jungle when I became frightened of the noises and screams far more terrifying than those any charael could possibly have made. The first time I heard this noise, I ran screaming to Mother, scattering the small bundles of grass, which she'd placed here and there. She embraced me tightly in her strong, moist arms. Her sweat fell on my face. Her white teeth shone in her wet, brown face. She laughed uncontrollably. I knew that she knew the reason for my fright. She always knew my fears. Pointing in the direction of the whistling monster, just visible worming away over the tops of the soft blowing saroot grass, from which she often made brooms for the house, she said, 'That, my sweet moon, is just a train.' Holding me up she said, 'And it's going to Karachi.' Pointing to small dots on top of the train she said, 'And see all those people sitting on the top and standing by the doors, they are all going to Karachi as well.'

'Is Karachi far, ammajee?' I asked.

'It is far, far away.'

'Even further than Dina?'

'Dina is only eleven miles away,' Mother kissed me on the head and said, 'We can walk to Dina, but Karachi is so far away that we have to go there by train. It takes a whole night and one whole day to get there. That is how far it is.'

'I don't want to go to Karachi.'

'I wouldn't let you go that far away from me, chhallayah,' Mother said putting me down. 'And if you went so far away from me, then what would I do?'

From that day onwards, whenever I heard a train go by I used to think of Karachi, a distant land, that consisted of lots of trains with people sitting on the top and dangling out of open doors.

Going up from the Pohai, we are fast approaching our turning. I can smell Mother's sweat and the scent of freshly cut grass of my childhood. No one has said a word ever since we crossed the Tarakki Bridge. And now we turn. Many people are waiting for a bus next to the jalebee shack. It still looks the same in its outward appearance as it had been when I'd last seen it. But today it stuck out like an unhealed scar. Oh, I had sat there, on the worn out straw mat and eaten jalebee with her. Accusing eyes stare at me from every direction. I know what some of them are thinking. He's returned now! All the leaves of all the bushes and trees become still. My pounding heart drowns out all other sounds, or perhaps nature has gone silent. Everything seems to have been drenched of life. There are no clouds in the angry blue sky – they too have deserted me. I wrestle with my simmering volcano. And then we go down the hill. I sink into a dull trance, pulled under by invisible currents swarming with accusations. And then we are over the bridge under which the trains went to Karachi. A bit further down, down a sharp sloping hill, just as we cross another small bridge, that squats over the shining waters of the kas, I see a little boy running after a woman who is carrying a large bundle of grass. A chill runs down my back, I lean out of the window and yell, 'Ammajee!'

The woman stops and slowly turns towards us steadying the weighty burden on her head. She grabs the little boy's hand and pulls him towards her as our car passes. Her kameez is stuck in patches to her moist body. Shock spreads over her face as she recognises me.

Coming out of the kas we pass a group of men playing cards under the shade of an old kikker tree. They stand up as we get closer. And then I freeze as I see a tent inside our graveyard. The volcano erupts. I scream, 'Oh, God, what have I done?'

And then the car stops. But I don't get out. There is nowhere to go. There is wailing all around. I rock to and fro. My sister, Shabnam, runs crying towards me. I now stand outside of the car and try to get back inside, but there are so many hands holding me, pushing me, caressing me. My legs shake or perhaps it is the ground underneath. I fight the hands and the crying and try again to crawl back inside the car. Shabnam calls out hoarsely, 'You can't make her wait any longer.'

I am inside the graveyard. A tent is shading her grave. It is surrounded by freshly dug earth. I open my mouth, the volcano explodes and the hills echo a cry so loud that it digs its roots deep in my head, splitting me in two. Then I see a body, deep inside the hole, wrapped in a white caffan. I fall to the ground clawing the earth. An uncle standing down in the pit, moves the caffan off her face. She is dark, almost black. This is not my mother; surely not I scream. I turn away from the grave. Someone asks me something and I nod. Men start hurriedly filling the grave.

'No. No. NO,' I yell. 'Stop. Stop. Stop. I have not said my goodbye yet.'

But it is too late. Men throw shovelfuls of soil into the grave, which is already half full. Mother has gone too far away now. A large man lifts me off the ground and hugs me and cries, 'I have become a widower.'

Snatching myself free from him, I run to the grave and jump in roaring, 'Get her out. Get her out. I haven't said goodbye yet.'

Someone pulls me out and I join the men hurrying earth into mother's grave with my hands.

High above in the sky, under which I grab fistfuls of hot, red-brown earth, an aeroplane takes its human cargo to some distant land. Rugged hills below garland us in barren silence. They stand still, those semi-naked, all-seeing hills with sprinklings of discoloured greenery, absorbing this inhuman human tale. And the bloodshot eyes of those standing round, where had they all come from, in this sun-soaked terrace of death over-grown with weed and wild jandhs stunted by goats? I throw my head back, narrow my eyes on the plane: why had you taken me away? Why had you held me back? To the hills: did you know you would see me so?

How many others have you seen, and remained silent? That dark, dark woman, draped in the white cotton caffan, how could you have been my mother? What have I done? How much pain have I made you suffer for you to go so black? And why have I let them take you away from me, so soon after seeing you so? Why have I not asked for another moment?

Men shake my hands saying: 'It is God's will.'

'Be strong. Almighty will help you get through.'

'She was God's creation and He has taken her back.'

'Be strong. Time will heal, my son.'

'We all have to go. Some go sooner than others do. But we all have to go.'

'May God give her a place in heaven.'

'We are all born out of earth and it is to this earth we return. It is nature's law.'

A man with a shining silver beard wearing dark sunglasses embraces me, weeping wildly: 'You don't recognise me, son. You used to play in my lap, but that was before you went to England.'

The word 'England' sends my body into spasm. The volcano erupts again and I scream. The hills sigh my cries back at me. Holding me tighter and tighter the silver bearded man whispers in my ear, 'You are lucky, my son. You could at least say farewell to her.'

'Is this my luck?' I point to the grave.

'I was working in Karachi when my mother died,' the silver bearded man says softly. 'All I saw was the earth under which she was buried.'

'But you must have cared for yours?'

'Everyone cares for their own mothers,' he says pushing away from me.

'But I didn't. I cared only for me. That is all that seemed to matter.'

'And look at you now. Silly boy,' the old man rebukes. 'If you didn't care you would not have come back so soon.'

Embracing me again the silver bearded man starts singing a baint,

> *Payoo maray, hik diya bujna*
> *Ma maray, muk jani sansaar ni lo*
> *Kuthay Ma tay kuthay Payoo.*

> When Father dies, a lamp extinguishes
> When Mother dies, the world plunges into darkness
> There lies the difference, in Mother and Father.

If there was an everlasting hell then surely it was trapped in this iota of time, where our prodigal son now basks, returned from the land where the streets are 'sonay nal sajain nay'.

Clasping a fistful of earth from my mother's grave, I brush past people whose faces prick my eyes like unconnected visions in a recurring dream. I stop before a flimsy tin gate that hangs precariously at the entrance of the graveyard. I hadn't noticed it on my way in. Light blue patches of faded paint struggle against encroaching rust. It moans loudly each time someone touches it. As a lost child is pulled towards the sound of its mother's voice, I feel drawn to the gate. Its metal groans sound like mother's lullaby. I am a little embarrassed, for this gate knows me, but I cannot place it.

Like a monsoon cloud that can quickly invade the brightest of days, bringing thunder and lightning in angry spasms, teasing and toying with the thirsty earth, threatening to drown it, only to disappear again, my mind stalls. Then, like a downpour, like a sideways swirl of wet, cool winds aching for the dry grass, my old friend finds me. Before making its way to this graveyard this gate used to hang at the entrance to my mother's house, attached to the outer walls, which she herself had built. When I saw it, it had just been hung, against Mother's protestations. She'd been happy with the original wooden one. Her father had given that to her when she had first built the outer wall and like my grandfather, that gate had been all but cracked with age. Rusty, star-shaped studs held the hardwood frame together. With time it had become increasingly difficult to shut. At night, even after fastening it with a thick metal chain it was necessary to prop it up by nudging a heavy log against it. Despite this, a slight push from the outside would create a gaping hole. Village donkeys, cows, buffaloes and goats all seemed to understand this. But it was the dogs that had mastered the art of getting past it with ease. Not that they needed to come through the gate in order to enter our courtyard, for the walls were so low that but for the crippled and dying, canines could easily scale them to scavenge their fill.

I had been in the house when my father called the carpenter to replace the old wooden gate with the metal one.

'But my father gave me this,' Mother had protested in a strung voice. 'In those days it cost over one hundred rupees and he said that I was never to remove it from this house.'

'Come on. Come on,' Father said to the carpenter who stood unsure of what to do. 'Women never let go of anything.'

'Lalajee had been so proud when this gate first went up,' Mother moaned as she made tea for the carpenter. '"Your house needed a purdah," he said to me. "I have been meaning to do this for a long time. And now, mind you never take this gate off. Gates like this don't come by every day and when they have gone, then that which they protected will be unsafe".'

'You can't live on memories,' Father said as the carpenter bashed out the old wooden gate.

I had sat bemused, thinking perhaps people always talked like this in the villages. For me the gate had no meaning. I was glad with the thought that my short stay here might see a reduction in the number of stray dogs who wandered into the house.

Reality comes storming back as Hamza pushes the aching

gate wide open for me to leave. Walking out I look right towards the car. It is parked near some soft-blowing blades of saroot. This is a child's stone's throw away from the gorian alla pul – the white man's bridge in whose shade flourish freshwater springs. As a child I had played under that bridge and during my last visit had sat in its coolness, which remained so irrespective of the heat around. I could still hear the echoes of that time. Once we had spent a hot day playing cards, our voices dancing off the damp, dark walls of the bridge. We had sat deep underneath the bridge, just below an arch through which light flooded in as though from a torch. We had played a game called 'bank', in which everyone put money into a kitty and then tried their best, through fair or foul ways to win the pot. It was an intensely absorbing game in which each ace or picture card was valued at ten points and the rest at their face value. We played with two packs shuffled together. Everyone was dealt 13 cards each. You could finish by making a running flush of four cards and the rest had also to be flushes of three. If you were unable to make a running flush of four cards then you were penalised with full points to the value of your hand and these were doubled. There was always a wild card and that was the opposite colour to the card that was turned over. If you were lucky enough to have more than one wild card, the others would be fined an extra 25 points per wild card. If two people had two wild cards each, they would be fined 50 points and the rest a hundred. The objective of the game was to avoid reaching the dreaded mark of 500. At which point you had to leave the game. You could rejoin by paying 50 percent of the kitty entry, but you had to rejoin at the numbers of the highest player. This could mean 499. There were constant arguments, which were peppered with the most colourful of rustic obscenities. But it rarely went beyond hot words. We played in dread of the police for it was illegal to gamble. As a precaution, we would always chip in and pay someone to stand and act as a lookout. Once our lookout had fallen asleep whilst on duty. Regaining consciousness when a police patrol was virtually upon him, he had managed to shout out a warning.

'Pulse! Pulse! Pulse!'

The bridge had echoed.

Everyone scattered through the opening at the top. Some grazed themselves on the sharp edges of the white man's bridge, others shredded their bodies as they dived through thorn bushes. I slipped and sprained my ankle. Had it not been for Hamza's quick thinking, I, too, could have been among those who were captured, beaten and forced to buy back their freedom. Hamza had hurriedly got me to lie down under the shade of an Afghan kiker tree.

'When they come over to us, just speak to them in English.' Hamza whispered covering his head under his parna.

We were of course pretending to be asleep out there in the sweltering heat. Through the corner of my eye I saw the policemen emerging out of the rear end of the bridge. They looked like hungry jackals coming out of their den. They were all out of breath. Some of them ran after the other players. A fat policeman huffed and puffed his way towards us. Inbetween catching his breath, he let out a barrage of obscenities.

'What sort of Pakhand is this?' the fat policeman thundered in an accent I barely recognised.

Sitting up I noticed his vulture eyes twinkling in the sunlight.

'What the bleedin' 'ell is this?' I protested in the broadest Bradford accent I could manage. The police officer was about to strike me with his lathi when he suddenly stopped.

Hamza lay as still as a corpse. I could hear his heart pounding in his chest.

The policeman looked over his shoulders towards an officer who had just come across the bridge. He was bent over out of exhaustion.

'Inspector saab!' the fat policeman shouted. 'Look at this drama saab. We have a desi angraiz here.' Turning towards Hamza the policeman kicked him on the soles of his feet and asked, 'Are you angraiz as well?'

'Jee saab,' Hamza replied calmly sitting up. 'What's the matter, saab.'

'You were in there playing cards, weren't you?' the policeman asked a little unsure of himself.

'Playing cards, saab?' Hamza replied. 'Not us, saab. Just relaxing with my cousin who has come over from England.'

'Relaxing in this heat,' the policeman cursed, 'you lying son of a ...'

'Don't you dare swear at me,' Hamza interrupted indignantly. 'My uncle is DSP and you'll live to regret every word.'

The policeman stopped mid-sentence. He turned and walked over to the inspector. A moment or so later he returned and asked,

'What is your uncle's name.'

'Choudry Akram Ali,' Hamza lied.

'Where is he based?'

'Jhelum.'

After a brief thoughtful silence the policeman said in a subdued tone, 'You must know names of gamblers.'

'We were asleep,' Hamza said getting more and more confident with each moment.

Turning to me the policeman asked, 'And you?'

'He doesn't understand,' Hamza said.

'And I was conceived by a pig,' the policeman cursed, turning away from us.

It was just as well for I was about to say in Pothowari, 'And you were too', but a quick glare from Hamza ensured it remained rattling inside me.

Walking away from the gate I can still hear the echoes of Hamza's roaring laughter after the police had gone in search of the gamblers. Hamza's laughter was bouncing around the broken hills in the middle of which was cut a swath of cultivable land. The Afghan kikker tree is only a teardrop away from where I now stand. I am unsure where my next step should be. Hamza tries to direct me towards the car.

An army of black ants, unconcerned with their own individual fate, marches up and down a dusty brown path that has recently been ripped out by the blades of a bulldozer. Hamza keeps rubbing his feet into the soft earth. His movements send countless ants to their death. Their colleagues, some carrying leaves twice their own size, move around the grave of ants and go about the chores of their existence. Their pathway is like the finger drawings of a child, but it is decorated with the paw marks of dogs, and deep imprints of cattle and deeper ones of buffaloes. Small marks of goats are mixed with human footprints – some barefoot, others with shoes. The path is cracked in parts and smooth in others. A few jagged boulders sit untidily in the middle.

Turning away from Hamza I walk up the path towards the village. The graveyard has all but emptied. A couple of men put the final touches to what Mother has become. Some women stand under a dead kikker, with dark outstretched limbs, not far from the gate.

A part of me wants to run to my mother's house, as fast as my feet can; perhaps then I can be rid of this nightmare. Another part wants to run in the opposite direction, back on the road from which I had come, back on the aeroplane on which I'd come, back to England.

But for one lorry wailing past where the woman with the grass stood, the road is empty. From where I stand I can see traffic moving on the Pohai. A screaming Karachi-bound train pops out from behind the hills. Memories of a life in Karachi slash into my head. This was not the Karachi clogged up by trains overflowing with human cargo, but one where I'd lived sometime before going to England. There was a bazaar full of people and shops overflowing with colours and voices. I was holding onto a tall woman. She didn't look like anyone I had ever seen before. She was someone very special. I knew that because everyone in the bazaar was staring at her and a man, quietly walking by her side, was taking photographs of things here and there. I had believed her to be a fairy, she wore a Pakistani kameez on top of red, white and blue trousers, striped with stars. He was a little smaller than her and wearing a hat with tassles swinging from the edges; he was an angel, the ones my mother used to tell me about, who came to children who were good and listened to their mothers and didn't stray from home. True, I had strayed and had got lost, but this fairy with her wide trousers had found me and I was safe and she was buying me all manner of toys. The bazaar had whispered:

'Angraiz.'

'Amreekan.'

I imagined these to be the names of the fairy and the angel. I could not understand what the fairy said to me. But each time I looked at something, she bought it for me. Mother had come charging out of the crowd, screaming like I'd never seen her before. Snatching me away from my fairy she had shouted, 'Give me back my son.'

Grabbing the toys out of my hand, Mother had thrown them at the fairy. The poor thing had been terrified by her. Mother kept screaming at the fairy and the fairy kept saying something back to her. But neither of them understood the other, or so I thought at least. I tried to free myself from Mother as some other children were taking my toys. But it was no good. Mother was not going to lose me again. A funny little man popped out of the crowd, which had surrounded us, and to my surprise he could speak the fairy's language.

'They are visitors to our country,' the funny little man said to my mother. 'You should not be so rude to our guests.'

'Why did you take my son away?' Mother asked pointing a finger at my nervous fairy.

'I was only buying him toys,' the fairy said through the funny little man.

'Just tell me,' Mother asked, 'how could you walk away with another mother's son?'

The funny little man whispered something to my fairy.

'He looked so lost and cute and I wanted to buy him something,' the fairy said through the funny little man.

'And you think he has no mother?' my mother had shouted, holding me even tighter.

The fairy's face had turned red right in front of my eyes. Perhaps she was a bad fairy, I wondered, for Mother hadn't told me of any good fairy, which changed the colour of her face like this one. Mother became even more enraged when the fairy put some money in her hand. Throwing the money in the fairy's face, she wept, 'I don't want this… and you can't have my son.'

I was shocked, watching Mother throw all those notes away; whenever I asked *her* for money for some sweets or kulfi, she always said we didn't have any and I should wait till the end of the month when Father got paid.

III

After whistling the broken fragments of its song across a fiery sky, the Karachi-bound train disappears behind a jagged line of hills. Its sigh is cleansed out of existence by a sudden gust of hot, keening wind. Small dead leaves and passing blades of grass swirl around in tiny tornadoes that scrape along the dusty ground. As though beckoning me on, the wind sweeps debris off a small path that leads towards two craggy centurion hills sitting at the rear entrance to Banyala.

The hills are now much further back than they used to be. Long twisted Palahi roots cling to the outer edges of the hills. A few grazing goats balance effortlessly on the overhangs. Below them and the roots, a path curves through a dark swathe of the hills' shadow. I stop just before the shade. Someone has stuck a thick, twisted root into the head of a snake. A crow nervously pecks at the flesh. I flinch nervously. Taking my eyes off the snake, I glance back across to the graveyard. Mother is now free from us. Knots of people are walking up towards me.

'Elder brother,' a young man cries hoarsely, 'and so you have come back.'

Turning towards the voice I am startled by the outline of a tall youth running out of the shadows. He embraces me tightly. Karim, my younger brother, has become a man and I am reduced to a child.

'My mother is dead,' Karim cries. Pushing himself away

from me he runs towards the graveyard calling, 'Go home, elder brother. Go home. She has left you a present.'

Slowly I begin to run homewards, jogging past falling walls, exposed rusting pipework, a cow dozing in the coil of its tether. A group of women walking towards me stop and step aside. Near the cobbler's house, the path narrows and is blocked by four children playing marbles.

'Move away, move away!' a child shouts grabbing a fistful of marbles from inside a large chalked circle on ground, 'Amma Shamim's son has come back from Valait.'

'You leave my marbles where they are,' another child, much smaller than the first, protests.

I stop and bend double, catching my breath. An old woman, with a cracked face, as dark as my mother's in her grave, comes out of a house, close to the children. Slapping the second child around the head, she chides, 'Shut up you little bastards.' She walks over to me and rubs her rough, moist hands across my face, tuts and sighs, 'Oh-kho! Has my son met his mother?' Hugging me affectionately she whispers into my ear in a cracking voice, 'And what was all that wealth you earned in England for? But Almighty be thanked, for she went finally to rest after you came back. No soil crossed her face until her son had come to her.' Letting me go she wipes my forehead saying, 'Go now, ma sadqay. It is hot. Go now into the shade of your home, built so lovingly by your mother.' As I pull away from her she adds sorrowfully, 'But who will welcome you now?'

Taunting snatches from my last trip to Pakistan keep coming back. As soon as Mother had seen me she had shouted a joyous note, which had risen above the din of the chaos in Islamabad Airport's Arrivals lounge. She placed a garland of jasmine flowers, with two large red roses at its end, around my neck and had then suddenly plucked a necklace made out of folded rupees from somewhere, and hung it round my neck as well. This one was embroidered with shining, golden tinsel.

'It is for good luck, my pardesi son,' Mother said, kissing me on my cheeks. Sensing my irritation at the necklaces, she added, 'You must leave it on till you get home.'

'I am not a mah-raja you know,' I protested.

'God willing you will be one day soon, my son,' she sang. 'And I will find you a pretty little bride, but for now you are just that, a little mah-raja.'

A drummer's loud rattle greeted my arrival in the village that day. A few people stared at me as I walked slowly homewards, past the corner of a house that filled me oddly with fear. But this didn't last long and I walked on through the winding streets, picking my way round a pile of buffalo dung. Turning into the tight galli that led to our house, I realised the drummer was playing in our courtyard.

The entrance to our house had a garland of red roses draped over it and judging by the smell of fresh lime, all the walls had been recently whitewashed. The whole house had been lovingly decorated with long lines of brightly coloured confetti. Young children stood close to a large oil drum, filled with iced rose sherbet and gulped quickly whilst inquisitively eyeing me as I walked past under the confetti. My father distributed sweets as thanksgiving for my safe return. The whole village seemed to have been crammed into our house. Later that day my father sacrificed a cow and distributed its meat throughout the village.

As soon as he saw me, the drummer started lashing at his tthol and limped forward. Tassels, that hung off the edges of the drum, danced from side to side as he moved. This had been the drummer of my childhood songs. He was a short, dark man. He seemed shorter now. His curly hair had thinned, and his round nose seemed rounder and wider with age. He looked at me and smiled. Though he'd lost all his teeth, it was still a youthful smile. Placing his right hand's drumstick in his mouth, he shook my hand, all the time continuing a rhythm with his left stick.

'Welcome home, my son,' Bava Abdullah said breathing heavily.

'And you are still playing this tthol, Bava,' I smiled.

Bava Abdullah took a deep breath, pulled the stick out of his mouth, smiled and replied, 'This is all that was written for my miserable caste and this is life, my son.' Turning his eyes away from me he started to beat the drum with both his sticks.

Three small women, smiling greedily, materialised from somewhere. They squatted close to an old hibiscus plant, with its red open-mouthed flowers dangling above their heads. Bava Abdullah stared at them suspiciously. The oldest among the women, perhaps older than my grandmother, had no teeth. She sat between the others and carefully started to unwrap something. A few moments later she held up a battered old ttholki and looked up towards Bava Abdullah, who turned round and continued on with his drumming. The old woman started to bash a rhythm out on the ttholki. Her companions joined her in a song. My father nodded towards Abdullah who stopped drumming. Most of the people ignored the singing. Irrespective of the song, their rhythm and tone remained the same. Abdullah hovered irritably around the women as they mixed Indian film and local folk songs singing,

Ghar aya ni maharra pardesi
ho-ho-ho ni ghar aya ni mahara pardesi
ho-ho-ho ni nimbooaan naan jorra as-saan baghay
    vichoon lorrayah
ho-ho-ho ni pardesi putraha rah pahlaan tera as-saan
    malay-ya…

Father, flushed with a huge smile, walked up to the women and offered the oldest one a ten rupee note. She stopped playing and stood shaking her head. Her silver-grey hair stuck to her head with sweat.

'We are not beggars, saab,' the old woman said indignantly refusing to accept the ten rupee note from my father. 'We have just come here to celebrate in your happiness.'

My father grinned and offered her twenty rupees. The other two women stood up as well and started shaking their heads in disagreement.

'Keep this, my son,' the old woman said to Father, 'I have told you we are not asking for this money.'

'Then what in God's name do you want?' Father laughed.

'Give them a thousand rupees each,' someone shouted mischievously.

The women went quiet.

'Come on, hurry up,' Father asked, 'what do you want?'

'One hundred rupees each, a suit each and a meal,' the old woman replied quickly.

'One hundred rupees for all of you,' Father said handing the old woman a hundred rupee note. Pointing to a corner of the house, he added, 'Eat over there and then go on God's road.'

The old woman shook her head in disbelief, taking the hundred rupees from my father. Hardly had the singing women started to eat when Bava Abdullah's ttholl burst into life again. Someone held a ten rupee note on top of my head. Bava Abdullah limped over, kept the rhythm going with his left hand and with his right he took the ten rupee note. Holding it up for all to see, he yelled, 'Vail, vail, a lakh rupee vail, Choudry Saleem ni vail.'

Every few moments someone placed a ten rupee note on my head and Bava Abdullah collected it and blessed them for making such a generous gift in my honour. Someone placed a hundred rupee note on my head for Bava Abdullah to take. He took it shouting so loudly I felt my neck being sprayed in his spit. My father lit some fireworks and these began fizzing perilously close to people. Apart from me, no one else seemed to notice the danger.

Like a well-read tourist I smiled through all this strangely familiar, yet oddly alien culture.

If ever a house had known happiness it surely must have been ours that day when I arrived. So much meat was eaten for once even the stray dogs had a feast, and whenever I opened my eyes on that starlit night, engulfed as it was under a silver-gold blanket of moonlight, there was the sound of bones being crunched. That night, long after my uncles and aunts, cousins and childhood friends – many of whom I only pretended to recognise – had left, I finally opened my suitcase.

The jumper I'd brought for my father had been too small. Despite this, and even though it had been a blistering summer, he had worn it all the same. It only just covered his stomach and so silly it looked on him.

'You should have brought a sweater factory with you Saleem,' Mother joked, pointing to his enormous stomach. 'Maybe then something could be made that might cover that great drum of his.'

I had also brought a Seiko Five watch for Father. This filled him with pride. To my mother's joy he finally took off his old wristwatch, one which had long since stopped working. I had brought this for him on my last visit. Taking the leather strap off the old watch, he tossed it into the fields at the back of our house. That night he went to bed wearing both his watch and jumper. How he slept in that sweltering heat was a mystery to me, but sleep he did.

I gave my sister an expensive suit and a cheap make-up set that I'd picked up in a market. She paid scant attention to the suit and started covering her face with make-up. I gave some chocolates to my young brother and he immediately hid them somewhere. By the morning he could not remember the hiding place. We found them eventually, stuffed behind a dressing table. The chocolates had melted and mice had mostly eaten what was left. My brother spent a whole week killing mice.

Father, Shabnam and especially Karim made such a racket, Mother shouted at them, 'Leave us mother and son alone.

We have a lot to talk about.'

When we were alone, Mother whispered, stroking my hair, 'Tomorrow you must get rid of this jath. For now tell me about life in England, my son.'

'Leave it alone,' I squirmed.

'Tell me about life in England,' Mother repeated, with a deep sigh, reluctantly taking her hand out of my hair.

'What can I tell you?'

'Just tell me anything.'

'It's very different.'

'I know that, son, just tell me what happens out there.'

I thought hard about what I could tell her, but could think of nothing that would make sense right now. I fell into a silence, which Mother broke by saying, 'Tell me what you did last year.'

'When last year?'

'Today last year,' she laughed.

The first thing that comes to me is the memory of being drunk at a punk gig with Karamata, one of my flatmates.

'Come on, come on,' Mother nagged.

'I went to listen to music with some friends,' I said, avoiding her shining black eyes.

'I suppose you must have big tape recorder over there,' Mother said.

'No, Ammajee, not a tape recorder,' I searched my limited Pothowari for appropriate words, 'It was a big get-together of people and there was a group singing on a big stage in a very big hall with lots of lights.'

'Like quali groups?'

'Yes, but they didn't sing quailis…'

'I know that!' Mother said exaggerating each word. 'They are Angraiz, how could they!'

'This group, Ammajee, was called...' I paused and smirked at the sound of it even in English, 'The Bad Boys.' 'It was a...' I searched my Pothowari for a word, eventually opting for, 'punk saaz.'

'Don't use Angraizi words son,' Mother protested. 'Talk with a straight tongue.'

'Their name means pharay murray,' I said, laughing at the absurdity of the translation. 'And I don't know what 'punk' means. It's like a swear word, I think.'

'Pharay murray and swear words,' mother said in bewilderment.

'Angraiz group names sound very silly in our language, ammajee.' I said, 'Maybe they don't translate well.'

'Well, doesn't 'pharay murray' mean 'pharay murray' in English?'

'Yes it does, but...'

'Tell me about other groups you like then,' Mother asked.

'I like The Beatles...'

'If you speak to me in English again I will slap you, son.'

'Well, in Pothwari they would be called poondhs.'

'Poondhs!' Mother exclaimed.

'And there were The Monkeys – Boojos... and The Birds – Pakhaeroo... and The Animals – Danghar...'

'Nobody would have names like this, son.'

'They even have names I can't repeat in front of you, Ammajee.'

'So tell me what were Pharay Murray like then?'

'They wear torn clothes with lots of zips on their clothes and chains off their trousers. They colour their hair yellow, red, green and whatever else may take their fancy...'

'They wear torn clothes in that rich country, and what do their mothers think about what they are wearing...'

'They don't care what their mothers think.'

Mother went quiet. The silence pricked me. I continued, 'Their mothers don't like the music of Pharay Murray. It is youth music and only young people listen to that.'

'How can young people listen to young music? Music doesn't have age,' Mother said. 'What happens to young people's music when they get old then?'

'Anyway, Ammajee,' I said, snuggling up to her, 'they wear lots of safety pins. They wear these in their clothes, through their lips and even through their noses.'

'Oh for God's sake,' Mother threw her head back laughing. 'Just because I am a village woman don't think me stupid. I am your mother, you know.'

'I am telling you what really happens and if you don't want to listen then just go to sleep,' I insisted childishly.

'No. No. No,' Mother said, 'I'm not sleepy. You just keep talking.'

Mother stared at me with wide open eyes. The frantic, flashing lights of a noisy punk gig flashed through me. 'Sometimes when these singers get really excited they end up smashing their instruments.'

'How much do these things cost?' Mother asked in astonishment.

'Thousands.'

'Our money?'

'No pounds, ammajee.'

'Are they sad when they smash their instruments?' Mother asked.

'They do this when they are happy.'

'When they are happy they smash things worth hundreds of thousands of rupees!' Mother exclaimed, 'and what do they do when they are sad. Start burning buildings?'

'Sometimes,' I giggled. 'And when they are really, really happy, they spit at their listeners.'

'And I suppose,' Mother said in disbelief, 'their audiences, well when they are *really really* happy then they spit back at those singers, eh?'

'That's exactly what they do, ammajee!'

'And you expect me to believe that white people are like that?' Mother slapped me gently around the head. 'Go to sleep now, my son.' She bent over and picked up a pair of slippers. Placing these next to my bed she said, 'Make sure you wear these if you need to go for a pee at night and remember this is the season of snakes and scorpions.'

'I've brought some shoes for you, ammajee,' I said pointing to the contents of the suitcase that were strewn across another bed at the far end of the room. 'They are under that mess.'

'I have you,' Mother whispered walking away from me. 'What need do I have of your shoes, but I will hold them, my son, for they are my treasure, and when you are gone, I will look at them and think of you as you are now and remember every word of your story. Even though I know it's all rubbish.'

Just like last time, I have brought Mother a pair of brown leather shoes, paid for by my uncle.

'Brown leather shoes,' I splutter pulling away from the old lady. 'Ammajee, I have brought you brown leather shoes. Now make a necklace of those shoes,' I curse aloud to myself, turning into the last galli that leads to our house. 'Wear them around your neck and parade through the village. Be laughed at by all who see you. What did you do in England when this is what you really are? Chastisements screech ahead of me, but the world either side of me slows right down, like a slow motion film.

I slide past more people coming from the direction of our

house. Eyes gape at me, some flutter uncertainly around. A white cockerel jumps up from behind a low wall and darts noisily over a shrub.

Each footstep becomes heavier the closer I get to our house. Every inch forward brings with it a flash of another stream of images of a faraway land flickering like childhood. The house is different now: large stones form the base of an outer wall, with a redbrick extension built on top of it. It is patchily plastered with cement, but most of it is padded with mud. I stop by the entrance. The images of the interior rush towards me: a large open earthy courtyard; an uncovered well; a guava tree; a gigantic jandh.

'It is hard for Pardesi sons to come into a house in which there is no mother to welcome them,' my mother's sister, Parveen says, coming out of our house. She hugs me gently. Her moist face pressing on my cheek.

IV

The last few days have been long. The nights seem to have no beginning or end. A constant stream of people go through the house. Some stay for the night, others leave after short, silent condolences. The men sit in the baethak at the front of the house. In spite of my father's requests I refuse to leave the room in which Mother died. The present she left me was a tape recording; a single cassette that she must have recorded over and over with her talk, layering and layering with gentle conversation. She kept a vigil with it and now, sitting in the same room, on the same floor, I keep a vigil back. Not wanting to play it, not wanting to let it out of my sight.

As I sit there cross-legged, arcs of light carry the whispers of women through the cracks in the newly painted door. Women who come to my mother's phuri sit on the veranda, sometimes wailing a long, slow lament, at other times quite unexpectedly laughing, only to burst into wailing as soon as a new woman or a new group of women arrive. They constantly talk of my mother:

'She came to my house,' a whisper sighs, 'and she bade me farewell as well.'

'Yes, sister,' a sigh whispers back, 'surely she is destined for heaven.'

'It is said, only those bound for heaven know when their time has come,' the first whisper pontificates.

'And that is why they are fortunate enough to be able to

say their last farewells.' The second concurs.

Someone walks onto the veranda. Sunlight coming in through the cracks in the door fractures to their movement.

I want everyone to disappear so I can be alone to play the cassette. I take it out of its player and hold it like a wild lalgarh bataera, half expecting it to talk to me. It weighs heavy one moment, the next seems so light. I set the cassette player next to me, and yet I'm terrified of hearing her voice. The idea makes me shiver. I take a deep breath and force my hands to slot the cassette into its cradle. Just then the door swings open and the thought of ever listening to it floods away.

'It is not good to listen to departed souls so soon after they've left us, my son.' The white bearded man I met at the graveyard stoops quietly, leaning against the doorway. He takes off his dark glasses and looks at me tenderly with eyes moist with age. My father stands behind him. Beyond him, past rows of women, the world basks in a blinding sunlight. 'Come now, son,' the bearded man says gently pushing the cassette player out of reach. 'So many people are here to see you and here you are sitting all alone. English people like to be alone at times like this, don't they? But we are not like them, we share our sorrows.'

'Do you not recognise Bava Sardar?' Father asks.

I shake my head, 'And I don't know you or anyone else either.'

'But we know you,' Sardar says stepping forward, 'and that is what is important. You can forget us, but we can't forget you, because you are a part of us.'

I am repulsed by the absurdity of Sardar's supposition. How could he know me when I didn't know myself?

'I know you as well as I know every single plant that grows in this land,' Sardar says sitting down beside me, blocking the wind from the pedestal fan. 'My eyes are not what they used to be, but, by grabbing a fistful of soil I can still tell you which plants will be growing when rains come.'

'What of those plants which are transported to different lands?' I lower my head, turning it away from him.

'Plants can grow anywhere,' Sardar replies, 'but they are only truly happy in that earth which gave them birth. It is only there they find life's true meaning, and it is earth, in one form or another, to which everything has to return. That is Nature's law.' Turning his face towards the pedestal fan, Sardar talks into a gusty wind that slices through his voice. 'I wouldn't recognise you by sight, even if my eyes hadn't failed me, but your voice and the way you speak, I can still hear your mother when you talk, Saleem.'

Sensing the tremor juddering through me at the mention of Mother, Sardar turns towards me. 'Grief, my son, is one of those things that all who live must face. It engulfs you when it comes. And come it must. It drenches you in a coldness you could never have expected. And come it must. It makes your skin dance, and your feet slide and everything you know cling flatly to you. And come it must. You have no home when it comes. And come it must. The nearest shelter is as good as anything you built or tried to build before it came. But come it must. Creeping and coagulating even in those driest days, gathering its tiny droplets. Growing more and more - through many - into one. Rising through us, from us, up into the sky's abeyance...' He breaks off.

'For some, Saleem, it falls when it should, when it is time. For you, for us, it is a monsoon.'

I sink to the ground and curl up, imagine being dry like a husk. Sardar stands up. 'Come on now,' he whispers pulling my arm with his old, rough hand. 'Drink it, breathe it in. It must happen. It has to happen.'

'Don't let anyone touch my tape,' I eventually snarl at my father, as he hands Sardar a walking stick.

'No one will touch your tape,' Father assures. 'Go and sit in your mother's puhri and send your brother out. He's been there all day.'

'I still don't know why she had to die,' I mutter stepping out onto the veranda.

'You've not let anyone near you since you came back,' Father says. 'How can you know, but there is plenty of time and you shall know every detail.'

'Go wash your face and come sit with me in your mother's puhri,' Sardar says turning towards the baethak.

A lost smile dances momentarily over my lips and then is blown away by the air from the overhead veranda fans.

After throwing some water across my face, I stop by the purple bougainvillea plant. My father is giving some money to a tall, thick set man who has just carried in a huge block of ice. Droplets of water slide down from his head, over his wet, clinging kameez and around the visible edges of his twisted backbone, collecting in a gap in the tiles by his bare feet.

'Abbajee, tell me what happened to my mother,' I ask Father.

Father looks at me with heavy eyes and then turns his face towards the iceman who, after counting the money, folds the notes into a small bundle and tucks them away in a pocket in his vest. The iceman then takes my right hand and holds it tightly in both of his. He looks me in the eye, releases my hand from his hard, wet grip and lowers his head saying, 'I am really saddened by auntijee's passing. She was as much a mother to me as she was to you.' He pauses, lifts his kameez, dips his hand into his vest pocket and pulls the bundle of notes out. Without raising his head he holds the notes up towards my father and says, 'I can't take this money from you. It is the least I can do for my auntie.'

'Oh Kamaldeenya,' my father says softly shaking his head. 'Death is to life what night is to day. But we all have to leave this world one day. Your words are enough support.'

The iceman continues to stare at the ground and carefully

puts the money back into his vest pocket. He turns slowly and walks out of the house, leaving behind him a dotted line of water drops, which stretches from the puddle in between the gap in the tiles, following him right up to the gate.

'Poor people have such big hearts?' I sigh.

'Only poor people have hearts, son,' Father replies. 'Rich people have holes that can never be filled.'

Father is a tall, fat man with a thinning cap of curly, silver-grey hair. He has a huge bloated midriff that lifts his kameez clear of his knees. Though now his face, like the rest of his body is round and puffed, it has still not lost its pinkish grey colour.

'Tell me what happened, Abbajee?' I ask.

'Look, your cousin has come,' Father points towards Hamza who walks in just as the iceman is leaving. 'You go and sit with him and we will talk when we have seen to our guests.'

'I want to know now what happened to my mother,' I insist, ignoring Hamza.

'What are you father and son whispering out here?' Hamza laughs.

'This chhalla son of mine wants to know everything.'

'Well tell him then,' Hamza says.

'Only Almighty knows everything,' Father replies. 'I only know what I know.'

'Just tell him what you know then,' Hamza says placing his arm around my shoulder.

'She was always ill,' Father says sitting down heavily on the edge of a bed which Hamza has pulled over. I sit down close to Hamza at the other end of the bed. Father's face twitches as he continues, 'She was always ill after you left for England. When your brother Karim and your sister Shabnam came along, she was a little better, but she never forgave me for sending you away. I did everything I could. I took her to specialists. I took her to lots of hakims and many, many shrines. There was only one she really wanted to go to, but Ajmair Sharif is in India and there was no way for us to go there. She never really got up after you left. She was always tired and always complaining and fighting with me. She used to swear at me even when there were people in our house. Doctors said she had kakri pathri and they said she had to have a small operation to have them taken out. But you couldn't use a word like operation to her. She hated doctors, always called them butchers. She used to say, "If you ever make me have an operation, it will be my death." Just over three weeks ago she started getting terrible pains in her stomach and back. It was around midnight when this happened. I took her to Dina, to Shafi hospital. Doctors there did a scan on her and said she needed to be operated on. They said it was painful but she was in no danger. But she was in such pain that I drove her straight to Mangla Fauji Foundation and woke up Colonel Hafeez. He examined her and said what the doctors at Dina had said. He said she needed to be operated on immediately and he said it was just a little operation. But your mother wouldn't listen at first and said if I wanted to kill her then go ahead. She only agreed to let them operate on one condition.' Father wipes his eyes and continues, 'It was I who killed her. I should have listened to her. She was always right, but I never listened to her about anything and now she is gone… Her condition was that we first come back home and I did that because she wanted to say her farewell to all her friends.'

Hamza adds in a soft voice, 'And Khalajee came back to our village as well. She went from house to house and bade everyone goodbye. I clearly remember her saying to my mother, "Only those with fate on their side can withstand the daggers of Pakistani doctors. I am not going to be so lucky." We all thought she had gone crazy again and that she was saying all this because she was just scared.'

My stomach tightens. I stop hearing Hamza. My ears twitch and begin to burn. Walking towards Father, I point at him, 'It wasn't me who did this. It was you. You decided I should go, you tore me from her. You killed her as much as you killed me 15 years ago. You decided to rid her of me; no mother could've done that to her son. It was you.'

He stands in silence.

'Go talk to her, my son,' he says eventually, as if he's heard nothing I've said. 'She was always sitting in front of her old tape recorder. She'd talk to you as though you were next to her. Then she had her operation and everything was well…'

'That's not true, Saleem,' Hamza interrupts. 'She got yarkaan from Mangla and that's why she died.'

'It is true she got yarkaan,' Father says, clearing his throat. 'But whatever has happened was meant to happen. Allah decides. Not doctors…'

'Allah gives life, Uncle,' Hamza interrupts my father again, this time harshly. 'It is our job to protect that life. How many people go for treatment to that place and come back dead? You can't blame all this on Allah. She got infected because of dirt and lack of cleanliness and care, and you lot didn't look after her properly when she came back here. She was up and about three days after coming out of hospital. I saw her over there,' Hamza says pointing to some chilli plants, 'she was clearing rubbish out of there. She should never have been doing things like that, should she?'

'But she was not one to listen,' Father chokes, lowering his head onto the palms of his hands.

'That's because no one ever listened to her, did they?' Hamza says angrily. Father sobs. 'It's not your fault unclejee, nor is it any doctor's fault either. It's this pig of a country. Those hospitals in Dina are not hospitals, they are shops, selling out of date medicines and promises of life to those poverty has already killed.' Turning to me sharply, Hamza adds, 'You come with me, Saleem, and I will show you shit, real shit in these places they call hospitals. Mangla is not much better, that's if you are lucky enough to have a fouji connection. There is nowhere for sick people to go. We're just two legged animals waiting for our turn to die whilst our government tries to build atom bombs.'

'I can say no more today,' Father says getting off the bed. 'And Saleem, go and sit in your mother's puhri. It is your duty.'

But it's too hot to sit inside, even in the evenings. And I have Sardar's words still ringing round: 'It is not good to listen to departed souls so soon after they have left us.' So instead I go up onto the roof and lay back under a cloudless sky, feeling the heat rising from my skin, imagining the tiny molecules of sweat, coagulating, coalescing, clamouring to get free.

For two weeks, maybe, a thick carpet of snow would cover Bradford's streets. Then it would rain, making the world freeze in an altogether new way. Chill winds, winding through park trees and telephone wires, would scratch against every window on Carlisle Road.

The first time I was arrested it felt like justice reining me in for the sins of the night before. Though the charges they read out, as I stood dazed in my underwear, meant nothing at all.

The night before we'd finally, as a house, established a few ground rules. Comprised of fellow runaways, many of whom, like me, had come direct from squats or living rough in Manningham Park, my housemates had taken to the place like an easily conquered palace. It had heating, windows, mattresses in the bedrooms and before too long it'd become a regular doss for friends, and friends of friends many of whom would turn up with their girlfriends, hoping for a free bed. At first we didn't mind, but the endless cleaning up of others' sexual exploits had brought things to a head.

Along with stricter cleaning rotas, a golden rule sworn – written on a scrap of paper that everyone signed: no one other than the residents would henceforth be allowed to screw in the house. This had held firm for three days, when all but Akber Shah had gone to college. Akber Shah's friend, Zaman Ali, known to most of his friends as Pedro, had turned up with two white girls. By the time I got back home that afternoon, Pedro and the girls were on their way out. I walked past them in muted anger, refusing to shake

Pedro's hand and as soon as I saw Akber Shah I shouted, 'You dirty painchoud bastard. What the fuck is Pedro dicking here, eh?'

'Yaar,' Akber muttered meekly, throwing up his shoulders, 'you know.'

'I am not cleaning any bastard's spunk!' I snarled brushing past him.

'I'm twenty-four years old, yaar, Saleem,' Akber said following me.

'Its not about *your* lulli,' I said turning around sharply, 'we'll have all t' lulls of Bradford here.'

'You know me, yaar,' Akber said clasping my hand in both of his.

'This is my *home*,' I said snatching my hand free, 'not a fucking brothel.'

That evening, when everyone was back, we held an emergency meeting. We sat around a large board that was placed on top of overturned crates. It served as our coffee table. We sat around drinking tea, trying to find a solution to the current crisis. I learnt to my horror that this wasn't the first breach of our historic decision. There had been Satnam, a.k.a. Gurnam, Aslam, a.k.a. Andrew and Kaz. Akber had allowed all these in, with the promise that they would find a woman for him, but only Pedro had kept to his word.

Akber Shah was not only the oldest among us, he was also the one with the most money, but he rarely paid his share of the food bill, cooked or cleaned. I resented him from the first day he walked into the house. He had managed to sow the seeds of discord among us almost immediately. He was a soft-spoken slimy man, who always blamed my problems on me 'leaving the path of Islam'. He was the only son of a mullah, who had made his fortune, according to popular belief, through drugs and dealing with the police.

'We can't go on like this,' I hissed amidst the acrimonious clatter into which our meeting had degenerated. 'This is all I have for a home. You lot can always piss off to your mum's...'

'I bloody well can't,' Karamata, the curly haired kid interrupted, 'Me fucking old man tried to run me over only today.'

Apart from Akber, the rest of us burst out in boisterous laughter.

'But me point is this,' I said as the laughter subsided, 'I can't scoop any more johnnies out of the bog. And what's more, if Akber can't stick to a decision 'cause he has a hungry dick, then I think he should follow it home.'

'Alright lads, so I fucked up,' Akber said raising his voice suddenly. He stubbed a half smoked cigarette into an overflowing ashtray. His eyes welled up. The rest of us fought to hold back our giggles. 'So now you all know. But it was me first time...' We all started laughing hysterically, slapping each other's hands and thighs.

'Saleem's a prat for upsetting you, our kid,' Karamata spluttered wiping his eyes. 'I think we can solve this problem like grown men. You know what I mean.'

'I don't want to live with you bastards any road,' Akber snapped.

'Kalya, yaar.' Karamata lit a cigarette, offered it to Akber and said, 'You have really fucked up.' Turning to the rest of us he added, 'Look lads, we're not gorays. We can't let Pedro's lull destroy our yaari, like. It's not like he's had my bundh but I suppose rules are rules.' Akber sat silently with his head bowed. Karamata took a deep breath, patted Akber on the shoulder and said, 'I have an idea. Will you listen to it?'

'OK,' Akber whimpered.

'Look, yaar, if we make a mistake, we have to pay for it. Right!'

'I suppose so,' Akber replied.

'You know we are all flat broke, and you being the putter of our imam, well you should go out and get lots of beer and get us pissed and also cook and clean for a full week.' Turning to the rest of us Karamata asked, 'And what do you think lads?'

We all nodded back.

'You leave me dad out of all this shite,' Akber snapped in delayed reaction. 'And if you think I'm cooking for a week, you can all kiss my thoo.'

'Not if it's been near that stuff Pedro hangs around with,' Karamata smirked.

'I'll tell you what I do for you bastards,' Akber chortled. 'I'll pay for the booze tonight but I'll be fucked if I cook for a day, let alone a week.'

After a short argument, we managed to get Akber to agree to provide the booze and also cook that evening meal and clean up afterwards.

That evening, a number of lafangas got wind of the fact that we were having a booze up and turned up uninvited. One or two of them brought some beer, but most came on the chance of a freebee. A few of them turned up with their girlfriends and sat around for hours in frustrated anticipation.

We drank and smoked into the early hours. One by one everyone collapsed into a stupor. Some of the guests rolled into a corner of the front room and crashed out.

The next morning, slightly before dawn, there was a loud banging on the front door. I tried to ignore it, hoping someone else would attend. But no one did so I walked sleepily down the stairs and turned the latch. The front door crashed open. Uniformed police officers, some carrying truncheons, rushed in. A hangover was raging in my head. I was pinned against a wall by two officers. One of them placed a truncheon under my chin and jerked me up onto my toes.

In the front room an officer shouted, 'Up you get, you dirty Pakis.'

Some of the lads screamed in pain, a few swore at the police. An officer from the front room called my name. I shouted back hoarsely. The officer who had called my name came out of the room and nodded to the ones who were holding me. They turned me around, yanked my arms back, handcuffed me, whisked me outside into a police car and with beacons flashing and sirens wailing raced towards the police station. On the way one of the officers told me that I was under arrest for attempted murder. The hangover was now gone.

I learnt later that five of us had been arrested. We were told that we had tried to break into Bradford College, where the security guard, a retired old constable had challenged us. One of us had hit him on the head with a sharp object and he was now in a coma, practically dead. This was the first I'd heard of it. I was terrified of what the officers told me, that should I not accept my role in this affair the judge would ensure that I was never released from prison. But should I admit my role, given that I had no record, it was likely that I would get a much lighter sentence. Over the next two days, I tried to plead my innocence. They kept me awake throughout, each time developing the story a little, claiming that one of the others had given more details implicating me. I had, they said, initially been the look-out and Karamata and the others had gone into the building. I had seen Mr Jacobs, the security guard and had run off to warn my co-accused. Mr Jacobs had given chase. He had blocked the exit door to the side of the college. The police said that, according to Karamata, I had hit Mr Jacobs on the head and that is how we all managed to escape before they arrived. They now wanted me to tell them where the weapon was. By the end of the second day, I began to believe every word the police said. A police officer read me a statement detailing my role. I agreed to sign it. He pushed the paper in front of me and gave me a pen. I was trying to work out where to sign when another officer walked into the room. He looked at me and shook his head and took the statement off me before I could sign it and walked out again.

I was left alone for a long time to sit in perplexed silence. I concluded that Mr Jacobs had died and that I would now be charged with murder. The officer who had earlier read the statement out to me returned some time later. He was beaming with a smile. He gave me a cigarette and said, 'Well, Saleem, we know you didn't do it, lad.'

'I fucking told you so,' I said with relief, 'and neither did the others.'

'We know that. We've got the bastards who did.'

'Can I go home now then?'

'It's not that simple.'

'We found some stolen university plates in your house.'

'But they were there when we moved in,' I protested, remembering something our landlord had said about the previous occupants being students.

'Now listen, you little shit,' the officer said firmly, 'be smart.'

Along with the other lads, I was charged with stealing property from the University of Bradford. The police told us we had to plead guilty and that we would be fined fifty pounds. We were hauled in front of a small, fat, woman magistrate and pleaded guilty and true enough she fined us fifty pounds.

A week after Mother's death I am waking in the soft dawn of jaith: the gentle sound of the azaan, floating over the sleepy village; cockerels answering each other, now loudly in our yard, now in a house close by, now a distant one from higher up in the village. Our cockerel, called Major, is an unsightly bird with flaming golden feathers. Mother had been fattening it for my return. She used to do this all year round, every year, just on the off-chance of me coming back home. Major was one of those rare birds that somehow manages to survive the frequent outbursts of rani kheth, the Newcastle disease which regularly wipes out entire flocks of chickens. Were it not for Mother's death, Major would almost certainly have been digested by now, if for no other reason than the fact that it suffers from a non-conformist sense of time. It starts cock-a-doodling loudly in the middle of the night and in our village this is considered inauspicious. Auspicious or not, it's certainly very annoying. Among other virtues, that have taken it closer and closer to the pot, is its ability to attract just about every hen in the neighbourhood, with the result that the ground is almost always covered in droppings.

'I'll put a knife to that bastard's neck today for sure. This sister fucker thinks he is a Valaiti king,' Father shouts, his head covered under a thick, white, dew-stained sheet. Major is boasting non stop to village cockerels.

'How is a cockerel a king, Abbajee?' I joke.

Sitting high on the tall branches of our jandh tree, Major continues on unconcerned.

'It is not an ordinary cockerel,' Father says, lifting the sheet off his head. 'He is Major Saab. A sarkaari saan and doesn't care if it is day or night, he just does his thing. But today is his last day on this earth…'

'No one touches Major,' Shabnam says sitting up from the bed next to father. Tying her hair she adds, 'My mother raised him from a small chicken and I won't let anyone touch him. I'm going to keep him forever and ever.'

'I raised you from a small chicken and am I going to keep you forever and ever then?' Father chuckles.

'I'm just a burden on your shoulders, aren't I?' Shabnam says, dropping her sleepy eyes. 'You don't need me now that elder brother is back.'

'I'll send him back…' Father chortles.

'You know I didn't mean that!' Shabnam hollers like a goat that is about to have its throat slit open.

'What did you say that for, Abbajee,' I ask.

My father sits up coughing and laughing. The more he laughs the louder Shabnam yells.

'No crying now, my sweet beautiful daughter,' Father says

placing his big hand on her head. He roars with laughter as my sister pushes his hand away. She jumps off the bed and runs, bawling, inside the house.

'You've upset her for nothing, Abbajee,' I protest.

'The crying of children like this,' father says, wiping his eyes with the back of his hand, is sweeter than heaven's music itself.'

Just then Major lets out another deafening cry.

'Major's baang is worse than Mullah Afzal,' Father says leaning over the bed to pick a stone from the ground. After locating Major in the tree Father lobs the stone at the bird shouting, 'That's enough, you son of a donkey.'

The stone whooshes through the air, cracks through the branches before reaching its target. Letting out a startled cry, Major scuttles through the branches and lands near the wall.

At this time in the morning, when the yolk of the sun is about to steal through the remnants of the night, clouds of mist rise up from the hills at the feet of which sits Banyala. The air fills with the scent of roasting parathas. Women carrying tokras of rubbish move like ghosts through the mist. A sweet, moist air clings to the body, made all the sweeter by the knowledge that soon, too soon, it will be replaced by hot winds and a blistering sunshine. Then just before the first rays of the sun begin to fan out across the fading darkness, doves begin to coo and sparrows pop out of trees and crows sing from the top of rooftops, eyeing morsels of food. The brave among them, swoop down and make off with whatever is within their reach. Voices of children, reciting the Quran, drift overhead, in the early mornings of the village.

As far as I can remember, this is the first time a child from the village hasn't come to read the holy Quran in our house. My mother had taught the Quran to many people in Banyala. Some of these had grown up, married and had sent their offspring to her as well. She had been a gentle teacher, rarely raising her voice and always ensuring that each Arabic word was pronounced correctly, just as she herself would pronounce it. But woe betide any child who misbehaved. Her gentleness only stretched to teaching. And children knew this well, for all who came to her had tasted not only the coolness of her love, but the heat of the back of her hand as well.

The children stopped coming the day my mother died. But against the advice of my sister, Father has now insisted on getting them back. He said he was going to keep alive all that she had loved. And so now the children come back. They leave their shoes and slippers by the front gate and pad barefoot towards my father. He is standing in the veranda sipping tea from a steaming mug. His eyes swell at the first sight of the children. 'Come on, come on,' he beckons them in the voice of a drowning man. 'Read your lessons just like you used to do.'

The children perch themselves on the side of a bed and, rocking to and fro in time, recite in Arabic. 'Babbly' and 'Baby' are twin six-year-old sisters. They wear identical bright red shalvar kameezes. Qamu, their younger baby brother sits squashed in between them. A little distance away from this trio, on the farthest corner of the bed, squats the frail figure of a little boy called 'Chinga', the prawn. Dried snot is stuck to the upper lip of his unwashed face. The sisters begin to recite melodically. Every now and then one of them elbows Qama. Each time they do this they giggle to themselves. Following each nudging, Qama raises his voice and utters something unintelligible. Poor Chinga rocks his sleepy body and mumbles something which no one can understand.

'See, Saleem,' Father nods towards the children, 'how blessed we are to hear our holy Quran read in our house by such angels.'

'They don't know what they are reading, Abbajee. They are learning to read in Arabic and they have no idea what anything means. It's pointless.'

'What do you Englishmen know about this knowledge's value?' Father replies. Turning abruptly to Chinga he shouts, 'Ohy, Chingaya. My wife has died. Not your mother. Read loudly-loudly, so that I can hear what you are saying.'

'What use is it him reading loudly or quietly, Abbajee? He doesn't understand and I am sure God doesn't care.'

Father ignores me. Chinga starts twitching nervously and goes completely silent.

'Did your mother not feed you a paratha this morning?' Father thunders at Chinga.

'I give this little bastard a paratha every morning,' Chinga's mother says walking in through the gate, 'and he is no better than my other herd which I am raising. Like their autr father, they are good for nothing. They only know how to eat and crap.'

'Welcome, sister Doalto,' Father waves to Chinga's mother. 'Come have some tea. It is fresh and hot.'

'God be gracious on your house and all who live here,' Doalto says, taking hold of a mug of tea from Shabnam.

'Son of a shagbag,' Father roars at poor, shaking Chinga. 'What did I ask you to do?'

'Abbajee, don't swear so much,' I protest.

'They only listen if you talk to them like this,' Chinga's mother says sitting down next to me. She is a large woman. The bed groans under her weight.

'Come on, my little babu,' my sister encourages Chinga from next to the chulla.

'Babbly' and 'Baby' struggle hard to stop themselves bursting with giggles. Chinga tries to read aloud but instead starts crying.

'If I see a single tear come out of those squint little eyes of yours,' Chinga's mother threatens, pointing a fat finger at her son, 'I will gorge them out with my bare hands. Now you read loudly-loudly like you have been asked to do.'

'Bay. Alaf. Jeem…' Chinga hollers.

Everyone in the house bursts into laughter as we hear poor Chinga repeatedly recite his Arabic alphabet in the wrong order. Chinga's recital grows louder and louder.

'Come here, you little mother fucker,' Father orders, getting his breath back.

Chinga sits with bowed head for a few moments and then clutching his sipara close to his chest, walks nervously towards my father, but stops just out of his reach.

'Come forward,' Father orders.

Chinga takes a few butterfly steps, still out of reach.

'Come forward, I'm not going to eat you.'

Without raising his head, Chinga inches forward. Father grabs him by the ear and pulls him close.

'Read now,' Father orders.

'Bay. Alaf. Jeem.' Chinga's words stumble out of his mouth and dissolve into tears around his feet.

'Open your Qaida,' Father demands.

Chinga opens it with slow, nervous fingers.

'Lift up your head,' Father barks.

Chinga raises his head, avoiding our eyes.

'Read now,' Father suppresses a smile.

'Jeem, Alaf, Bay,' Chinga mumbles.

Pointing to the Arabic character for 'Bay' Father says, 'This is an Araby Bay and not *your* mother fucking Bay…'

'Abbajee! Tobaastakfaar!' Shabnam huffs. 'How can you talk like this to children when teaching them Quran paak.

'Son of a Sowri,' my father swears at Chinga ignoring Shabnam. 'It is Alaf. Bay. Pay.'

'Alaf, Bay, Pay,' repeats a slightly relieved Chinga?'

'Shahbash,' Father says, pinching Chinga lovingly on the cheeks. 'Excellent. Now go and learn it properly. And if you learn properly, one day, when you grow up, unlike your tribe, you may be able to write a letter to your mother when you go away and get a job.'

'And what would his mother do with that letter?' Chinga's

mother says, getting up off the bed. It sighs with relief. 'Who, out of all my children, would read it to me?'

'I'll read it for you, auntie,' Shabnam says, tossing a paratha on to the hot tava. It sizzles over the gentle flames of the wood fire. The scent of butter burning on the tava drifts onto the veranda.

'Blessed you be, my daughter,' Chinga's mother says affectionately. 'Blessed must those mothers be who can read their own son's letters.' Turning to me she adds, 'and a lucky woman your heavenly mother was to have had a son like you, who wrote all those letters to her when other valatiay forget us as soon as they leave our village.'

'My letter!' I whisper.

My father turns round with bewildered eyes. I lower my head in shame.

'Yes. Indeed, she was blessed,' Chinga's mother says strolling out of our house. 'She used to tell me how well you were doing, especially after coming out of jail and winning your court case and how you wrote to her every other week.'

As the children leave I try to remember the teachers at Mount Pleasant Comprehensive in Bradford. Whilst most of them did their best just to get through the day, becoming faceless blurs even before I reached my twenties, one stood out. Mr Tower, our RE teacher, was a weatherbeaten old man who seemed to have chosen that time in life that best suited him and then stayed there, never ageing further. Twice a week he would march into the classroom, tumble a pile of books onto the desk and begin another half-hour attempt to convert us to Christianity. Then one day I remember he came into class without his usual beaming evangelical smile. He stood in front of us, Bible in hand, and with a concentration on his face that hushed the room. His green eyes picked over us. Then holding his head high, he said, 'Muslim souls cannot be saved. Perhaps all souls are lost. I am retiring.' He marched out of the class and the school, never to be seen again.

The resignation of Mr Tower left an indelible mark on our class and on me. Though we always saw him as a bit of a clown, trying in all earnestness to convince us that God had a blue-eyed blond-haired human son. To us Jesus was a prophet; but news that God needed to sire a human heir came to us too late in life to be taken seriously. It seemed blasphemous even to those who were already beginning to question their faith. Even so, we respected the old man whose faith couldn't be shaken. And such a dedicated man's failure to convert us set in motion the first of many questions.

It was shortly after Mr Tower resigned that another Angraizi set doubts raging through my teenage head. I was getting off a bus on Cecil Avenue on my way home from school, when a pack of six white kids jumped me from behind the shelter. They surrounded me and started kicking and punching. As one of them pulled a knife, I had that not unfamiliar thought that this time I might actually die. I started lashing around and accidentally hit one of them on the nose. It bled and he started to cry. I was hurt and bleeding but kept my feelings to myself. Then all of sudden a father of one of the boys ran shouting towards us. The boys moved away. The father was a giant of a man and came straight towards me. I covered my head with my arms, he grabbed my wrists and lifted my arms away. I screamed. His son laughed. The father pulled me off the ground and as I closed my eyes I heard him shouting, 'You stupid little bastard.'

I waited to be hit, but he released my hand. The father shouted hoarsely, 'What the hell have you done?'

I opened my eyes. The father was holding his son by the neck in his other arm.

'It was the Paki who started it,' the white boy yelled.

The father let me go and slapped his son swearing, 'I am ashamed to have fathered a racist piece of shit like you!'

The white boy wrenched himself free of his father, moved out of his reach and said, 'You're a soft bastard dad, and you're a pussy when it comes to these black swines. You fucking Commies are all the same.'

'If you weren't me own son, I'd kill you.'

'Lay a finger on me again, you cunt,' the white boy shook his fist at me, walking backwards towards his mates, 'and I'll knock your bollocks up your arse.'

The white boys ran off noisily, leaving me with the father.

'Come on, son,' the father said wiping the blood off my face with a handkerchief, 'I'll drop you off home.'

I had never met a white man like this one before. Some of the teachers were very kind and always smiled at us in school, but they weren't real men, for they existed only at school. 'Why did you help me and not your own son?' I asked.

'He's just a racist pig,' the father replied despondently. 'I don't know where I went wrong.'

'Are racists like Paki bashers?' I asked.

'He is something much worse,' the father replied, choosing his words carefully. 'He is a Neo-Nazi.'

I told him my address and pretended to understand as we walked towards his car. Sitting on the back seat I asked, 'Are you a Commie?'

'That I am, son,'

'Do all Commies hate their sons?'

'I don't hate my son. I hate what he has become.'

'What's a Commie then mister?'

'A Commie is another word for a communist,' the father said speaking slowly so that I could weigh each word. 'And we believe that every man is equal. A man or a woman's colour should not be used against them.' Pushing his hand out of the car window, the father waved towards a large mill on our right hand side. 'You see that. There are hundreds of these dotted around the towns and valleys of Yorkshire, and around the country there are thousands of people working in them, round the clock day and night. My father died working in one of them. Many people die because of them. The thousands of workers who spend their lives in front of their machines only just get through life. But a very few people get very rich. They take the wealth produced by the workers. A Communist is someone who believes all the wealth belongs to the workers who create it. In a capitalist world there is so much hunger, yet there is so much food around no one need sleep on an empty stomach, or live without a roof over their head or be sick without enough money to buy medicines. A communist is someone who believes in a different kind of world, a different kind of system, one which is based on respect for life, not on individual greed. Not one where the son of a worker can attack another, just because of his colour.'

I listened intently to this vision of a different world, though most of what he said didn't make any sense to me. My uncle worked in a mill, but he felt eternally grateful for the privilege.

'In a world like yours,' I asked, 'children wouldn't have to leave their mothers and go to faraway lands, would they, mister?'

'No, son,' the communist replied, 'they wouldn't.'

'How can we get to this world, mister?'

'It's a long way from here,' the communist laughed pulling up in front of our house. 'We have to fight for it.'

With our house now emptied of children, Father and I sit and eat breakfast in silence. I find it hard chewing on the crisp, hot parathas which my sister keeps putting in front of us. Each mouthful sticks stubbornly to the sides of my dry throat.

'How long does post from England take to reach here, Abbajee?' I ask interrupting the purda which hangs between us.

'Oh, about five to ten days,' Father replies wiping paratha grease off his hands. 'Are you expecting a letter from someone?'

'Yes.'

'It may come, or it may not come,' Shabnam says clearing

the food off the small coffee table where we've just had our breakfast. 'If postoffice staff think there is something valuable inside it, then they keep it. Especially if letters are fat, these get opened and then don't turn up.' She stops, smirks and asks, 'Whose letter are you expecting, elder brother?' It must be a girlfriend, eh?'

'Stop this baqwas,' my father reprimands. 'At times like this people write letters of condolence.'

'Go on, elder brother,' my sister chides, walking over to me, 'Tell us. Am I going to have a sister-in-law?'

'Didn't you hear me?' Father says, clearing his throat.

'Go on. Tell us,' she insists, stroking my hair with one hand, a teacup in the other.

'It is my letter,' I lower my head. 'I sent it to Mother before I knew I was coming back.'

'You finally wrote her a letter!' Shabnam roars, tea slapping the floor. Striding off towards the chulla she cries, 'He finally wrote to her!'

I sit with my eyes tightly closed hoping for something to strike me, hit me, to squash me flat till I'm not there anymore. A crow crows somewhere above the house and its song echoes everywhere inside.

'I will go and ask at the Tarakki sorting office,' Father says, lifting my chin with the tips of his fat fingers.

'No,' I protest, opening my eyes. 'It doesn't matter. I don't want that letter to come to this house.'

'But your mother would want it,' Father says, standing up, 'and she would want it read.'

'I just wrote rubbish in it, Abbajee,' I mutter. 'I wasn't thinking about what I was saying.'

'No words of a son are ever rubbish for his mother,' Father declares.

'Even if she's dead?' I cry.

'Especially when they are dead,' Father replies, 'and try to listen to your mother's message. By not listening you are carrying a heavy burden around with you. And I want to hear her voice again, but I can't do that until you have listened to her.'

After my father leaves, I lock myself in the room in which Mother had breathed her last and perhaps for the first time, for as long as I can remember, I pray to the Almighty. I pray for my letter to get lost in the post and I beg Him to give me courage to listen to my mother's message.

Mohammad Zamman, the village postman usually comes in the afternoon around 3.30pm. I have spent the last few days in dread of this Gabriel. Our postman is a tall bony man with a long, silver, goatee beard. Come rain or shine, in illness or in health, Mohammad Zamman walks the seven miles to the sorting office in Tarakki. He goes loaded with outgoing mail, from our village and a number of others that are dotted around in the small valleys in between the ragged hills that envelopes the area, and returns with incoming mail as well as bags full of shopping.

It is a little past 4pm and I'm relaxed for the day, knowing Mohammad Zamman's calling time is past. Of course, it's now he suddenly strolls into our yard shouting, 'Janaab!'

My sister runs towards him and collects a number of letters. The edges of those cold words I wrote to Mother race around my head. When Shabnam turns round I relax. My letter isn't among those she's holding. Mohammad Zamman disappears but then like a stubborn ghost, reappears again saying, 'I forgot to give you this one.'

Shabnam stops, looks across at me coldly and walks back towards the postman. My body tenses as I stand up.

'Let me see this letter,' I say.

'It's from Uncle Zaffar in Dubai,' Shabnam says waving the striped envelope.

'And Saleem Saab,' Mohammad Zamman shouts over to me in his frail voice, 'your father has been to Tarakki and they will keep an eye open for your letter. Whatever arrives there, will inshahallah arrive here.'

Like listening to Mother's voice on the cassette player, I find it impossible to look at any of her pictures. Each time I go into the sofa – a large, newly built room that runs at right angles to the one in which she died – I become drained of all strength. Something terrifies me in this room. For some reason, there is one picture of her I can't look at without being overwhelmed. I have had all the others taken off. Maybe I have become inured to this one. It is a picture I know well, for I am in it, imprisoned in a black and white snapshot of the day I first went to England. Even in that flat, depthless, posed picture, my mother's face is taut with anguish, and the little boy standing to attention, dressed for the first time in those ill-fitting western clothes, is caught on a wave of adventure, in lands where the song says *sarkaan sonay nal sajain nay*, like in the English Dick Wittington, where the lights shined brighter than any star and darkness never came.

The day loses its fight with the dark. Birds sing and twitter, jostling for position in the trees of our courtyard, and a wondrously warm soothing cacophony of sounds it is.

All I have to do is to press a button and she will start talking to me. One little button that needs only the slightest of force. One I cannot come to touch.

'If you can put soil in her grave,' Hamza says softly, 'you can certainly push this button.'

I look up towards his shining dark eyes. Drops of sweat slide out of his thick hair and roll down his dusty face.

Apart from my grandmother, who is lying on a bed at the other end of the veranda, Hamza and I are the only ones in the house. As is her life-long habit, my grandmother is mumbling something, which no one in our family bothers trying to understand. Some joke that she's casting spells, others that she's praying. There are some who still maintain she's singing, though she will never say which herself. Whenever anyone asks, she turns her face away, laughs and replies in a hoarse whisper, 'And what will you do if you do find out?'

I wonder if my mother ever found out. Or if, with Mother there, they formed a whole conversation – my grandmother muttering and Mother listening. Slowly, like the after-shock of an earthquake, or like the second splutter of a volcano that's done its worst but not quite finished, I explode. The house becomes too much, the rooms, the sweating walls that korkillees shiver up like bad memories, it all becomes another prison cell, a grave and I have to burst out leaving Father and Shabnam and Hamza to find the answers.

I crash outside striding towards the gate. Just then a large she-buffalo pokes its head through the gap and stares blankly at me, stopping me with enormous, black eyes. A crow rides on its back, while a smaller, lalgarh bird perches on the rim of its left ear, carefully pecking inside. The buffalo scans me for a moment, then flicks the ear. The lalgarh flies out, hovers a moment, then settles back down in the same position. The crow keeps eyeing me apprehensively. A dog yelps somewhere close by in the galli to the back of our house. As I get closer the crow dashes off noisily. The buffalo licks its nose, flicks its ears, blinks its deep, blank eyes and moves gracefully towards a pile of old rocks, swaying past thorns, to stomp down the slope and graze in the field beyond.

The cries of the dog are now doubled by the excitement of children. An emaciated dog, followed by a pack of children runs past me. The dog squeezes itself through a gap and hides behind the pile of rocks. The children excitedly collect an assortment of sticks, bricks and stones. Two of them rush into our house and come out with an axe and a shovel. Some children prod the dog with twigs. Each time it yelps for mercy. A few children start taking the rocks off the pile. The dog jumps out, running carelessly through the thorns, under a hail of missiles and disappears into the field. Some of the children place a few stones on the thorns and chase the dog.

Grabbing hold of the boy nearest me – he is around ten years old – I ask, 'What has this vachara done?'

'This dog is a real painchoud,' the boy replies, staring incredulously. The other children surround me. 'He's just killed Bawa Bagha's seel cukkar.'

A number of children start speaking at the same time: 'Unclejee, it was a beautiful cukkar'

'It was King of the Chickens'.

'There will never be another cukkar like that one, uncle.'

'It was a Valaiti cukkar.'

'No it wasn't, desi rubbish.'

"Don't you say that about my bava's cukkar, you bastard.'

A pakora vendor sings his presence.

'Unclejee, can you give us ten rupees for chatni pakaroy?' the boy I'm holding asks.

I give him a note and, followed by the other children, he races off to the seller. The two who had gone after the dog scramble over the thorns and rush past me to join the others. The pakora seller has already sensed a big sale and has placed his wares under the shade of the twisted branches of an old jandh tree.

The jandh was there, as it is now, even when I was a little boy. It now stands in front of the ruins of a house. I had spent my youth next door in my grandparent's house, now in ruins. It too has decayed and collapsed now. My uncle and his neighbours live in Bradford.

'I say you should not stand under this tyrannical sun,' a young man says, clutching my hand tightly. He is a tall man with sharp eyes and shining, black hair. 'You foreigners always forget us.' A smile blazes across his moist, dark skin. His white teeth shine out from gums that have been coloured with walnut bark. 'You don't remember me do you? I am Barkat. We went to Ramdayal School, we used to walk there every morning.'

'Yaar, Barkat,' I apologise. 'Your voice sounds familiar, but in truth I do not recognise you.'

'Just tell me, brother,' Barkat says pulling me towards the thin shade of a young kikker tree. 'I say, why do you Valaitis always forget us? I mean, what is it in that country that you just don't remember people you grew up with?'

I try to think of an answer…

'I know why,' Barkat chorkles. 'I say, its those pretty gorian, isn't it, eh? Who wouldn't forget themselves surrounded my beautiful, fair white women?'

'No. No. That's not it,' I laugh.

'I say, it's pretty gora boys, then?'

'No, yaar.'

'Well, it can't be the kotian, I mean unlike us, you lot ride donkeys for fun over there, eh,' Barkat offers me a cigarette. I shake my head. 'Not good enough for you, eh!' Putting the cigarette back into its box he asks, 'Give me one of yours then, eh!' I do. He lights it, inhales deeply and continues blowing smoke out of his nostrils, 'I think something must happen to you lot when you leave home, eh.' I say nothing. 'I worked in Saudi. I was there for ten years, you know, and during all that time I only came back once. And that was when bayjee passed away, but I swear on my Maker, none of us over there ever forgot home. I mean to say, I still remember you when you were at school. You didn't once cry when Marsterjee's cane snapped.' Tugging on my hand, Barkat adds, 'I say, jull yaar. I am going to Ramdayaal on a bus. Some rahmis have arrested my goats…'

'Arrested your goats?' I laugh.

'Yes, yes,' Barkat nods. 'They are in a bakra pathak, a goat jail, in Ruppar. I will have to pay haeri to get them out. Nowadays safarsh is no good, they only listen to money. What a country Pakistan is, eh? I mean, wolves run our government and goats go to jail.'

'Yaar, I am going to my mother's grave,' I protest, trying to free my hand.

'I say, she is not going anywhere,' Barkat replies.' My bayjee is buried not far from her, but how would you know that? Come, let's go, we will pass our old school as well.'

Barkat yanks me forward towards the ruins of my uncle's house. A pathway has evolved through what used to be a window. The wall through which it leads hangs in broken parts. The ground below has hardened under the hoofs of animals and the feet of children.

Ramdayaal school is around 20 minutes' walk from Banyala and, needing the air, I let myself be dragged into Barkat's rescue mission. During my childhood, we spent many an hour chatting and play-fighting with the thick leaves of the ak plant. The school stood on the banks of an old kas and sat opposite flowing hills, which in those days were adorned in a blanket of green trees and bushes and the red-brown earth. Trees, in whose welcome shade we all had our lessons, lined the outer courtyard as well as all the inner lanes. The gardens were beautifully arranged, growing all manner of fruit, flowers and vegetables, courtesy of the children's hard work, all for the pleasure of the headmaster.

We have hardly covered any distance and I'm already exhausted. Barkat skips happily in front. A forlorn smile strays across my lips as I recall how he had done just this as a child. An incomplete memory creeps up on me.

A devil of a teacher, Master Hussein, brandishing a cane. He held it up for all the boys to see. He struck the air. It cut through the wind with a loud whoosh. The schoolboys held their breath. The cane slashed through the air again and cracked against the backside of a young boy.

Each year, when the headmaster introduced new students, he would shake the cane and stroke it all the while twisting his long, bushy moustache with his other hand.

The cane had been an integral part of schooling as far back as memory stretched in these parts. It was called Be-Jamaloo. It was claimed by the few who could read and write, that had it not been for Be-Jamaloo there would no literate person around these parts. The cane had been at the school long before the school had become a part of Pakistan. It cared not what the religious background of the backsides it struck. Nor, for that matter, did it discriminate against caste. Before Pakistan, it had graced the backside of many a Sikh and Hindu arse, and since 1947 it had exclusively struck Muslim bums.

'Remember Be-Jamaloo?' Barkat asks.

I nod. We are passing a junior school. Lots of children squat on the ground, under the shade of a tali tree. Pointing to the kids, Barkat says, 'Our fathers went to this school, you know.'

'Don't children have chairs?' I ask.

'Neither did our fathers. But they had mats then.'

A child is being punished by being made to bend over in the cukkar position. Squatting on the floor, he has pushed his arms through his legs and is holding on to the tips of his ears. I too learnt this lesson.

At school we were forbidden from speaking in our own language and had to speak in Urdu. The problem for the school was that hardly any of us spoke the language, this included most of the teachers.

All day, with the other children, I would shout out the letters of the alphabet as loudly as I could. How the teacher had heard me mispronouncing 'Alif - Aam' in the din created by 50 odd children, I'll never knew. But this is what I said, and in truth so did everyone else.

'Mother fucker!' Master Hussein had said, pointing to me with his long finger, 'How many times I have told you bastards to leave your junglee language at home.' The class fell into a shocked silence. For a moment, the silence of the boys silenced the birds in the trees. A few crows started calling out to others. Mastar Hussein slowly walked towards me, Shouting, 'Alif sey Aam! If you do not get this right, I will strip your skin and feed it to dogs.' The boys close to me froze. 'Except Saleem, everyone else sit down.'

The class obeyed. The crows stopped. A slight wind rustled through the branches.

'Now let me hear you,' Master Hussein said, walking menacingly towards me.

'Alaf nal Ambh, sir!' I replied.

The class burst out in laughter. Master Hussein stopped, put his arms behind him and clasped his right hand into his left and smiled. He looked at me with his cold, cold eyes.

'Alaf Ambh, sir.' I said again.

Each time I said 'Ambh,' the class burst out in raucous laughter.

'Cukkar!' Mastar Hussein ordered.

I went into the cukkar position as quickly as I could. The boys closest to me moved away a little as Master Hussein came forward armed with an old tarrapar, a well worn flip-flop, Be-Jamaloo's regular replacement. He dangled the tarrapar close to my bottom. I felt its tingling heat. Blood rushed to my head. Sweat trickled. My arms began to ache.

'If you cannot get Alif right,' Master Hussein retorted, rubbing the tarrapar across my bottom, 'what chance have you got in this life? Now let me hear you say it.'

'Alaf Ambh, Masterjee,' I cried.

Master Hussein's tarrapar cracked against my bottom. I tried to pronounce the word as Mr Hussein had requested but for some reason the sound would not come out and instead I kept saying, 'Alaf' and 'Ambh.' Each time Mastar Hussein hit me harder and harder. The class had sunk into an angry silence. In the upside down world I saw Barkat standing up. He shouted, 'That's enough.'

Master Hussein rushed towards Barkat, grabbed him by the ear and dragged him to where I was cukkaring.

'Wait here,' he thundered, stomping off towards the classrooms.

'Be-Jamaloo, putter,' Barkat whispered. 'And don't let Masterjee hear you cry.'

I nodded. Master Hussein stormed back, Be-Jamaloo in hand. The class held its breath as Master Hussein cracked Be-Jamalo across my backside.

'Do they still beat children like they used to?' I ask Barkat as we pass the playground.

'If they didn't these little bastards wouldn't listen to a word,' Barkat laughs wiping his brow. 'That was Master Hussein's son who was teaching back there.'

'And what happened to Masterjee?'

'You saw him yesterday,' Barkat replies.

'Where?'

'I saw him walking into your house.'

'I still remember Be-Jamaloo,' I grin.

'You should, it signed its name on your arse.'

We stop by a well, in the shade of an old banyan tree. A blindfold buffalo is walking round and round, a rod tied to its back, which turns a wheel that brings canfuls of water out from the well. The water tips into a tray and flows down two small gullies dropping musically into a small tank.

'I hear teachers don't hit you in England, eh,' Barkat says dipping his hands into the tank filled with cold water. He scoops some water in his hands and says throwing it over his head, 'It is a *gentalman* country, with rules, yes. Not like this hell, full of cutthroats.'

'It's different, yes, but there are lots of cutthroats there too.'

There were around a hundred of us at Mount Pleasant Comprehensive, with nearly a thousand white children. At break times we stayed together, in assembles we stayed together, often increasing our numbers by linking up with other schools, bandying together on our morning routes, when we were most vulnerable to attack. We learnt to survive attacks by staying together, but also fared well in fights because most of the boys in our class were much older than their official age. I remember the sight of one lad, Shafiq Ahmed, dwarfing his desk each morning as our names were read out. We called him Lala, and he spent most of his day in the toilets, shaving. The immigration rules had changed, which meant that anyone over 18 could no longer come into the country. Shafiq Ahmed's solution to this was to shave several years off his age. He had a full beard by the time my voice broke. The poor lad spent his life trying to convince us he was in fact a boy. By 15, he was balding. I remember the bewilderment of our teachers at the fact that so many of us shared the same birthday. We had birthdays like 5/5/55, 3/4/56, 4/4/55 and 5/6/56. Some of the boys made up stories about fertility festivals and sacred dates, and our teachers believed them. The real reason was that we could remember the dates on arriving in the country. We'd all heard about children being denied entry on not being able to remember their dates of birth. We didn't care much for birthdays anyway.

'Your father said you have won your case?' Barkat asks, resting a foot against the playground fence.

'Oh yes, I won my case,' I lie.

'What are English jails like, tell me, yaar.'

'Jail is jail.'

'Is it true you get colour TV in there?'

'In some prisons.'

'And English police, I hear, they talk to you really nicely,' Barkat says standing back up and stretching. 'Now these Pakistani police, well, now English police can't be as bad as these sons of wild bitches. Can they, eh?'

'These are the bastard children of Britain,' my words roll out quickly.

'Yes. Yes. Sons of pigs can't change into milk-giving cows, I suppose,' Barkat reflects. 'But did you have telephones inside your cells?'

'My dick! You have telephones in there, you don't worry about it.'

Seeing how I'm struggling with the heat, and distracted, Barkat waves me farewell, throwing some words after him about meeting again, on his way to the bus stop. Closing my eyes where I sit, I drift towards the disinfected floors of Bradford's Nelson Street Police Station. I was being frogmarched away from the charge room two weeks ago, through a labyrinth of corridors; up and down numerous steps, until I was pushed into a plain room with thick plate-glass windows, through which filtered a hazy light. Just enough to let one know it was daylight outside.

There were three chairs in the room. Two of them on one side, the other set a little way from the table, near the wall. This one was obviously for me. I walked over to it and sat down and scanned the word 'mum', etched decoratively into the table.

'Don't worry me ol' flower, they've nought on yer,' I said aloud trying to amuse myself.

Hardly had I said this when the door crashed opened. DS Gower and two plain clothes from my flat earlier, stomped in. A few moments later, an elderly officer joined them. Gower offered me a cigarette, placing the packet on the table in front of me, just out of reach. I took one out. He flicked his lighter. I leaned over, lit the cigarette, leaned back against the chair and blew out a plume of smoke. The elderly officer pushed a well-used metal ashtray towards me. The two plainclothe officers sat down opposite. A few policemen glanced into the room. Eight eyes stared at me, silently. I was desperate for the interrogation to start. But the silence continued for what seemed like a day, in which I polished of the best part off Gower's cigarettes.

'I'll 'ave chips, beans, toasts two well-done eggs and a cup of chah,' I said, trying to break the ice.

No one replied. The intensity of their eight-eyed gaze seemed to get stronger. I could hear the faint sound of footsteps in the corridor. The eyes flashed messages to each other. A tall, uniformed officer stepped into the room. Everyone suddenly stood to attention. I almost did the same.

The uniformed officer's stony gaze ran over me for a few moments. He nodded to Detective Sergeant Gower and walked out without saying anything. He was followed out by Gower and the two plain clothes. After they'd gone, the elderly officer walked over to one of the chairs and sat down sighing with relief. He introduced himself as Sergeant White. He took a cigarette out of Gower's packet, looked over his shoulder, pulled out a lighter, lit the cigarette and inhaled deeply, asking, 'Do you take sugar in your tea?'

'I was only joking.'

'I'm not.' Sergeant White, smiled blowing the spoke out. 'Even the hardest nuts break, you know, son.'

'I'm not hard.'

'But you're a bloody nut though. Otherwise you wouldn't be in this bleedin' place.'

I looked into his green, experienced eyes. Thick stumps of greying eyebrow sat on a wrinkled forehead. The fluorescent light reflected off a bald patch that ran down the centre of his head. Two thinning mats of hair clung to the sides of his head. A cropped moustache sat on his upper lip and harsh wrinkles zigzagged through the loose skin of his face.

'Now, son,' Sergeant White said after a contemplative silence. 'I've been told to sit here. I don't know what you're in here for, but I've been around for long enough to know that the Chief does not come down to see every thief, prick and Harry who passes through.'

Sergeant White had such a warm, fatherly tone that for a moment I felt like hugging him.

'Am I under arrest?'

'Not as far as I know.'

'Can I go home, then?'

'Now don't be a cheeky cunt, Sergeant White said, flicking ash into the ashtray. The pupils in his eyes momentarily contracted. His eyebrows flickered upwards. Shaking his head, he continued in the fatherly tone again, 'You're up shit creek. I suggest you help yourself.'

'Are you the soft selling bit of the force, then?'

'You really don't understand how deep you're in it, do you?'

A large, boldly numbered wristwatch on Sergeant White's silver-haired arm showed it was nearly 7am.

'I should be at work in half an hour,' I said.

Sergeant White tightened his lips and nodded politely. After a brief pause he looked me in the eyes and said, 'I've seen 'em all you know: rapists, murderers, thieves, everything. I'm nearing the end of my service, and I know enough to know they're going to throw the book at you. My advice to you, me lad, is not to play the clever cunt.'

'You've got fuck all on me and you know it.'

'You're not dealing with coppers like me,' Sergeant White laughed. Placing both his bony hands on the table he pushed himself up, turned around and said, walking out of the door, 'Times are different now.'

I was left alone for a long time to stew in a cold silence that bounced off the walls, sometimes it mixed with the sound of muffled voices, or footsteps, some of which were sharp metal on tiles, others plain thumps of leather. The fluorescent light started to intermittently buzz.

I have forgotten how magical sleeping on the open rooftops can be. It is the night of a full moon and its light rains down on us in torrents. It's as though a gigantic torch is shining from high in the night. I am lying on my back, smoking and listening to the village. Hamza is fidgeting on a bed next to me. A cool breeze is blowing softly, washing over us the songs of the crickets. A jackal howls close by making chickens flutter in the trees below. Stray dogs growl occasionally at the back of the house.

'Isn't it amazing, cousin,' Hamza says blowing smoke circles into the night and pointing to the moon. 'During daylight, it burns and at night it does this.'

'How about a peg-sheg, cousin?' I suggest after letting out a contented sigh. 'Life has got to go on, eh.'

'You have said words to cool my heart, yaar,' Hamza replies dejectedly. 'But we can't do this yet, Maulvi Deenu is on his deathbed.'

'What is us having a few whisky pegs got to do with his death bed, yaar?' I protest.

'This is a village and we don't do things like this,' Hamza replies.

'He will never know,' I offer.

'Everyone in Banyala knows you have whisky with you.'

'How!' I sit up in shock. I haven't let anyone near my luggage.

Turning onto my side, I stare at the long curving shadow of the hill that arcs round the back of the village. My thoughts wander back to the house of my childhood and the voice of Maulvi Deenu. He was a tall, thin man, with a tapering black goatee on a long face which never smiled. With stick and slap he had taught me to read the Quran. Contrary to the belief of my father and uncles, I was not led astray from the path of Islam by the infidelities of the

West but by the antics of Maulvi Deenu. A mischievous smile crosses my tired lips as I remember the day he put the fear of death into me. He had come to our house early in the morning as usual. I had overslept and my mother had made a paratha and egg for me. Along with everyone else she had gone off to a funeral somewhere. I was just about to start eating my paratha when Maulvi Deenu came. Without saying a word he snatched my breakfast away from me and by the time my tears had fallen onto the dry ground, he had managed to scoff most of it down. I was around eight years old then and the only protest I could make was to cry. Unperturbed by my noise Maulvi Deenu finished off my breakfast and said the sentence, which he often used to say, 'Now if you say a word about this to anyone you will be severely punished.'

'But I am hungry and my mother made that paratha for me,' I cried.

'That is how it is meant to be,' Maulvi Deenu said, wiping his lips.

'I am going to tell my mother you ate my paratha,' I said. Maulvi Deenu slapped me around the face. My ears burnt, but as the heat of it faded it took with it my fear of Maulvi Deenu. I said, trying to hold back my tears, 'That was my paratha and I am going to tell my mother.'

'If you do that,' Maulvi Deenu warned in a voice that filled me with terror, 'if you tell anyone what has happened here, then as surely as I am standing in front of you, you will burn in hell. Demons will gouge out your eyes. Your tongue will be pulled out of your mouth. Your limbs will be torn from your body. And if you are lucky then demons may eat your heart, otherwise it will be tossed to dogs.'

After saying this he stormed out of our house, leaving me all alone. Long after he left, images of demons and ghouls and other evil creatures followed me around the house. I wet myself with terror. By the time my mother came back I had a raging temperature. I was dumbstruck. Mother called Maulvi Deenu to say a prayer. The sight of him made me faint. That night I stayed awake, expecting to be carried off by demons as predicted by Maulvi Deenu. Each shadow of the shadowy night filled me with terror. Slowly I saw the night marching on and heard the roosters beckoning the new dawn. The first ray of the sun filled me with such joy that I stood up and confidently pronounced, 'It is all a lie!'

'What is my son,' Mother shouted, running into the room.

'Demon-sheeman koi nee,' I shouted, 'Maulvi Deenu is all a lie.'

Later when Maulvi Deenu arrived to give me my lesson I whispered in his ear, 'I know you are a liar now. They never came.' Maulvi Deenu ignored my words and taught me as though nothing had happened and went on his rounds.

But all that is a long time ago now. I am dozing off slowly when excited voices begin to fill the street below. Sitting up, I realise I'm alone up here. Hamza's head pops up from the stairwell, saying 'Maulvi Deenu is about to go.'

'Up or down?' I ask.

'He can only go down,' Hamza laughs.

'Is he dead?'

'Nearly.' Hamza sits down next to me. After a moment he adds, 'He wants to see you.'

'Me!'

'He has said his farewell to everyone else and you have not been to see him.'

'He was such a bastard, let him go meet his demons.'

'In death we always forgive,' Hamza shakes his head.

'Stop this phalsapha, yaar.'

'You must go to him,' Hamza orders.

'I will when it's light.'

'You must go now.'

Not wishing to disappoint my cousin I walk sleepily down the stairs and follow him to Maulvi Deenu's house.

It is strange how memory comes alive. As soon as I walk into Maulvi Deenu's house I feel as though I was here only yesterday. The stone steps leading down into his house still wobble as they had done when I'd last stepped on them as a boy. The stone walls look as they did in my childhood. A throng of women sit around a bed that is placed close to a large jandh tree, its thick trimmed branches curving skywards. A couple of young women rhythmically keep mosquitos off Maulvi Deenu with hand held fans. He is an old, overweight man now with a silver beard shining in the moonlight. Opening his hollow eyes he beckons me. Walking closer I shake his hand. It is cold. He strains to say something. I lean closer and he whispers in my ear between heavy, laboured breaths, 'May God praise you for coming to me, my son. Forgive me for anything I may have done to you.'

'What are you talking about, bavajee?' I try to reassure him.

'I never did manage to digest that paratha, my son,' Maulvi Deenu says.

'I don't remember any parathas bavajee,' I lie, 'and I am truly grateful for you for teaching me to finish our holy Quran.'

'Don't talk baqwaas,' Maulvi Deenu coughs. 'You were not a child to forget.'

'Let old things be gone now, bavajee,' I reply sitting down next to him.

'Now, my son, was Valait good to you?' Maulvi Deenu asks.

'I have passed some years.'

'It is good you have returned to your mother,' Maulvi Deenu says, 'only those fated are lucky enough to meet their mothers, even if it be for a farewell by their graveside.'

I make no response. Maulvi Deenu starts coughing painfully. Regaining his breath he says, 'My son, I am about to leave this world, but before I do, I have one request of you.'

'If it is within my power I will certainly try to help,' I am filled with a familiar and uncomfortable dread.

'Don't worry, my son,' Maulvi Deenu says, spitting phlegm into a crumpled rag that seemed glued to his weak hand, 'I am not going to ask you for money.' Lowering his voice to a whisper he continues, 'I have heard that you have brought some whisky with you. Is this so?'

'Yes, it is,' I moan.

Handing me a small, empty, cough syrup bottle, Maulvi Deenu says, 'Fill this for me and bring it now.'

'Bavajee!' I protest, 'What sort of a thing is this you ask for?'

'I have always wondered what it would taste like,' Maulvi Deenu smiles. 'Now go and get me some, before it is too late.'

Placing the bottle into the side pocket of my kameez I make my way out.

'What do you mean he has never tasted whisky?' Hamza whispers amazed back at the house. 'What sort of a thing is that for a dying Maulvi to say?'

I sneak into our back room. On my first night here I hid my shoulder bag at the bottom of a large, metal trunk normally used to hold the family linen. After pouring the whisky into the small bottle, I switch on the ceiling fans to disperse the smell and return to Maulvi Deenu. His eyes glow when he sees me. He takes the bottle from me and hides it under his pillow. I sit with him for a few uncomfortable moments, swear at him under my breath and then politely take my leave.

The next morning Maulvi Deenu makes a miraculous recovery and comes to see me later in the afternoon. He sits around waiting to catch me alone but I give him the slip. Two days later he dies. I feel guilty for begrudging him so little a thing as whisky, but comfort myself with the thought that at least he went contented.

Over the next few days a number of friends, ground down

by poverty, come to our house and plead for money. I give all of them a little each until I am down to just over a hundred pounds. At the current rate I will be out of money without having spent a penny on Shabnam or my father.

I decide that the best course of action is to avoid meeting anyone, just as I avoided meeting my mother in the shape of that cassette – now locked back in her room to everyone's dismay. No one tracks me down the following day. The sun is fierce; heat raining down and the earth dry. The electricity goes off again and I am lying in the shade of a tree trying in vain to ward off a particularly persistent fly. Someone rattles the rusty old chain of our gate. A tall, dark man walks in towards me.

'Janaab!' he shouts walking closer. 'May Allah bestow wealth and peace upon you!'

'There is no one at home,' I say dismissively. 'Come back later.'

'I have come to see you, kind sir,' the tall stranger says walking ever closer. He squats a few yards away from me just outside the shade of the tree and says, 'I last saw you when you were a little boy. I used to carry you around on my shoulders, but you won't remember that, you were only a child then.'

I don't answer, thinking of the little I have left.

'My name is Tanveer Sultan and my village is a day's walk from here beyond Tilla Jogian,' Tanveer says, rummaging through his pockets. He has short, greying, curly hair and a dark, shining face, which is covered in perspiration. He takes out a small packet of cigarettes, lights one and continues, 'I am a poor man and I have a wife and three children. All young and there is no one in this whole world who I can turn to.'

'God will look after you, Tanveer saab,' I reply. 'There is nothing I can do...'

'But please, saab, just listen at least,' Tanveer interrupts. His eyes swell up and he continues with a quivering voice, 'I am a Jat, sir, and we are a proud people. I do not come to your house lightly and my God knows how hard I thought before coming to you. My wife has been ill for many months now. She never recovered after giving birth to my daughter. God knows I have done all I can for her. I have taken her to some of the very best doctors, and you know, sir, they are like butchers, each time I go they just give us lots of medicines and charge lots of money and she doesn't get any better. I have now no more money to spend on her. I have sold all our animals and spent every paisa on her treatment and still she does not improve. I have been to all the pirs and still she does not get better. I now have no more money and, God forbid, should anything happen to her then who will look after my small children.'

I begin to resent myself for even having money. I am about to offer him some when Tanveer clears his throat and says, 'I know everyone is asking you for money. People here are such chackarbaaz. I know. But believe me, as God is my witness, I have not uttered a single false word. I would sell my soul to get her any medicine that would make her better…'

'Tanveer saab, I am not a rich man and I am not a doctor.'

'But I have not asked janaab for any money,' Tanveer replies. 'All I ask is a few drops of Valaiti medicine. I am convinced only that will make her better.'

'You tell me what medicine it is and I will try to get someone to bring it over for you.' I let out a sigh of relief.

'But kind sir,' Tanveer says, 'I know you have some medicine already.' Handing me a small bottle he adds, 'I only want a few drops.'

I snatch the bottle out of his hand, stomp inside and return a few moments later with a small amount of whisky. Tanveer's eyes flash with happiness. He kisses my hands, takes the whisky and leaves singing my praises. Hardly has Tanveer been gone an hour when another man walks into our house. He is a short, round fellow, with bleary eyes.

'I have nothing left to give you,' I shout. 'Go away from here.'

'You used to call me Uncle Sheeda, and now you want to send me away from here. Your father and I are like brothers. I have walked for six hours barefoot, just to see my Valaiti son and this is how you talk to me,' Uncle Sheeda says angrily.

'I am sorry, Uncle, I don't recognise you.'

'I will wait for your father and then he can tell you who I am,' Uncle Sheeda says stroking my head. 'Just because God has been kind to you, doesn't mean you should be cruel to poor folk like me. My son, if it was not for an utmost emergency I would never have disturbed your rest. She has been ill for a month and is now on her last legs. Should something happen to her I am done. All I have is her and without her there is no future for me. Please help me, my son.'

'What can I do for you, Uncle?' I curl my lip in disbelief. From the tone in his voice, I conclude he is going to ask me for at least one thousand rupees and there is just no way I am going to agree.

'If you had seen her skin before she fell ill you would have gasped in awe at her beauty. And now alas she is dying. God willing though, and with your help, she will be saved.'

'You should take your wife to a doctor, Uncle,' I suggest.

'It is not my wife who is ill,' Uncle Sheeda replies. 'It is my majh. And there was not a prettier buffalo than her around, giving a katti each year.'

'I know nothing about animals.'

'Ah yes, my son,' Uncle Sheeda holds out a bottle. 'But you have some Valaiti medicine and all I ask for is a few drops.'

I reluctantly give Uncle Sheeda, or whatever his name is, an inch or so of whisky and resolve to drink the rest before the village goats started falling ill too.

Later the same day my father comes home all in a huff. He stomps around the yard muttering something under his breath and intermittently glaring across at me. He is a tall, proud man, my father, who rarely misses any prayers. I suspect that I am the cause of his present discomfort. Eventually he stops muttering, points to me and shouts, 'You have brought such shame upon me. How can I face anyone? I spend my life sorting out people's problems, helping them cleanse their souls and here you are bringing such evil into my house. Especially at a time like this. You have your dead mother's dying words waiting for you in that machine and still you won't listen to them. Instead you do this. Is this all you've learnt? Maybe God is punishing me.' Sitting on the side of a bed next to me he lowers his head and starts crying.

'I don't know what you're talking about, abbajee.'

'And now you lie to me. Your own father! How could you?'

'But I have done nothing, I swear, Father, I don't know what you're talking about.'

'You have sharab in this house!' Father says.

I don't respond.

'Where is it?'

I lower my head.

'Here it is, Abbajee,' Shabnam, who has been sitting quietly in a corner, says holding out my bag, 'He keeps it in this.'

'Give it to me,' my father orders. Turning to me he asks, 'Key?'

'Here, Abbajee, I have his key as well,' Shabnam says gleefully handing father the key.

Father takes both bottles out of my bag and holds up the half empty one, and exclaims, 'Allah forgive me. He has drunk all this in my house!'

'Not a drop of this has passed my lips, Abbajee,' I protest.

'No,' Father replies holding both bottles from their necks. 'You managed to get Maulvi Deenu to drink, and that just before dying!'

Just as father is about to hurl the bottles against the outer wall I see Hamza walking into our house. He runs back out again. The bottles fly through the air. They seem to move in slow motion, turning in mid-air, over garlic shoots, over a nervous goat who follows the line of flight until the two bottles finally smash, one by one, into the stones.

This being Friday, a maulvi is giving a sermon over the Banyala mosque's speakers. A strong smell of whisky drifts towards me as Father stands up, wipes his hands and, making for the bathroom orders, 'You will go and, read your Friday prayers.' My sister says in a mischievous voice, 'Here elder brother, I have ironed your clothes already.'

'I will deal with you later,' I hiss, nodding my head vindictively.

'Abbajee!' Shabnam calls out, 'he is going to beat me up.'

Father stops, turns around and glares back at me, shakes his head and disappears into the bathroom. I sit impatiently waiting for him to leave the house so I can vent my anger on my little sister. He comes out of the bathroom a few moments later, turns to leave the house and shouts towards me without turning his head, 'Do your voozoo, and if you lay a finger on my daughter, I will kill you.'

My sister bounces around the house confident in her new safety. I smoke a cigarette and listen to the sermon. Hamza turns up a short while later. Turning to him I say bitterly, 'You are such a coward.'

'Cowardice had nothing to do with what I did,' he replies earnestly.

'You just ran.'

'Yes I did, but not because I am a coward.'

'Coward,' I repeat holding back a smile.

'Yaar, I was actually running because I know Unclejee has no aim and behind that wall I could catch the bottles. I don't know how he managed to get it right this time.'

'Well it's all gone now.'

Keeping my promise to Barkat, I set off for a gap-shap with the village lads. Long shadows stretch out over the galli which runs at the back of our house. A powerful bulb throws down a circular cone of light. Either side of it is abandoned to darkness. A cool breeze breathes out across the land. A few lads are sitting on some well-worn gravestones in the shadow cast by the mosque under the moon. One of the lads intermittently flashes a torch onto the ground. Somewhere in the hills beyond the last house of the village, jackals howl; a train rumbles past against a backdrop of loud thuds echoing from the direction of the old shrine.

The graves the boys are sitting on lie just across from a handful of shops that make up a road I've been told was bestowed on the village by General Zia-ul-Haq, the current ruler of Pakistan. A second huddle of lads squats in the courtyard of one of these shops to my left.

'Welcome, yaar,' Barkat shouts across from this second group, some of whom are sprawling across two abandoned beds, while the others either perch on the edges, or lean on the walls of the courtyard. 'You have become like a brooding hen.' A few of the lads stand up making room for me. After shaking various hands I slump down next to Barkat.

A palm reaches out from behind some lads sitting opposite me. My hand meets it. An emaciated face, with beaming eyes and a thick drooping moustache follows it saying, 'He is a Valaiti cukkar, not a hen!' The voice stirs a few faded memories from somewhere in my childhood, but the name fails me. 'You lot just always forget us,' he adds.

'Let it be, yaar,' I say pulling my hand away, embarrassed. All of a sudden his name surges to me. I stand up and embrace him smiling, 'This sisterfucking voice can only belong to Raju.'

'How did you remember him?' Barkat laughs.

'Friends and lovers always know each other,' Raju interjects.

'More like bastards are hard to forget.' Barkat says.

The lads snigger.

'Yaar Saleem,' Raju says, slapping my shoulders. He somehow manages to wriggle next me. 'Tell us something about Valait.'

'Tell him something about white women,' Barkat says.

'Don't *tell* me about gorian,' Raju replies. '*Find* me one so I can go there.'

'I thought you were married,' I say brushing Raju's hand off my pocket. He tries to grab my cigarettes.

'People like Raju will always be looking for gifts from whiteman's world,' a young lad with large firing eyes, says.

'Yaar Khurshid, be quiet. I just want a Valaiti cigarette and a gori for a wife, at least my dreams are attainable,' Raju replies forcibly taking my packet of cigarettes out of my pocket.

In the distance the thudding continues sporadically.

'You must stop dreaming about this life and join our jihad,' the youth with the eyes says.

'I am married, Saleem, but I still have a lot of life in me,' Raju says ignoring Khurshid.

'This bastard has more children than he can count already,' Barkat says nodding towards Raju.

Khurshid recites a few verses from the Quran. The lads sit up in respectful silence. Khurshid says 'Infidels are razing Afghanistan and you can only talk about women and cigarettes.' Turning to me he adds, 'And brother Saleem, you too should shoulder your responsibility and help our Afghan brothers. Should kafirs be successful in Afghanistan then it will be our turn next.'

I am thinking of a reply when Barkat says, 'All Raju is asking for is a British cig and a white woman. He can easily smoke his cigarette and he has much to offer the white woman. Now you Jamaatias are being paid to fight this jihad of yours by mullah Reagan.'

'It's true,' I add, perking up. 'General Zia is nothing but an American pawn and all these jihad outfits are run with American money.'

Khurshid goes quiet for a moment and then starts shouting in Urdu, 'Communism Ka Kabristaan – Afghanistan–Afghanistan.'

'Afghanistan will become the graveyard of communism,' I translate inside my head.

Barkat looks Khursid in the face and says, 'Now behave, or else I will stand outside your house and tell every neighbour what you used to do with bava Bagga's donkeys. And not just the pretty ones.'

A young lad comes running out the of night, towards us, shouting, 'Soldiers!'

Everyone goes quiet. The faint thudding sounds continue as they have done throughout the night, but now they seem to be much closer. Hundreds of soldiers march past us in single file.

'Are this lot off to fight the Russians as well?' I ask after the last soldier is out of earshot.

'No,' Barkat replies. 'These are our reserve troops for Indian offensives in Kashmir. That border is very tense again and it is only 30 miles away from here. There are rumours that India is about to attack.' Barkat lights one of my cigarettes and continues, 'But it's all bullshit, you know. India won't attack unless America says "OK". And they can't say OK because these bastards have loads of bases over here as well and then there are their illegitimate children,' nodding to Khurshid, 'like these jihadis! Just who would India attack?'

'Kashmir does not belong to India or Pakistan,' I say. 'Neither should we be fighting over it.'

Khurshid says patiently, 'When we have liberated Afghanistan, we will free Kashmir.'

'That's if you can keep your dick out of Bagga's donkeys!'

'Problem with this world is all this politics,' Raju says pinching me on the shoulder. 'Salaam, yaar, my brother, can't you find me any old white woman?'

'So long as we have momins like General Zia,' Khurshid snaps, 'God willing we will be victorious.'

'I'll tell you about General Zia saab,' Barkat smiles. 'One day he was sinking in some quicksand and he starts shouting, "Help! Help save me." A voice beamed down and said, "This is God here. I will save you, but on one condition." General Zia replies, "Yes, yes. Almighty gee I will accept any condition." Voice said, "You have to speak truthfully." General Zia replied, "Is there anyone else who can save me?"'

Apart from Khurshid everyone else bursts out in laughter. Someone hands Barkat a lit cigarette. He inhales until the end glows. He looks around grinning, 'Get me a bottle-shottle, you sister fuckers.'

'Give him a bottle, yaar,' I shout across to the shopkeeper who has been standing all night leaning against a large freezer.

'You keep bottles flowing and I will keep screwing Zia until he regrets being born,' Barkat says.

'Yaar Saleem, we are all Muslims here as well you know,' Raju adds.

I nod at the shopkeeper, who opens the lid of the freezer, leans in, and comes back up with a fistful of fruit juice. We sit sipping the cold juice. Raju nudges even closer to me, letting out an exaggerated burp as he does so. 'Saleem, let us leave all this baq-baq and get back to our gap-shap,' he says.

'Shut up and accept your lot in life,' Barkat reprimands Raju. 'And stop dreaming about white women. You are not going to get a better-looking one than the one you have.'

'I am talking to my mate, Saleem,' Raju replies handing a bottle of drink up to a hand that lurches out of the shadows behind him.

'Raju, even if I could find one,' I smile, 'not that I can anyway, I mean I do not have white women pickled, ready for the picking, but suppose I could, they are not going to be Muslims are they?'

'Hunger has no religion,' Raju replies.

'You mean as far as you're concerned all holes are made by God?' Barkat chides.

'I may not be able to find you a gori, Raju,' I say, 'but you know there is a law in England that says men can treat other men like their wives.' Raju puts his arm around my shoulder listening intensely. 'If you like I can try to find a man for you?'

Raju goes into thoughtful silence for a moment and then asks, 'Will I have to give or take?'

'You shameless bastard, Raju,' Barkat chastises.

Raju ignores Barkat and starts twisting his moustache.

'Well if you take, I suppose you have to give as well,' I say patting Raju on his thin shoulders.

The lads laugh. Barkat hands my cigarettes around saying, 'Let us all enjoy some Valaiti nasha.'

'It's just poison,' I protest vainly trying to retrieve my fags.

'But it's Valaiti poison,' Barkat smiles lighting up.

Everyone goes silent for a moment. Matches crackle and flash in the moonlight. As the night has progressed the thuds have grown closer and closer, though still muffled by the hills around the village.

'That, Saleem,' Barkat says reading my thoughts, 'is our army in Tilla Jogian. They don't normally do this at night but these are dark times. They say India is about to attack from this side.'

Barkat nods to his left and then nods to the right saying, 'And Russians are going to take us over from over here, so we have to be ready to defend this country of ours. What would anyone want from here. I don't know. There is only hunger and more hunger. This is all baqvaas, big people's games so us little people just keep on going hungry. This is all a big drama being played out by that maulvi Reagan. But what really hurts me is what they have done to Tilla Jogian. They practice artillery there and are making a big facility so that big, big rockets can take off.' He stops mid sentence. His moist eyes shine in the moonlight. Marching footsteps approach us. Columns of soldiers march silently past us, in the direction of the border.

Tilla Jogian was a magical place deeply ingrained in my mind. I had heard about it in countless Punjabi folk songs. It was a place where Ranjha, the mythical lover of Waris Shah's heer had gone for his sojourn. But until now I did not know that this place was so close to our village.

As the last soldier disappears, Barkat says, 'See, Ranjhaya, no Jogi could sit under these bombs…'

'I have thought very hard,' Raju interrupts. 'I accept your conditions, Saleem.'

'Which ones?' I ask puzzled.

'If that is what it takes to get to England then I accept,' Raju replies.

The lads shout with laughter.

'Uncle!' A young lad protests, 'Are you willing to sell your honour, just to get to England.'

'Listen, son,' Raju replies, 'our country is run by these generals, who have sold their arses to America, what is my pathetic bum worth?'

'You have spoken well for once,' Barkat says placing his head across someone's thighs and stretching his legs across a few lads. 'You know I get around, and recently that no good Sheeda, who works in GCHQ, he told me that there was a meeting going on where all Pakistan generals were present along with an American CIA man, a big general or something. As this meeting was going on, a great big, ugly woman barged in. This American whispers to General Chisti, he is general Zia's righthand man, and this American asks, "Who is this woman?" and General Chisti replies, "Sssshh. Sir, please be quiet, that is General Zia saab's wife." Our American says, "My god if General Zia can fuck her than Pakistan is no problem."'

Khurshid stands up in protest saying, 'Only kafirs and communists can sit and enjoy this sort of conversation.'

'Oh, go get a donkey-shonkey,' Barkat waves dismissively towards Khurshid.

V

The image of two whisky bottles tumbling through the air seem to distract me for several days. No one comes to see me about their illnesses or asks for money, and the tape remains unplayed. One morning a letter arrives from England and for a moment my heart stops beating. I don't recognise it though and when I tear it open, it reveals a single scrap of paper from one of my co-defendants. It reads: *Don't do the dirty on us, you bastard.*

Early next morning an announcement is made on the village mosque's loud speakers. Haji Abdullah, son of Haji Nowab Din, it explains, has been martyred in England and his body is arriving at Islamabad airport tomorrow. I had grown up under the shadow of Haji Abdullah and was well aware of the reasons for his 'martyrdom'. He was one of the permanently rising stars among the mullahs of Bradford and lived only a few streets from me in Southfield Square. He was one of those inarticulate community leaders who the British media always manages to wheel out whenever anything to do with Muslims makes the headlines. He was the father of a flock of girls, who almost all the young men of his mosque were determined to court. At one time in his life he was a renowned boozer, one who was regularly seen with white women clinging to his arms. But as his girls began to grow and increase in numbers he discovered Islam. Until the invasion of Afghanistan by the Soviet Union he had spent a large part of his life raising money to ostensibly build a new mosque, in some part of Pakistan or other. After the invasion, he dyed his beard with henna and, along with his friend, Mohammad Azam joined a Wahabi sect who ran a series of Quranic classes on Blenheim Street. They stopped going door to door to collect money from people's houses and started to praise Shah Faisal, the Saudi King. Their meetings now were always followed by food and I attended a few of them and heard their new plans for the building of a major new mosque which would be called the Shah Nowaz Mosque.

It was now an open secret that the Americans were channelling money through Saudi Arabia to recruit Muslim youth to fight against the Soviet Union in Afghanistan. The Blenheim Street classes quickly became recruiting centres for young men wanting to go back to Pakistan to fight against the communists. As we were from the same village, Haji Abdullah had cajoled me into a few meetings. On one occasion I noticed a white American man sitting in on a session. He was said to be a convert, committed to fighting for the freedom of Afghanistan. But he talked only to Haji Abdullah and Maulvi Azam. Over the next few months each of them began to drive round in a new Mercedes Benz. Mohammad Azam would disappear for long trips and we'd hear of large amounts of money being sent to his relatives in Pakistan enabling them to move to the city.

As the work on the new mosque in Bradford progressed the two men began quarrelling. It was clear to all who still attended their classes that the fight was about who controlled the jihad funds, though it always reached us officially as some theological difference or other. The arguments came to a head on the inaugural sermon at the completion of the mosque. I had been forced to go along by flatmate Karamata, besides there was free food. Mullah Azam, who somehow had managed to avoid going grey with age was arguing that colouring any part of a man's beard was akin to a corpse being draped in a multi-coloured cloth, and was strictly forbidden by Islamic law. Haji Abdullah stood up from somewhere and started shouting that, 'No bastard should be allowed to swear in this house of God.' Mohammad Azam returned with similar pleasantries and several people left in disgust. Mohammad Azam rushed towards Haji Abdullah unpocketing a penknife as he ran and proceeded to stab Haji Abdullah. The latter being the stronger of the two then wrestled the knife out of his former colleague's hands and stabbed Abdullah back. At the time of my leaving England both men were still on life support machines in opposite Intensive Care beds of Bradford General.

A few hours later, along with Hamza and a busload of villagers, I find myself for some reason waiting in the car park of Islamabad Airport. The body of Haji Abdullah is being conveyed towards us across the tarmac, its weight shared between two airport trolleys. On the way back to the village, I sit in the front seat of the van carrying the coffin. Police and customs officers along the GT Road, on seeing our cargo, wave us through automatically.

As we approach the graveyard, hundreds of faces step out of the shadows. The wooden coffin in which Haji Abdullah's body was freighted to Pakistan is laid on an open stretch of grass and rows of men form neat lines behind a maulvi. I am in the first line. A man rushes past sprinkling everyone with rosewater. Just before the prayers begin an old man steps out of the first line, turns towards the gathering and shouts, 'Brothers! This funeral cannot take place like this.' Clearing his throat he raises his voice, points to the coffin and continues, 'This is a wooden coffin and it was made by infidel hands. In order for us to read funeral prayers, we must first remove this body, cleanse it, wrap it up in a new caffan and only then can we send him to his maker.' The gathering looks on in silence. The old man pauses and says, 'And then we must burn this wooden coffin.'

The coffin is made out of beautiful polished oak. An idea jumps into my head and I shout across to the old man, 'Babajee what you say is right.' Hamza, who is standing next to me, tugs on my arm and hisses for me to keep quiet. 'Haji Abdullah was a great, God-serving man,' I continue. 'He taught me all I know and I think you should bury him in the manner most befitting for a man like him. But I beg that you let me keep this wooden coffin so I may remember him. It is only wood and it comes from that land where I lived with Haji Saab.'

'Well spoken, my son,' the old man replies, 'and may Allah grant you a long life.'

In the next few minutes Haji Abdullah's body is taken out, and readied for burial. During this time my cousin curses, 'You sometimes talk out of your arse, Saleem.'

'I will explain, just listen, yaar,' I whisper back.

'You have an arsehole for ears; may you shite all over your shoulders,' Hamza swears as the prayers start.

After the funeral I find a donkey wallah and load the coffin onto the back of his beast, for a slow journey home. Cousin Hamza refuses to walk close to me and instead joins a horde of children who follow our progress along the winding road. The whole village watches on bemused. My father who must have got wind of what I was doing is waiting at the entrance of our house with arms folded across his chest, 'You are not bringing that thing into my house,' he says.

'But, Abbajee, it is only a piece of wood.'

'It had a dead body in it for God's sake, son.'

'I will get rid of it in a few days.'

'You will get rid of it now.'

'If it is that important to you then let us take it to Dina,' Hamza intervenes. 'I know where we can keep it.'

After loading the coffin into the back of a clapped out Suzuki van, we head up the winding road towards Dina.

'I swear England does things to you lot,' Hamza says blowing smoke out of the window. 'What in, God's name, are you going to do with this thing?'

'I'll tell you later, but tell me, do they always take bodies out of coffins when they're sent back from England?'

'I have been to many funerals where bodies have returned

from England, but no one has ever taken them out of the coffin – they have been buried as they arrived,' Hamza nods to the back adding, 'But what *are* you going to do with it?'

'I have only one hundred pounds left,' I reply. 'This coffin may be my salvation.' I am squashed next to him, squeezed in against the driver.

'A hundred pounds is a lot of rupees,' Hamza says.

'I'll tell you my plan when we are alone.'

'You can say what you like brother,' the driver whom the villagers call Pastoal – The Pistol – says, 'whatever you say will remain locked behind your lips, yaar.'

I look into the reflection of Pastoal in the mirror. He has sharp beady eyes and a leathery skin.

'We can trust Pastoal,' Hamza assures. 'He is an old driver and drivers have seen all there is to see, you know.'

'Well, Cousin,' I choose my words with care. 'When we came back from Islamabad, did you notice how no one stopped us?'

'Even police are human,' Hamza replies. 'They don't arrest dead bodies.'

'Precisely. And since I've been back, there has hardly been anyone who hasn't wanted booze. Even buffalos want booze here.'

'And what of it?'

'Well, as I see it. If we can get some booze then there is no shortage of customers. And as I still have a few rupees left I've been considering a small business venture. Just till I can get back to England.'

'And the coffin?'

'Well first of all, where we could get booze from?'

'What sort of a question is that?' Hamza tuts. 'I haven't spent half my miserable life wandering these streets for nothing.'

'Does that mean you can get some?' I ask.

'As much as money can buy,' Hamza replies.

'I have one hundred pounds.'

'That can buy some,' Hamza admits.

'And that's where Haji Abdullah's coffin comes in.'

'You can't be serious!' Cousin Hamza laughs.

'No one arrests coffins. We just have to make sure we go and buy on those days when flights from England come. There is always a coffin or two on them, isn't there?'

'You cannot find a better person to drive than me, sir,' Pastoal says placing a hand on his chest. 'But you know apart from money, if you could spare a little for me.'

It takes me a little while to convince Hamza but eventually he agrees. In two days' time there is another direct flight from England due in at Islamabad airport. That morning we load the coffin into Pastoal's van, cover it with old rags and set off to Islamabad. For added authenticity we hire two old women professional wailers, both at three hundred rupees. They do not ask any questions about what we're up to and agree to cry eagerly at any moment should we be pulled by the police. Hamza drives us to a street in Sector E5, near Blue Area, the business district of Islamabad. I stay in the van while he goes into a large house and comes back a short while later, smiling broadly. He leans over and whispers in my ear, 'I've bought 160 bottles of Murree beer at 25 each and also have one dozen bottles of whisky. We have to pay what we owe, it is on my honour.'

The booze comes out of the house in boxes marked *mangos*. Pastoal and Hamza load the booze into the coffin whilst the women squat under the shade of a large rubber plant. We set a heavy coconut under the frosted plate glass viewer of the lid. On the way back the women tie their dupattas round their heads and sit with the coffin in the back. And after only two stops on the roads from Islamabad to Jhelum, we arrived safely back in Dina. Cousin Hamza pays the women and they quietly melt into the side streets. By evening, we've managed to sell all the beer at three times what we paid for it and get four times as much for the whisky. Over the next few weeks we make regular trips to Islamabad, quickly acquiring enough money to fill most of the coffin with whisky.

We have become expert at packing the coffin in such a manner that none of the bottles rattle. On one trip, turning off the Islamabad Highway onto the GT Road I see a number of people standing beside a Suzuki van identical to ours. Drawing closer I recognise a few of them. They are returning from Bradford and as one of them recognises me, he flags for us to stop. Our routine well-worked out, Hamza flies into the back and covers the coffin with planks and old rags.

The returners, it turns out, are accompanying the body of Mohammad Azam, who too has succumbed to his injuries, and the van they travel in has managed to get one of its well-worn tyres blown. As time is getting on and they're running late for the funeral, we are asked to take his coffin in our van. Mohammed Azam's coffin is placed on top of ours and we set off towards Mirpur in Kashmir. Pastoal drives in terror of our coffin being discovered by the accompanying passengers. When we get to Mohammad Azam's graveyard, an enormous crowd of mourners gathers round our van. Before I've time to say anything they hoist both the coffins out and set them on the ground.

'Which one is my uncle's?' a middle-aged man with bloodshot eyes asks.

'This one,' someone points to the nearest.

A group of men step forward, place the coffin on their shoulders and disappear into the crowd reciting the Kalma.

'Where is this coffin going, my son?' a tired voice asks.

'Jhelum,' Hamza replies quickly.

A few men lift the coffin gently and place it back in the van. Pastoal who has been standing next to me has finished off a whole packet of cigarettes. His clothes are drenched with sweat and he is shaking visibly.

By the time we get back to Dina, it is almost dark. Hamza

pays the criers and they disappear into the city. Pastoal helps drops us off and leaves shaking his head, 'Toaba, toaba, and toaba.'

We sit around in the yard for a while too tired to consider what we may have just done. As I summon the energy to start unloading, it hits me. Hamza is lying under a ceiling fan and I run back at him screaming, 'We're dead, yaar. We have Mohammad Azam in there!'

Hamza jumps off the bed and rushes to me. He looks at the coffin in disbelief. He turns deathly pale, silently shaking his head from side to side.

'Go get Pastoal and let us take this body to Mirpur now,' I say.

Cousin Hamza does not reply.

'I said we have to get this body to Mirpur.'

'And what do we say when we get there, "Sorry, but you've buried our whisky!" '

'What are we going to do then?' I ask.

There's a pause as a skinny dog makes to leap down from next door's wall.

'He was a real bastard, you know,' I say nodding towards the coffin.

'You can't say things like that about dead people,' Hamza explodes.

'No point shouting at each other.' I try to calm the situation. 'We have to do something.'

'What?' Hamza asks.

'We should call Pastoal back and ask him to do something with this,' I suggest. 'We have plenty of money and we could pay him well.'

'I'll get him. You ask him and then you should go back to England.'

'I am happy to go now, but let us sort this thing out first.'

Cousin Hamza lobs a small stone at the dog as he leaves. The dog jumps behind the wall yelping. Hamza comes back with Pastoal a short while later. I explain the mix-up and Pastoal thinks for a while before saying, 'We have to give this man a Muslim funeral and then we have to bury him.'

We wait around till midnight then set off into the jungle. Following a dirt track into the hills north of the village until there are no tracks left, Pastoal pulls on the handbrake. We climb out and find ourselves on a new track of headlights fading into the night. We take turns to dig. I ask Pastoal to do the honours but he protests, saying he doesn't know any funeral rites. After a lot of discussion Hamza agrees to say the prayers, while Pastoal and I stand in a line behind him. Just before he starts, Pastaol shouts, 'Hamza saab, show this sisterfucker some dignity, yaar, and throw your cigarette away.' Hamza takes a few quick drags before stubbing it out – and we raise our hands in a strange kind of mime.

We bury Mohammad Azam before dawn, placing some freshly cut branches around the spot to make it indistinguishable from the terrain around.

When we arrive back at the house, Pastoal leaves us muttering, 'May Almighty ensure that our paths never again cross.' Hamza and I head up to the roof, but although we are exhausted we cannot sleep.

'Yaar, Hamza,' I say, 'that bastard is dead, and we can't just let all that whiskey go to waste.'

'I don't want to hear anything, just go back to where you belong,' he spits.

'But yaar, we have to sort this mess out.'

'This is not a mess. Everything else is a mess.'

Come next morning, Pastoal, Hamza and I are driving to Mirpur. A few young girls are sitting in the graveyard as we arrive, reading the Quran to what they think is Mohammad Azam's grave. Seeing us walking towards it, they stand up and leave silently. We sit around for sometime surveying the place.

'My son, you have come back so soon,' a man who introduces himself as Mohammad Azam's nephew exclaims. His shadow falls across my back. A fearful chill tiptoes up my spine.

'Yes, uncle,' I reply.

'Come now, son, you must be hungry. Come and have some food.'

We make many visits at different times over the following few days, to wok out an opportune moment to rescue the whisky. Intrigued by the regular visits of strangers, the local imam proclaims that Mohammad Azam must have been a saintly soul to attract such attention and, to my horror, he declares that the grave will be transformed into a shrine. He claims that he has seen Mohammad Azam in a dream and that he would sit for the rest of his life by this grave, offering amulets for those who could bear no children.

That evening, for better or worse, we decide to raid the grave. It is dark and the graveyard is deserted. I stand guard, whilst Pastoal and Cousin Hamza frantically rip into the grave. A short while later Hamza screams. I run down towards the grave and am relieved to see our coffin intact and surfacing. As Hamza prises the lid open he seems to moan with it. 'Some bastard has stolen our booze!' The lid falls back to reveal a row of boulders.

After shovelling the earth back into the grave we quickly make our way back to Dina. 'Yaar, I'm not a graverobber let alone a thief,' Hamza moans as we cross the Pakistan boarder. 'What did you learn in England?'

I don't answer.

After pleading guilty to the plates theft, the West Yorkshire Police regularly dragged us in for any crime in the area where Asians were suspected. Our flat became a weekly stop-off point for them, and the sound of the door being half-kicked in more regular than the alarm clock we never set.

I found myself pleading guilty to three further charges:

Twocking a blue Hilmann Avenger I had described to me so many times I began to think I *had* caused that dent in the passenger side door; assaulting a policeman who in actual fact assaulted me when I interfered with him assaulting someone else at Friday night throw-out time; and on a third occasion for simply being on the wrong street – on my way from the Central Library to Sunwin House – as a group of Asian youths ran past me. One of the police officers in pursuit grabbed me, threw me to the ground and handcuffed me, eventually charging me with possession of cannabis that he pulled from his own pocket.

In all three cases they had nothing on me and I held out each time, refusing to sign their pre-written statements. But the crunch came on the second night of interrogation when I could be relied upon to sell my soul for sleep. The last time I left the station broke and hungry, as well as raw all over. Karamata met me. 'Fuck it, yaar,' he said, 'we might as well *be* thieves.'

'As long as it's a white cunt,' I nodded.

We began stealing clothes and radios from shops and selling them for whatever we could get. It didn't take long before I started to get arrested again. This time though, knowing what they were talking about for once, it felt better.

One night, it was one of those nights when we didn't have a penny between us, we came up with another foolproof idea. There were four of us: a tall lad, much younger than us, called Mushroom, a small South Indian lad called Teddy, Karamata and myself. It was Karamata's idea. The previous night we had all gone to a disco at the Student Union building. When it came to leaving, Karamata had been nowhere to find. We assumed he'd scored and gone off home, but when we got back he wasn't there either. He turned up around 4am, carrying a sackful of cigarettes and a few bottles of spirits. He explained that he had been so drunk that he had fallen asleep behind some chairs at the back of the hall. When he woke up he was all alone. He took what he could carry and walked out of the fire escape.

'It's not even alarmed,' Karamata boasted, 'and I made sure it was locked after me. They won't even miss the stuff I took. The cellar is full of it.'

It was a Thursday night when we finalised the details. We would hit the place on Friday. Mushroom, the only one of us who could drive managed to get his hands on an old banger. Karamata and I stayed behind, with Teddy acting as lookout.

The plan worked better than we could have dreamt. We turned up at the dance hall, an hour or so before the end and hovered around, till just before the last song was played, then slipped behind some chairs and lay there as still as we could until the building was empty.

We first raided the fruit and cigarette machines of their money. We shoved this into two leather satchels. We were about to make our way to the cellar, when we heard a door creaking. We should have stopped in our tracks, but instead grabbed the money and ran towards the fire exit. It was at the bottom of a spiralling corridor. The exit door was chained. Still clutching the money we rushed up the stairs. A torchlight flashed. This was the only way out. We ran frantically up the stairs. An old guard blocked our way. He was panting. Karamata ran past him. The old man grabbed Karamata's arm, but he wrenched it free and ran out shouting, 'He's only a painchoud buddah.'

As I ran past the old man, he whacked me across the head with the torch. I didn't feel any pain and kept going. He grabbed hold of my jacket, shouting some unintelligible obscenities. I kept running, dragging the old man behind. Somehow he managed to latch on to my legs. We fell down and started to wrestle. The old man started coughing violently.

'Let go, you barmy old git,' I laughed. The old man coughed and tightened his grip. Each time he coughed his eyes seemed about to pop out of their sockets. 'Let me go or I'll fucking crack you one,' I hissed wriggling to free myself.

'For fuck's sake twat him,' Karamata shouted from

somewhere in the shadows. 'Mamays'll be here soon.' His footsteps became fainter.

I was scared of hitting the old man. Perhaps he was Mr Jacobs. Within a few moments of Karamata's words, the police arrived and I was once again in the cells. This time I was in for attempted burglary and I was sure to do time. The police tried to get me to name my accomplices. I maintained that I did not know them; we had only met in the hall that night and had done the job on the spur of the moment. I stayed in the station for the weekend and was brought up in front of the magistrates the following Monday. Karamata, Mushroom and Teddy along with Bava Payara Singh, were sitting in the public gallery. Seeing Payara Singh filled me with shame.

I pleaded guilty. My solicitor, a bored, grey-haired man, recommended to me by the police made some sort of a mitigating plea on my behalf. The magistrate was the same old, fat woman I had been in front of before.

Standing to attention before sentencing, I thought over the predictions of experienced cons, with whom I had spent the night in the cells. They had said I would get two months, at the very least. The magistrate peered down at me through her bifocals, lecturing, 'People like you bring shame onto your community. We consider your crime to be an affront to all that is decent in our society. Were it not for one thing, which you have done, I would not hesitate to give you the maximum sentence prescribed in law. There was no violence against the courageous security officer. In view of this fact, I have come to the conclusion that you shall go to jail for one year.'

My legs started to shake. The magistrate continued, 'Suspended for two. Do you understand?'

I nodded with relief.

When I walked out of the courtroom I swore at my mates for not rescuing me. They laughed at me. Bava Payara Singh ran his hand in a fatherly way across my head and said, 'Putter, you let them do this to you.'

I didn't reply. We walked out of the building towards a small, grassy mound opposite the town hall on the edge of what for some reason was called Norfolk Gardens. It was a bright, sunny day, one of those days when visitors to the city for the first time could almost mistake it for a pleasant place.

Payara Singh was a regular visitor to our house in Horton Park Avenue. He turned up like clockwork, every Sunday and brought us halva, purri and cholay from the temple. He was a tall, bulky man, with a clean-shaven, oblong face set with radiant green eyes. No matter what the weather, he always turned up in a long overcoat, the collar upturned. He'd spend the whole day with us, smiling now and then, but hardly saying anything. Yet we looked forward to his weekly visits, as this was a guaranteed meal.

Sitting heavily down in the middle of the grass mound Payara Singh asked, 'Do you know why I came today?' I shook my head without looking at him. He continued, 'I heard about you and thought these gorays had made another criminal out of one of my sons.'

Karamata, who had been fidgeting close by, winked at me and walked off with the others. Another machoud mission, I thought.

'Do you know why I come to your house every Sunday.'

'You have never told us.'

'You have failed to understand when I have,' Payara Singh cleared his throat. 'I long to hear the sounds of those words you boys say in your language. But you say them less and less.'

'Why so, bavajee?'

'More than your sounds, I love where those sounds come from.'

'We're just a bunch of jokers. Not serious like,' I said.

Payara Singh had a seriousness about him that day I

hadn't seen before. He said, as if in a trance, 'My son, I even know your village's name. Banyala.'

'Who told you?' I was surprised.

'You did.'

'I never,' I laughed, waiting for him to excavate one of his famous pearls of wisdom.

'You told me so with your own tongue.'

'But I only really speak English.'

'But when you don't. When you talk, even in those childish sentences. I hear flutes, wailing over those hills at whose feet Banyala sits.' Payara Singh took a deep breath and continued in a voice tinged with sorrow, 'I was born not far from there, in Katarian. Without your knowledge, off your tongue has rolled Pothowar's ancient music.'

Payara Singh's eyes brimmed with tears. Oh fuck, bavajee's off, I thought. Something in his voice made me feel a deep sense of loss.

Payara Singh continued in a voice that seemed to sing a lament, 'You come from a land of heroes and lovers, my son. Ranjha went for his sojourn in Tilla Jogian. But your heroes are not only those of myth and legend. There were those who spent their lives fighting their colonial masters. And they all suffered so much. There was Baba Mir Haider. I knew him well. He came from a place close to your village, but you don't even know he existed. That's OK. How could you know? These Angraiz are so clever. They make you feel, especially you youth, that somehow nothing existed before them. People like Bhagat Singh, and Udam Singh, they will never really die, they laid down their lives for you and you should know about them. If you don't know about your past, how can you understand your present? And if you don't understand that, then what hope is there for your future? These people are your history. They live in our memory. Memory never dies. It is reborn with each generation, always rejuvenated, full of past light, waiting to shine. You just have to learn to see it.'

'Who was Mir Haider?' I wondered aloud.

'That's not important now. I knew him well. Before 1947, when I was like you, before I left your village, I shared a dream with him. We wanted to be free not only from being ruled by this nation of thieves, but also from its illegitimate offspring. We wanted a country without hatred, a country of Heer, not one of Kaido. We never once doubted that some day, we would be rid of white man's Raj. But not in our nightmares did I think that I would have to leave my beloved, to come here. Perhaps we did not fully understand the power of Kaido's venom and how easily it could be used by these white snakes. It is still stinging all these years on, tearing Panjab's soul to pieces.'

'Did you have a girlfriend back then?' I laughed. Much of what the old man was saying didn't make sense.

'Girlfriend?'

'Your beloved, I mean who was she?'

'My beloved is still there.'

'Is she alive.'

'She is wounded and still young and will never die.'

'She must be very old now, bavajee.'

A smile flashed across Payara Singh's face. For a moment, he seemed to have become a youth again. Throwing his head back, he laughed, 'She is very old but still a child.'

'As old as you.'

'Much, much older.'

'Come on then, spit it out,' I mischievously tugged Payara Singh's arm.

'She is thousands of years old,' Payara Singh said shutting his deep green eyes. 'She is in all those red hills, and in those streams that flood during monsoons, and she is in each drop of rain, and comes out of my earth when it rains. She is in your voice. She is in those songs that echo through our valleys, sung by shaer-khwans and she is now here as well.'

'Bavays really do lose their marbles,' I laughed.

'It is where I was born and where I long to return.'

I was trying hard not to admit it, but Payara Singh had opened gaps in my own heart too and I was hungry to fill them. 'I think I understand, but where were you born?'

'Not far from Ramdayaal School,' Payara Singh said lying down, his eyes still shut. 'Do you remember it?'

I nodded.

'I knew your grandfather and raised your father in my lap.'

I felt strangely naked. Payara Singh continued, 'When I was young, Mir Haider used to say, "Dacoits have no colour". We must not let these white thieves, be replaced by those who look like us. Do you understand what I am saying?'

'I do,' I lied.

'How our simple folk believe in white lies. This country has done us no favours by bringing us to this land.' Payara Singh stopped, turned over towards me, adjusted his leg and asked, 'Was your grandfather a thief?'

'No!' I was taken aback.

'Your father?'

I shook my head.

'Thieves are not born, are they?'

I shook my head again, eager to get this lecture out of the way.

'Why are you here, in this country?'

A longing clawed at me. 'My mother couldn't afford to raise me,' I growled.

'Why?'

'I don't know.'

'You came here to grow up quickly and work. Now, I am but a passing visitor in this life. I am but a sigh from the past. But you, my son, in you are buried the dreams of our future. Yet you have let them turn you into a thief, a chour. A bandit. Everything is made by men, hands of men and women, those that live and those that have long since died.'

'I don't know what you're getting at.' I suddenly felt a pang of longing for my mother, for a mother I never had.

'A child taken from a mother is poverty's scar, a curse on this world,' Payara Singh said. 'How your mother must have loved you. How much is that love worth? How much did it cost her, even in her poverty to raise you? Imagine how much it costs to make a young man like you.'

'Perhaps we ought to have a pint, bavajee,' I said trying to wrench myself free from some invisible weight.

'We can have a pint-shaahint, later,' Payara Singh said dismissively. 'From day one, when a human child is conceived, how much do parents do? You are a child yourself. Imagine all that time and healthcare and food your mother and father spent on you. And when a baby is born in our country so many of them die before they get a chance of life. How devoted your mother must have been to save you from poverty's illnesses. And by your age, imagine, our countries pay for raising strong workers like you. How many times you must have gone to see a doctor? Your parents paid for that. If you were born and raised here, this country would have paid. It would cost them lakhs of pounds to raise just one worker. The Angraiz got millions of us to come here and work, and it cost them nothing. How much did they save? And these houses where we live, they may be better than where we lived before coming here, but you have to judge each place according to itself – these are not fit for white people's dogs, yet we live in them...'

Payara Singh continued his monologue, while I tried to add up the figures I'd seen quoted for how much Britain had saved itself by getting each foreign worker to come here. 'Painchoud thieves,' I whispered trying to come to terms with a figure too large to make sense.

'Yes, they are and you let them make you into a petty one,'

Payara Singh chided. His tone became more serious, 'My son, all that is made is made by man and you are a son of man. You are a young worker, who does not even know his own worth. They have stolen your world and your mind and you go and steal cigarettes, and think you have achieved something. Do not dishonour your ancestors. You should work, and only then will you find strength. There is no power in being alone. And this world belongs to us, workers and toilers and it really doesn't matter how long it takes, but one day we will take it back. When I was young, I used to think I could blow my oppressors away with one big phook. Youth has josh but no hosh. It has courage but no wisdom. Now I have hosh, but no josh. Each generation has its own role to play. We kicked gorays out of our homeland – what will you do? Steal from pubs and...'

Payara Singh stopped mid-sentence. A distant thudding sound, which I had assumed was coming form a building site not far from where we were sitting, now became clear as the banging of drums. A white police riot van drove by and parked a few yards away.

'Your family came to Banyala around 1890 because of what England did to Kashmir. That is why Kashmir is still bleeding today. In 1846, when England ruled India, they sold Kashmir to a Dogra called Maharaja Gulab Singh. They sold all your ancestors for three hundred thousand pounds. It is a lot of money now and in those days it must have been an awful lot more. But they sold everything. Our jungles, our people, our animals, our rivers, our lands. Everything.

'Maharaja Gulab Singh was a Hindu ruler who, like any businessman wanted to get his money back from his investments. There used to be a law which said that if you killed a cow then you would be sentenced to death and if you killed a Muslim Kashmiri then you would be fined a few paisas.

'In those days they used to have a thing called begar. It was a system of forced labour, not much better than slavery, where young men were forced to build roads and work for Maharaja often till death. Your grandfather's father used to say that his father told him that during his father's time, even a whisper of this word used to fill everyone with terror.

'Back then Maharaja was always fighting wars. The place most Kashmiri Muslims were conscripted to was called Gilgit, and it was a place few returned from. It was a long way from Jammu and the Kashmir Valley, and in those days there were no real roads. Everything the Maharaja's army needed was carried on foot, through mountains in snow and rain. His soldiers used to come and take Muslim men as a part of begar and these would act as carrying mules for Maharaja's army to Gilgit. Those that didn't get forced to go weren't that much luckier either. They used to have to pay all their harvest over to Maharaja Gulab Singh's men.

'You may not know this, son, though we call ourselves Choudry, we are really all Kasbis by caste. Before leaving Kashmir your ancestors used to weave cloth. But some time back, machine-made English cloth started flooding into India from Britain. Those British rulers were clever, they took raw materials from India and brought them to Britain, made them into industrial products and sold them back to India. In places like Bengal, they couldn't compete with the local cloth, a soft fabric they called muslin, not matched by anywhere else. They said it was so thin and soft that 20 metres of it could be folded into a matchbox. This cloth had been produced in India for 3,000 years, or maybe it started during the Indus Civilisation which is nearly 5,000 years old, and though many invaders came to our lands, it survived everyone. Everyone but the British that is. The East India Company destroyed local production thread by thread, by cutting off supplies to any weaver found still plying his trade. Weavers across India starved to death. A decade or so before they sold Kashmir, it became so bad even the Governor General, William Bentinck, declared "The bones of cotton weavers are bleaching the plains of India."'

The white police van suddenly screeched away from us, cutting Payara Singh's words in its roar. I was hyponotised by this history. He paused for a moment and stared thoughtfully in the direction of the police van.

'Your side of your family comes from a buzzrg called Sona Shah. They used to say that Sona Shah was a bit of a rebel in Kashmir. Maharaja's men came to take him away for begar but he managed to escape. Some say that he then got work in a clothing factory of some sort. He became a leader of workers there and led a strike about something. He was arrested and sent to jail. But he managed to escape from there and he went to his village. There was then a raid on his village and he was taken with other able-bodied men for begar to Gilgit. He was one of those lucky one who made it to Gilgit alive. When he got there, one of Maharaja's officers swapped him for a dog and he was taken to some place even further north than Gilgit. But he escaped from there and went back to Kashmir. When he got to Kashmir, there were no men left in his village. During this time there was also a terrible drought. There was no food to eat and it was then that he is supposed to have left Kashmir. But they say that up till that time when his legs would no longer carry him, along with a few others, he used to go back to Kashmir and fight Maharaja's soldiers. And look what you've turned out into?' Payara Singh sighed pushing himself awkwardly upright by pressing his hands into the freshly mowed grass mound. There was no traffic on the roads.

'You are not a thief, chall putter,' Payara Singh beckoned, taking a slow step towards the noise, 'let's march with some workers.'

I was filled with shame. I was tired from my time in the lockup and wanted to have a pint before going home to sleep. 'Bavajee, I am finished today.'

'Jump on my back,' Payara Singh laughed, 'I am still young.'

I decided to walk with the old man for a while. By the time we reached the police, the front end of a noisy demonstration had crossed down the hill and was slowly inching forwards. As soon as Payara Singh joined the march he started chanting, 'Workers… united… will never be defeated.' All frailty left him. His heavy voice lost its age. His limp disappeared. A few paper sellers came up to me. I shook my head at them, but Payara Singh bought some editions and a few magazines and gave them to me. Someone gave me a leaflet with the headline: *Victory to the Valley Strikers.* The demonstrations snaked, as far back as I could see, almost everyone was white. The Asians were mostly at the front. I didn't recognise any of them. This was the first large, white crowd I'd known that didn't feel hostile. There was a strong sense of some purpose, which I didn't understand.

From being just a speck in the sky high above us, a helicopter grew louder and larger until it roared just overhead. Mounted police blocked the road leading back to the police station. The drumming subsided. Some people, wearing armbands, ran up and down both sides of the demonstration, urging everyone to link arms and remain calm. Hordes of people shouting angrily, rushing forward. I felt a rush of adrenaline race through my body and joined them. Two rows of people wearing armbands stood in front of us. Not far behind these, behind mounted police, penned in by a line of uniformed officers, stood a group of white men waving Union Jacks.

We stopped. The demonstration went silent and then a huge roar rippled through the crowd and the drums beat back into life. The demonstration inched forward, away from the racists and slowly crawled round the town hall, heading towards the steps that led back towards the magistrate's court.

I let myself be swept along, listening to all the chants and megaphone speeches, and learned that a group of Asian workers had been sworn at by the management, denied masks, forced to bring their own protective clothing, and in attempting to set up a union 30 of them had been summarily sacked. By the time I learned what everyone was protesting against, I realised Payara Singh had done one of his disappearing acts again.

VI

It is two weeks since I last heard the voices of the children singing their *Alif sey aam*, and Barkat still doesn't have his goats. We are waiting for a bus to take us to the Jhelum district magistrate, to whom he is to deliver a letter from the village's Union Council in support of his claim. He is convinced that, being a foreigner, I would help his case by being present and increase the likelihood he won't have to pay a fine.

Sitting under the tree's shade beside the well, I begin to doze, only opening my eyes to see Barkat drying his hair with a scarf. A group of women, with water pitchers on their heads are walking away from us, into the blazing sunlight beyond the trees.

'It's too hot for us lot, and for you Englishmen it must be unbearable,' Barkat sighs, sitting down next to me. He offers me a cigarette. As soon as I take a drag I feel as though a burning match has been thrown down my throat.

'How do you smoke this thing?' I cough.

'We desis are sun-ripened,' Barkat says, letting out a hearty laugh.

A bus announces its approach through a pressurised horn. A musical tune of, *When the Saints Go Marching On,* rings out across the hills, its echo bouncing gently back.

Pointing to the approaching noise of the bus I laugh, 'This

is a Christian song.'

'You Englishmen worry too much about Islam,' Barkat replies nonchalantly.

'Couldn't they get a desi tune?' I wonder aloud.

'What's in desi things?'

'This tune is ridiculous!' I chortle.

'This is bus 1971. Raja Ajaib owns it. He looks after it better than he does his woman. He has built this bus up from an old wreck and treats it like a proper maim.'

'Christian war songs,' I smile.

The loud roaring of the bus's engine soon drowns out its own music.

Barkat stands up, shakes a few ants off his arms and says, 'See God listens to even *my* prayers. 1971 will take me to my goats.'

'Let's go later, yaar,' I mutter. 'It's too hot for me.'

Barkat thinks for a moment and sits down again. 1971, a rusty old wreck of a mechanical monstrosity roars into view, throwing up a huge dust storm. A cloud of smoke follows its progress towards us. Men are packed together on the roof. A few rags for curtains flutter out of its broken plastic windows.

The bus chugs past us without stopping. Men cling precariously off some wobbly steps to the ceiling.

'How do you work in this heat, yaar?' I sigh.

Looking up into the light flickering through trees, Barkat replies, 'What does a man not do for his stomach?'

Some small insect of the earth bites into my leg. I sit up in pain. But Barkat is standing now and looking off towards a group of men who seem to be running towards the village. A few women are following them barefooted.

'What's happening, Barkat?'

'Allah knows,' Barkat replies stepping out of the shade.

I follow him out into the blazing sunlight. The heat is so

intense I have to stop after a few steps. Barkat disappears round the corner. A few moments later, above the stomping of countless feet, a body is being carried up the road on a bed. The carriers come up the hill and solemnly pass the glowing trees, caught in the madness of the blistering sunlight in raining showers of heat. Mirages ripple along the semi-tarmacked road. The trees seem to sigh. Barkat is carrying the front of the bed on his shoulder. A group of people follow the body in burdened silence. A man comes out of the crowd and relieves Barkat. Other men relieve other carriers every few yards. Women come out onto the roofs; a few children dangle their legs off the edge of the outer mud walls of their houses.

The body is close enough for me to see, ferrying towards me on a charpaee. A white shirt, spotted with blood, is lifted of its head. A group of workers in bedraggled clothes, with bloodshot eyes walk close by. The men carrying the bed turn towards the well and set it down gently in the shade. They quietly drink water and wash their faces.

'Jamil Jat was crushed under stones in Tarakki,' Barkat says placing his sweaty hand on my shoulder. 'He was his family's only wealth.' His eyes swell up and he adds, 'He was our class fellow, Saleem. We used to play together before you went away… they said a truck overturned and Jamil Jat was trapped under a rock and now he is no more.'

'Why did it overturn?' I ask.

'Saab! Why do they overturn?' a young man with a dusty face scolds me. 'Saabjee, this is Pakistan, not England. No one cares about poor folk. Contractors, truck owners, police and all those big saabs, they just want money. They don't care. I was there. I saw what happened. Who cares about poor folk?'

'How did he die?' I ask.

'Does it matter? Vachara is dead,' the worker says, his tired eyes ablaze with anger. 'Poor man dies. Dog dies… who cares?'

'How did the truck overturn?' I ask again.

'Yes. Yes. It overturned.' The young man wipes sweat from

his brow, his voice relaxes a little, 'Well, not overturned, sir. You see… no one listens to us workers. We are paid a few rupees to load a truck. Truck owners earn by weight. Perhaps Jamil knew today was his last day. 2040, it was an old junk box really. It had no life in it. Its sides creaked even when it was empty. It groaned under a little bit of weight. We warned Naik Saab, the owner, but he just laughed. After we finished loading 2040, we sat down under a kikker's shade and I started smoking a beedi. As 2040 went past, its side just fell off. Thanks to Almighty, I am still here, but two big rocks landed on Jamil. I can't remember whose scream was whose after that. We moved one of those rocks off him. Blood was everywhere. He opened his eyes and stopped us from doing anything else. He had a look in his eyes, which mountain workers sometimes see. Jamil hated cigarettes. He used to say if our Lord had wanted us to smoke he would've put a chimney up our arses. But he asked for a cigarette. I lit him one. But he had no breath and it fell into his blood…"

The worker stares a moment at us then rejoins the carriers. The men carefully turn the deathbed around so that the head is facing forwards and, followed by the crowd, they set off in the direction of Jamil Jat's village.

Barkat and I are left alone at the well. We remain in solemn silence, broken only by the hoofs of the buffalo and the peaceful dripping of the well.

'Will his family get any compensation?' I wonder aloud.

'Compensation!' Barkat exclaims.

'From his employer ,I mean.'

'He worked for his stomach, yaar,' Barkat says screwing his eyes. 'What was Jamil Jat's life worth, eh? They didn't even bring his body back in a truck. His fellow workers will lose half a day's pay for carrying him back.'

'But why don't they protest?'

'Against whom?'

'Their boss.'

'And what will that do for Jamil, eh?'

'It may save another Jamil Jat's life.'

'What is written is written.'

'Who wrote Jamil's Jat's destiny!' I storm.

'Almighty.'

'Then why the fuck does he give less life here and more in England and to those who don't even believe.'

'You really are a gora.'

'Do you think white skin would be destined for a better life here?'

'Don't get technical yaar?' Barkat laughs.

'We have unions in England. Is there one in Tarakki?'

'And what good are they, eh?' Barkat asks interlocking his long dark fingers. He pushes his palms forward. The fingers crack. 'Working in Tarakki is not like working in England. Who knows where that bastard truck owner is now. If you get hurt in Tarakki, there's no medicine-shedicen. If you get hurt, you get hurt. There are no hospitals nearby. No doctor-shoktars. They are 15 miles away and no better than butchers.'

'This is terrible' I despair, my eyes closed.

'What is terrible, Valaiti saabjee?' Barkat chides. 'It is life. And if we protest then who against, eh? There is no government here. There are only mullahs or lullahs. Mullahs bark a new tune each time they need money and lullahs rule us. Valaiti babujee, you may have seen more of the world than a simple man like me, but I understand more. Politics is a game for those rich bangla-wallahs. Here if a poor man lifts his head too high, they chop it off.'

Barkat's words 'Valaiti-babu' follow my thoughts. I am still a child, I think to myself in English. I thought I understood the world. But Barkat is right, I am nothing more than Valaiti-babu, a gora, imprisoned in the skin of a Paki. A Paki in England, unwanted. A Valaiti in Pakistan, naive, arrogant, despicable.

'They carried his body all that way from Tarakki?' I ask unnecessarily.

Barkat doesn't reply. A child yells somewhere in one of the houses behind the well.

'Jamil Jats are lucky to be carried,' Barkat says walking into the sunlight. 'Will you try again with me tomorrow with the magistrate? I must rescue my goats. Jamil's funeral is at four today. Make sure you come. You went to school with him.' With a few quick strides Barkat is out from under the shade, melting into the day.

Barkat's words make me think of the comradeship I thought I'd glimpsed back in England, and of my first proper job. It was in an old spinning mill, past the leafy lanes of Oatley, making cloth for what we'd been told were uniforms destined for the Saudi Arabian Air Force. It was summer and the mill overseer had asked for volunteer workers to work through the holidays on a one-off order. Two of us, a shy young worker called Khalad, who had started at the same time as me, came forward. It was around 2am, when the overseer had asked. With hindsight, I should have followed the example of the older workers and kept quiet. We accompanied the overseer through the tight, winding staircase of the mill and walked up a few flights of steps when he stopped and said, 'Lads, all you have to do is to clean and paint the water tank at the top here. Do a good job as it feeds the sprinkler system.' It seemed straightforward and we nodded silently. The next Monday morning, the first day of the annual holiday when we came to work the machines were silent. The yard had a few cars of the officer workers who we rarely talked to. It was eerily quiet.

'Better you than me, son,' the guard – an old, constantly coughing man – said. He dangled a bucket in front of me. I grabbed it. Leading us to the base of the tall red-bricked chimney, he coughed, spat phlegm onto the ground, tilted his head back, looked up to the chimney and said, 'God help us if ever there's a fire. The shite in there... They should have built a new one long ago.' Leading us through the base door, he chuckled, 'Coming down's a bastard.'

A winding stairwell inside the building curved up for a few flights and then we came to a small door. This led us onto a metal staircase that snaked around the chimney. We were to climb to the very top and clean the water tank. As we got higher, the chimney began to sway in the wind. The staircase stopped short a few yards from the top. Here we had to lean up, without any protection, grab hold of the top ridge and pull ourselves up. Khalad followed me silently. By the time we got inside, we were ticklish with sweat. The wind howled angrily outside. A wooden plank had been placed across the water tank. A small, wooden pillow was placed on either side of the plank. Dead birds were floating in the water, along with all manner of other rubbish. A small brick ridge ran around the inside. A pack of cards, wrapped in a see through plastic bag was waiting for us in a hole in the wall. A sign in faded handwriting was pinned to the side of the tank. It read, *To the poor bastards who have come up to clean this tank. Do not stir the water. You will die of the smell. The bosses won't come here. Enjoy the cards. John and Mark. 1965.*

Comradeship is a language, I told myself on the 86 bus home from work that evening. A code set down in fragments, in ruinous runes, a trace signal that echoed of an alternative history – one that people actually take part in while being told they're merely spectators. Comradeship, I told myself that day as we lurched through Oatley, was a cipher, that now and then politicians and men of letters, tried in vain to *de*cipher.

Since the day of the Valley Strikers' march I'd read every leaflet and newspaper Payara Singh had bought me, stockpiling them under my bed after each Sunday visit. Every article felt like a new clue, a new suggestion at how to interpret this other-history.

One of the first I looked at had a picture of Asian workers on its cover under a bold yellow title *Don't Blame Immigrants*. It was only a few pages long, with questions and answers like *Why are Immigrants here?* followed by long, forceful explanations about the British postwar labour shortage and how each adult immigrant worker saved the British economy an average of £40,000 in education fees and the cost of bringing them up. Or headers like *Oppose Racism!* with arguments about division being a deliberate, calculated tactic of the bosses.

Another leaflet announced a demonstration about Palestine, condemning Israel as a capitalist European colony lubricated by racism, justified by Scriptures. Never had I imagined that white people would engage with this struggle in any way other than how we'd been taught it by the local mullahs and religious leaders, as a religious battle.

I began asking questions that I felt half ashamed to ask. Why did my grandfather serve as a soldier in the British Army for a country that now wouldn't let his daughter into it? Why did God make us, the Believers, so poor and these white people, who spent their time getting drunk, so rich? How come most of us believers in places like Pakistan died before we got to 50 and the unbelievers in the West lived long into their seventies.

A thrill ran down me the night I came to the heart of these interpretations. Communists, I had been taught by my Quran teacher, Haji Abdullah, are Godless creatures who were spawned by the devil. Though I didn't go to the mosque much any more, the fear instilled by the mullah remained. And there I was, in bed, with the most forbidden book of all in my hands: *The Manifesto of the Communist Party*.

The yellow flyleaf explained that the book had been published in China. I was confused. Why should something in English be published in China? Flicking over the first few pages I sat intrigued at a picture of a silver-haired white man with a thick beard, like that of a Sikh or a mullah but without a turban. The bearded man was wearing a smart jacket and looking away into the distance, a smile buried under his moustache. Underneath the photograph was a signature: Karl Marx. On the next page there was another picture of another bearded man, with the biggest, bushiest moustache I'd ever seen. He too was smartly dressed but, unlike the first, his hair was neatly combed. He was also staring into the distance. He had signed his name, *F Engels*.

The first page said, *Preface to the German Edition of 1872*. Lots of countries were mentioned over the next two pages. Whatever this thing was it was in lots of places, I concluded, flicking quickly over to another preface, this time of the Russian edition, then the English one, a French one, another German one, then a Polish one and finally an Italian one.

I couldn't understand many of the words and kept returning to a dictionary to decipher them, often failing to understand the dictionary as well. But then I reached a passage, which made me sit up in excitement. It was not so much that I fully understood the words, but that they created a kind of awe in me, the feeling someone was talking to me directly from a century before: *The history of all hitherto existing society is the history of class struggle. Freeman and slave, patrician and plebeian, lord and serf, guild-master and journeyman, in a word, oppressor and oppressed, have stood throughout history in constant opposition to one another, carrying on an uninterrupted, now hidden, now open fight, whither in revolutionary reconstruction of society at large, or in the common ruin of the contending classes.*

Three weeks after seeing my mother, dark in her grave, her tape is still rattling in my pocket. The wound-up spools of her message knock against their casing as I tap the thing, pacing from kitchen to sofa to veranda. Outside I can hear grandmother's words, floating in on the evening's breath, blending with a chorus of dog barks and the sound of a far off car. Finally I sit down on Mother's flowery, cotton-covered bedsheet and press the play button and the whole thing comes to life.

The birds in the trees seem to be singing of daytime, though it is now night.

'Yaar,' Hamza sighs, having followed me in cautiously, relieved to see me finally sitting down with her. 'Khala must have started the recording at noon.'

'I know,' I croak.

My father's voice hums faintly from inside the speakers, floats over the songs of the birds and slithers into my head. He is saying something to someone. Someone clears their throat. My stomach tightens to a warm, burning pain and a chill runs down my spine. It is distant at first, but gets louder as she closes in on the microphone. She is saying to someone: 'Is this mother fucking machine working now or do I have to do something else to it?'

'Turn your head the other way and speak,' comes the fainter reply of my father.'

'Hallo. Hallo. Saleem, my son,' Mother's voice fills the veranda. 'Assalaam Alaycum… So, how are you? Where are you? Where-ever you are, I pray that Almighty Allah looks after you. Ahmin.'

My sister is shouting something to Mother from somewhere in the background. But Mother continues, 'And if you were at home with us today, you could eat these lovely mangos with me.'

Mother laughs. Her voice is weak. From the loud clattering sound, which the cassette lets out, I guess she may have just knocked the tape recorder over. She says, 'Your father brought these huge mangoes home. We put them in a bucket and lowered them into our well and they have been in there all day and now they are lovely and sweeter than honey. Everything would be so perfect if only you were here, sitting in front of me, eating them, wiping the golden mango mess from your mouth. You have always loved mangos,' Mother pauses.

The sound of a match being scratched into life tells me she must be lighting a cigarette. She begins again slowly, her voice gently swelling and subsiding. 'There is so much I want to say and I hope God gives me time and strength to say it all. But if He gave me another life to live all over again, even then I wouldn't have enough time to say to you all that I would want to. If I live long enough, then I shall post this cassette to you myself and I will pray that you come back to me after hearing it. But I don't think I will live to see your sweet face again, my son. I feel my time is up. I hope Almighty grants me a place in heaven and looks after you…'

'You are not going anywhere,' Father interrupts jovially. 'You'll bury me before you go anywhere. That's our family tradition. You women always manage to outlive your husbands. You women have got life too easy, sitting at home and chatting all day.'

'It's not I who has eaten, and eaten and become such a sandah, with a drum for a gut. I'm just a walking corpse,' Mother hissed.

'She eats two parathas every morning, Saleem,' Father giggles back at her.

'Stop this baqwaas. I'm talking to my son,' Mother scolds, her voice cracking. 'I have no teeth left and I have not eaten a paratha since you last left for England. My taste buds died when your plane took off. Because I couldn't make parathas for you, I couldn't make them for myself…' Mother sobs.

'What are you crying for?' Father asks. 'He's probably out there chasing white girls.'

'I'm crying at my fate and I want you to go away and leave me to talk to my son,' Mother replies firmly, sniffing back her words.

'I'm going to sit here and make sure you don't fill my son's head with women talk nonsense,' Father teases.

'You never listen to me. Women twice my age are running around. But they don't have drums for husbands.'

'Come on now,' Father's voice changes to a softness I've never heard before. 'We'll soon have you fit-faat and you'll be running for our Pakistani Olympic team.'

'See Saleem. Your father is always making fun of me. I've

told him a hundred times that I don't want this operation. But he wont listen to me. My operation is in two days' time, but I know my time is up…'

'Oh yes. She's got a direct line to God. Truth is this, son. Your mother is a coward.'

'Get up from here this minute. Go away you big, fat sandah you,' Mother says chirping like a little girl. 'And for God's sake let me be with my son.'

'Alright. Alright. But leave a little space for me.'

There is a little pause in which the bed creaks and my father's footsteps fade away. Then Mother clears her throat and continues in an animated voice. Though a little weak, her old voice is back, 'He's gone now. He calls me a coward. But you will never meet a weaker heart than your father,' Mother laughs loudly. 'Most men zabah their own goats and other animals, but your father can't even manage to do a chicken. He is such a drama. When he is forced to, he will just about manage a chicken. But when he is just about to run a knife across its throat he will always close his eyes and turn his head away. I am not sure he even reads takbir, so he may have even made us eat haram! But that's your father. When he goes out to fields to do his shit, he has to first work out which direction the wind blows. For if ever he smells his own crap, he just starts vomiting. Sometimes it is so bad, that men have to carry him back home. And if you ever want to find out how weak he really is, then when you meet him next, just lick your finger and place your wet finger into his ear and watch what he does. But don't do this in public, Saleem, for he'll make such a mess and go red like a tomato. I don't want him humiliated.'

Mother laughs and sighs to herself. Another match is scratched into flame. She inhales audibly. The birds in the background fade away in unison. Night marches on. She clears her throat. 'I could tell you a thousand things, my son, a lifetime of things, but for some reason right now all I want to tell you about is our house. We built with our own hands, you know. You English wouldn't call it much. It was not a pakka house. It was just one room to start with. I built a little basaar from tree branches like we used to in those days, before these cement monstrosities came along. I was so proud of my little house, I was. We made a huge pile of gara which your father was supposed to mix. You make it by mixing soil with hay and buffalo pah. We plastered all the outside walls with it, and it dries as good as cement. No matter how hot it gets outside, inside it's always cool like a fridge, and in winter it's always warm.

'I remember your father was mixing this stuff. He pulled his shalvar up and, holding his noise with his other hand, he walked over that gara. Unlike nowadays, then he wasn't such a big drum. He must have walked around for several minutes before he noticed that his feet were crusted with pah. As soon as he did though he started retching. You should have seen everyone laughing at him and calling him names. I can't talk about your father vomiting and swearing back at them, without tears rolling down my cheeks. He was retching so much he got dizzy and slipped and fell into it. After that he was ill for two weeks and most of the house was built before he got better.

'And what a beautiful little house it was, Saleem, standing there all alone, far away from other houses. We only had two rooms and these were built with neela pathar, a blue stone brought here on donkeys from Tarakki.

'I used the leftover stones to build our courtyard wall. I did this all by myself. We had no gate then and at night I used a mat of thorns. But at least we had some purda. And just outside where we now have stairs, I made our first tandoor and a chullah. I built these with my own hands as well.

'In our yard we used to have a great big jandh tree. I built a thallah round its trunk and filled that with sand which I always kept moist and on top of this we used to keep our water pitchers. Our jandh was very old, it was even older than me, and its shade was so sweet, it kept our water cool.

'Children used to come in when our jandh's fruit was ripe to throw sticks into its branches then run around picking up ripe baers that fell down. One of its branches grew away from our house and children tied a swing to it.

'As well as the jandh, there was an old, tattered grape vine sprawling around our yard, and against your father's wishes I saved that from the axe as well. It nearly died when we built the house, with all the dust and dirty flying around, but thanks be to God, it survived. I trained it so it ran into our basaar, and that year it gave so much fruit even your aunties couldn't eat it all.

'When we first dug the foundations of our house, Saleem, we dug them so deep a man could stand inside. We came across some round boulders, which we thought were just rocks, but when we dug around them they turned out to be the lintels of another house. See, son, how deep our foundations are here. We found coins buried in among them too. Some were British Raj mint, others far older with indecipherable writings on them. Your father's friends quarrelled over how old they were, some said they were from Buddhist times, others said they were from the days of Alexander. Either way we buried them again, with some of our own, so that someday, when you rebuild here, you or your children, or your grandchildren may find them again.'

Mother goes on to tell of the mischief I got up to when I was a child, the incessant questions I nagged her with, the chickens I once killed by accident, thinking they had sunstroke. 'You won't remember now,' she whispers, 'but when you were a little boy I used to sing you *Saif-al-Maluk*. She cleared her throat and started singing. It is a deep, laboured voice shaking slightly through the night. As she sang my father came into the house. Over her voice he says,

'I didn't know she sang *Saif Maluk* for you, Saleem.'

I pause the tape and make my way onto the veranda where dinner is waiting. I eat without speaking. Today is Shabraat and the village has been preoccupied with festivities. Sweetmeats have been distributed to bands of boisterous children. We all sit, subdued, listening to a visiting mullah singing through the village mosque speaker:

'Today is when Angel Jibraeel comes down to earth and brings with him all that will happen next year; who will live; who will die; who will be born and when they will be born.'

There is a short pause after which the mullah mumbles something about how we're all privileged to have Imam Zaffarullah Khan visit our village. A few moments later, the new mullah starts to speak. His voice is full of authority. It echoes menacingly against the hills. The mosque's PA system is turned up and there is the loud screech of feedback. I stroll inside, hoping the noise of the fans will drown out the speech. But there's no escape. I can still hear the unintelligible din from the speakers. Khan is warning the village against lighting candles on graveyards saying this is not part of Islamic faith. There is a thunderous roar of approval.

After everyone has gone to sleep, I pick up the cassette player and walk out of the house. It is a moonlit night pregnant with the songs of crickets and the howling of jackals. Shadows cling to the hills. Keeping a safe distance, a pack of stray dogs barks angrily at me. Their eyes blaze in the moonlight. I pick up a small rock and lob it at one of them. The dogs yelp and run a bit further back and start barking again. Walking nervously past the dogs, I head towards the two hills that overlook the graveyard. Way beyond the GT Road is a twisting river, ablaze with headlights. Like a giant snake with hundreds of eyes blinking from its body.

Our graveyard is dotted with lit candles. A little beyond, in the next village, more candles flicker, and beyond these yet more flames cut into dark swathes of the night. I stand momentarily paralysed by these eyes in the darkness. I have no idea there were so many graves dotted around these hills. A comforting blanket of tranquillity wraps itself about me, pulling me towards Mother's grave.

During my years in England I lived in dread of graveyards. They were places of bodysnatchers, ghouls, vampires and other creatures of the night. I spent years watching late night horror films in which women were ritualistically deconstructed, first by the evil vampires, then by the vampire hunters brandishing stakes. Graveyards were filmsets for gaudy-coloured fear. Hammer horrors. Christopher Lee's running lipstick. But here I'm not scared. Something inside me edges me on. What can there be to fear from your own village's graveyard? I, too, will one day be buried here. Why should I fear the spirit or ghost of my mother or that of my grandmother, at whose feet she now lies, or that of my grandfather, or my dead uncle, who I've never met, and because of whom I went to England? Why should I fear the graveyard of my ancestors, who never dreamt of harming me in life? The spirits of my ancestors would only awake to protect me.

Mother's grave is covered in candles, some of which have been blown out, others flicker on, swaying gently in the breeze. After relighting Mother's unlit candles, I pick about the other graves and light more. Some flames vanish as soon as I light them. I chase dying candles until I stop suddenly – lighter in hand – in awe of the flickering on Mother's grave. I sit down by her feet. And as I do I think I hear a voice, riding on a gust of wind touching my head. It whispers, 'It is not safe to sit so close to a grave so late in this night.'

I smile to myself. The whisper is nothing but a passing thought, a shadow from those horror films in England. But then I hear a sharp rustle in the wild grass not far from me. I jump up startled. Something moves, a snake perhaps, maybe a lizard.

'You never really know what is happening in a graveyard.' The whisper returns, now laughing a warm laugh deep in my head.

I bend and kiss Mother's grave. Dried rose petals have melted into the earth. The scent of earth mixed with those of the rose petals lulls me in a motherly embrace.

A large flock of glowworms are dancing around in front of the entrance of the hills that leads into the village. All around, in almost every cranny, in the wild bushes, are throbbing particles of light. They blink over the dips and hollows that lead back down towards the graveyard where candles fight for life. The glowworms hover over the shining waters of a twisting stream in which the full moon floats. In the distance, below the lights of the GT Road, a Karachi-bound train worms, rattling, through the hills. Its lights garlanding sections of hill as it plays hide and seek.

On a bit of clear ground not far from where I stand, some pebbles flash out from the grass like cat's-eyes. They are encircled by the glowworms. Here, among the eyes, I sit down and play Mother's message. She is singing *Saif-al-Maluk*. Perhaps the glowworms know her voice and cannot bear to hear it again on this night of nights, or perhaps they know where she is now, for they fly over the falling hills to fuse with the candle lights. The flickering grows brighter and the songs of the other creatures of the night seam to blend. It is as though the land itself is singing. And my mother is singing.

She stops and the tape abruptly cuts out and cuts in again. The birds have faded from the background and it's clear, with her, it's daytime now. Mother says, 'I hope you liked what I sang for you. I used to sing it for you every night when you were my child. I used to sing until you were so deep asleep that I could hear you snore and even then, sometimes, just when I stopped you would sit up and say, "Ammajee, you have not sang me about Hunter and Dove." Even if I had, I would always sing it again for you.

'I don't know whether you know, but your date of birth on your passport is not your real date of birth. You are about one year younger than what it says in there.

'You were born during a very cold night. We had terrible winds that winter. My body still shudders thinking about them. Everyone in our village lived in kacha houses then. But we built fires and huddled up under big, warm quilts. There was plenty of firewood in those days as well, not like now. Our jungles were blessed with God's greatest creations. Our pallahi tree we can burn even when it is still fresh and wet. Our jungle was tight with so many trees then. Nowadays we have to walk for miles before we can collect firewood…'

Mother starts laughing to herself, the telltale sound of a striking match and another long breath. 'In those days Massi Patho and Massi Pago, two twin sisters, they always used to argue. It didn't matter what happened, to who it happened, or where, but they would have an opinion. And both of them always had the opposite opinion. It didn't matter to them who was right or who was wrong, they just had to be different from each other. One day, when Gama Kamhar's donkey gave birth to an ass, Massi Patho said, "Have you heard Gama's donkey has given birth to an ass?"

'And Massi Pago replied, "What do you know? I was at his house a few minutes after it gave birth and it was a donkey and not an ass."

'Massi Patho said, "What are you talking about? I was there. I saw it being born with my own eyes and it was an ass."

'Massi Pago wouldn't have any of this, "How could you know what it was? You couldn't see a camel even if it was standing next to you."

'Massi Patho always had an answer for everything, "I know because I was with him when he bought this donkey. And it was not a desi donkey he bought, but it was an English donkey. It was a white donkey and it gave birth to a baby that was also white."

'There was only one thing the pair didn't fight over. It was a bitch called 'Gultern'. Sometimes they would not eat themselves and give their share to this animal. But each time Gultern gave birth they would argue with each other, especially over who would get which pup.

'There must not have been a night colder than that winter's night when Gultern gave birth again. Massi Patho and Pago came rushing over to our house to tell me their good news. It was just as well. I was on my own and you, Saleeem, were ready to come out into this world.

'Those twins were strange creatures, if ever any walked on God's earth. It was from them I learnt *Saif-al-Maluk*. When they sang they used to sing together and there was magic in their voices.

It was as though Mian Mohammad himself was singing through them.

'Against everyone's wishes each year they always went to Khari Sharif mela. But Massi Pago and Patho were no ordinary girls. We couldn't go to Khari Sharif on our own, what with all those men and so many hoodlums there, but no one dared to turn a stern eye towards Massi Pago or Patho. They were braver than any man I met. They were so beautiful that even a prince would not have been good enough for them, but they never married. They always said they would only marry a man that the other approved of. And of course they could never agree and both of them left this earth without ever getting married. They used to laugh saying, "No man has yet been born who is worthy of us." But as they grew older, they didn't always argue like they used to. For a long time they hardly said a word to anyone apart from, that is, to recite *Saif-al-Maluk*. They weren't from our village. They weren't even born Muslims. They became Muslims after coming to Banyala.

'They came to our village in 1947 when Partition happened. It was a terrible day that day. We heard such tales that even now my blood curdles to think of it. Thanks be to God that nothing happened in our village, or in any other village around here. And yet people talked of murder and massacres and rivers full of bodies.

'I can still remember when all the Sikhs left our area. We didn't really have any Hindus around here. They mostly lived in Jhelum and other cities. They were rich people – at least that is what our elders used to say. We Muslims owed them a lot of money.

'But those days when Massi Pago and Patho came here were days filled with fear and nights when no one slept. When Sikhs left our area, everyone came out to bid them farewell. So many people were crying, so many tears were falling into the ground it could have made a river. Sikhs had to go to Domeli train station. Hundreds of people accompanied them to Domeli, where they caught a train to Hindustan. Your grandfather carried me on his shoulders and never once put me down.

'There were thousands of people there. I didn't know there were so many Sikhs living around here. They all got on a great big train, more crowded than anything you'll ever see. And they went away. After they left all those who had gone to see them off waited till they could no more see that train, and then they all walked back in complete silence. All you could hear was the sound of people walking. I've never heard our jungle so quiet. No animal or bird uttered a single sound that day. There was no wind either. No one stopped to drink water or take a rest. Everyone just walked with their heads down. No one really understood why all this was happening. It was just happening.

'But when we got back home women and children were all standing together, waving towards us. Our young men began running homewards. Everyone was pointing towards Tarakki Bridge.

'Some men collected weapons from around the village and ran off towards Tarakki Bridge, where a train had been forced off its tracks. Others stood guard all around the village. There was talk of dead bodies littered like dry grass everywhere. At first I thought that all those people we had just seen off had been killed. But their train had not gone in this direction. What had happened was this.

'A train coming from Peshawar with Hindus and Sikhs had been carrying nothing but dead bodies. We'd heard of a lot of Muslims getting murdered in India but, as God is my witness, nothing of this sort happened round here. At first I didn't believe all that talk about a train full of corpses. You heard so much talk about so many horrors then that it was hard to tell what was true and what was a lie. But when some of our men came back they said it was true. Dead bodies were everywhere and the vultures were almost blotting out sunlight. Your grandfather went along as well. Right up to his dying day, he never slept properly after that. Many, many years later, even on his deathbed he said he could still hear the groans of dying men and women. "Someone give them some water," your grandfather said just before dying. "In Allah's name give them some water."

'It was a hot August day when that train of death derailed.

All the men who came back from it came back covered in blood. There wasn't one of them who wasn't weeping. Some of those that died were buried there, but most were taken away by another train. God knows where those poor souls went.

'Bava Fazla – he is still alive and when you come you should ask him about this day – he recognised one of those who had been killed as his old friend. Against our imam's advice Bava Fazla brought his friend's body back with him and he refused to let his friend be buried. He kept saying, "My friend was a Hindu and I will give him a Hindu funeral". Our imam threatened Bava Fazla with a fatwa. And a special imam who was passing through our village that day said what Bava Fazla was doing was a terrible sin in God's eyes. That it was every Muslim's duty to try to convert nonbelievers towards Islam. This imam, I forget his wretched name, said that we should just dig a hole as far away from our village as we can and throw this body into it. That no one was to touch this Hindu body. Fazla was so angry he nearly killed this special imam with an axe.

'Just about everyone in our village collected wood and they built a huge pyre. People brought ghee with them from their houses and gave this to Bava Fazla. Bava Fazla covered his friend's body with ghee and started reciting some Hindu prayers and then lit his friend's pyre with his own hands. He waited until next morning and collected his friend's ashes and covered his own body in them and then ran around everywhere naked. People said he had gone mad, but he used to say, "How can *I* be mad, when I am covered in all this madness."

'Aside from Bava Fazla, some other people brought some injured men and women back as well. But they were so badly hurt they all died. Before dying, though, some of them told us what had happened.

'The killing had started just after their train left Peshawar. They were forced out into a great big field and that is where it all started. Some Hindu men were kept alive. They were made to throw dead bodies back into that train again and then were themselves killed. Those killers all wore masks across their faces, but they seemed to be following some sort of orders, from another masked man who spoke in English. They stopped killing only when they were exhausted and only had strength for robbing dead bodies. How anyone survived such butchery is a miracle. But you know, son, you can never kill everyone. Someone always survives to tell their tale.

'Killing took place in many other places until this death train fell off Tarakki Bridge. They said robbers had gone through each compartment, killing anyone who seemed to move, stabbing corpses as the train swayed them. Though all the adults on the train were killed – hundreds, maybe thousands… no one knows – some children did survive.

'This is how Massi Pago and Patho came to our village. These two were brought to our village.

'At first Massi Pago and Patho were kept hidden for their own safety. Sometimes large bands of strange men speaking strange languages would come wandering around here asking for non-Muslims. God knows where these devils came from, but they filled us with terror. We girls used to lock ourselves inside when they came. Not one of those children who were brought from that train was ever given up. The men would come like a hurricane and then disappear just as quickly.

'This was a parting present you English left us with, eh.

'But I hope you aren't bored with me yet, son, and you're still listening.'

Mother stops. A match cracks. The railway line is quiet now. Where are the corpses of mother's story buried, I wonder, staring back at the flickering candles.

Mother clears her throat and stops my thoughts trundling backwards. She says, 'I am supposed to be telling you about when you were born. I must be going crazy. Massi Pago and Patho came just as I was going into labour. They helped to bring you into this earth. Just after you were born, they started arguing with each other over who will give a gurrutti to you. We do this when a child is born. It is your first taste of a sweet thing. Anyway, after a lot of arguing they decided to do it together. They dipped their chichi finger into some honey and then put that honey into your mouth.

'I can't tell you what date it was when you were born but it was the last month of 1957 and winter had just started and that is when you were born. On a cold, windy night, but it was my warmest and happiest of nights. You won't know today what I felt like. Maybe men will never know, but when you have children, even if I don't live to see them or hold them or tell them stories, even if their own children never learn to call you 'dadi' – for such was written for me – even then, you can't know how much joy they give you.

'You were pure joy for me then, as you are now, and though I've never stopped crying since that day when I lost you, you must never forget: never for one moment did I hold one wrong thought about your actions.

'I know you are angry with me and you have every right to be angry with me. Sometimes I have been angry with your father and my father and I have cursed them, especially him, I have cursed him to his grave for taking you away from me. I curse you, England, for robbing my motherhood, for leaving this cursed separation on my shoulders, which is now pushing me into my grave. I want to know of you, England, and you English mothers, how could you think you could take my son and keep him?

'And I have been angry with God himself. He may punish me and I will find out soon enough, but why did he make us so poor? But God has never answered my prayers, Saleem. I have asked only for the simplest things in life, and they have never been granted me. Maybe God has a reason for not answering my prayers, maybe he is testing me. But how much more can he test me? All I ask now is a glimpse of your face, a word from your lips before I die.

'I have met many mothers who also had their sons taken to England. Not one of them is happy. All England's wealth is not worth a single tear of a mother.'

The heat from the ground rises into the night.

'Those few times you did come back to your mother, those were the only moments of happiness since you left, Saleem. I still have some of your clothes. They are still as they were when you took them off all those years ago. I wouldn't let anyone wash them. When I was really, really missing you, I would just sit and smell you.

'You were so clever as a boy. But you're my son, so I'm bound to say so, even if you were as thick as Reema Kamhar.

'You went to school first time in Karachi, when your father was posted there. I lost you once when you were a little boy there. Even then some Angraiz nearly took you away from me. You got your father into a lot of trouble that day.

'We used to live in Cantt and your father's unit was being inspected by some big officer saab. They were inspecting big, big toap guns. But that day someone had deflated all the tyres on every single gun. War with India was about to break out and military men were moving a lot of things all over. When they came to move those heavy guns, of course they couldn't.

'A big officer said Indian agents must have sabotaged them. All soldiers were made to stand in a long line and some very, *very* big officer came. Your father was one of those who stood in those lines. I don't know what this big officer said to those soldiers, but they looked really terrified. We women were standing by a gate through which this officer had to leave. You were holding my little finger. As he was going past us, this big officer said to another officer, "But who could have managed to let air out of all those tyres without ripping any of them or being seen?" You heard this officer say this and snatching your hand free from me you ran straight towards him shouting, "I know, uncle. I know how to do it."

'That big officer stopped and asked you, "You do, do you?"

'You said, "Yes I do, uncle." And then you started running towards those guns with the officers following you.

'I ran after you as well. I didn't know whether to shout

after you or what. When you got near a tyre it was nearly twice as big as you were. This chief officer said to you, "Go on then, show me." You looked around and found a tyre that still had some air in it. Then you climbed on top, lay across it on your stomach, swung your head down until you had its valve in your teeth. Then you twisted it and pulled until it started letting air out.

'You should have heard all those men laughing. That big officer asked you, "Why did you do this?"'

'You said, "Because I like hearing them fart and they can fart longer than my father."

'The officer picked you up and asked, "Whose son is this?"'

'Your father stepped forward. He looked like a corpse he was so scared.

'Holding you up that officer said, "Here is your Indian agent."

'Your father pointed towards you and said, "Wait till I come home tonight. I will make mincemeat out of you."

'You must have really got scared that day. As everyone laughed, you slipped away and I couldn't find you anywhere.

'You were missing for nearly four hours and I ran about like a mad woman. I ran through bazaars screaming and shouting and if it wasn't for those crazy people who followed those gorays who had you, I may never have found you. There was a tall woman. They said she was Amreekan, but I don't know where she came from. She was buying you all sorts of things. She said you looked so sweet she had to buy you something. I think she had no children of her own otherwise she would never have walked away with another mother's son. But still, years later, I still lost you to gorays.

'Maybe if your Uncle Shabir hadn't died when he did you may never have gone from me. He was a little older than you and it was he who was supposed to go to England. But such are God's ways. He was such a happy boy, so healthy with big round eyes and a smile that never stopped shining. Then one day he got a temperature and they took him to Doctor Kassam in Dina. He gave him an injection and sent him home. That night his body swelled up like a balloon and by morning he had left this world and gone to meet his mother.

'Do you remember your naani, Saleem? No! How could you, I suppose, how could you when you don't even remember your mother, eh? You're such a silly boy for hurting your mother so. But no matter how much you hurt me, I will always love you, and your naani used to love you more than she loved her own children. She used to say, "You must never let Saleem out of your sight or else he will be cursed with someone's evil eye." Perhaps that is what happened and that's why you went away. I don't know.

'Maybe your grandfather would not have gone to England were it not for white people coming to build Mangla Dam. That is how we got electricity so early in this village. You know that road which goes to Domeli? Well, our graveyard used to stretch way back there in those days. They needed stone for building Mangla Dam and had to make a wide road up to Tarakki Mountain where they blasted it out. Your grandfather made them electrify our village in return for giving them land for their road.

'It was around this time when all the roala started about going to England. Your grandfather was a schoolmaster in those days and it was he who supported us. Your father had just become a sapaee and we had no land of our own to live off. Your grandfather and his brother were our family's first two to go to England. In fact they were our village's first. They borrowed money to buy their tickets. All of us women sold what little jewellery we had to pay for their journey. Then getting to England wasn't like what I hear it is now. Agents used to come to villages, with great big drums and used to call people together. They used to say what English people wanted them to, "Valait jullo… sarkaan sonay nal sajain nay" – Come to England, where the streets are paved with gold. Other people talked of the fantastic machines you had in England. You could put a goat in one end and mincemeat would come out the other, or if you put mincemeat in the other end, a goat would come out the first! They must have thought us village folk stupid, eh son?

'Your Uncle Shafqat went shortly after that and when my father came back after a couple of years he said he would like to take you with him as well.

'At first I thought it was all a big joke and I used to laugh and say to him, "He's your son anyway. His naani merely raised him for you! Besides he is too naughty and never lets me rest." How these words haunt me now. I never knew how much you let me rest.

'I soon realised that my father was very serious, but still I laughed at him for I didn't really believe you would go. Then a few days before he went back to England, your father, your grandfather and your Uncle Khadim sat in our house. Your Uncle Khadim agreed with me saying you should not go. But he only said this because he wanted *his* son to go in your place. I was happy with that but your father and grandfather wouldn't listen to me. Your father never said an angry word to me, but my father told me to leave men to their business. And that's when they decided you would go.

'My father took you to England as his son. In place of your Uncle Shabir. Before you left you had to learn to call your grandfather *father*. But you were very quick and sharp and no one doubted you would fool Englishmen when you got to London.'

An owl hoots somewhere close by. It is a haunting sound, filled with the emptiness that seems to bounce off the hills. A moment later a second owl replies. A shadow passes down over the hills.

'Have you ever noticed, Saleem,' her voice asks me in the darkness, 'when you break a branch off a plant, drops of water seep from its wound? Well, it isn't water, son, it's tears. And if you look carefully at the droplets as they well up, you'll see this scar will never heal. But who listens to cries of plants?'

The owls call out again to each other. Further off the multi-coloured lights of passing trucks and busses mock the darkness. 'When you left, all our village came to see you off. We stopped in Gujarkhan and there you met your dada. You never saw your father's father again after that. He died a few years later. But that day he was so angry. He shouted at your father, "How dare you pluck this flower out of the earth and send him away without his mother?" He was an educated man your dada was. I don't know why your father didn't inherit any of these things. But he didn't say a word back. I just cried and told your dada you were leaving against my wishes. Your dada started sobbing too and said to your father, "Do you know what will happen to your wife when she goes back home after sending her son off? And do you know what you're sending your son to, to a land without parents."

'Your father kept quiet, but I cried and I always cried after that day. I have shed so many tears that you could make a river with them. Your dada gave you a glass of milk which you drank. You left and when your plane took off, I felt I'd been buried alive. Your father and I said nothing to each other on the way back. When we got home he started chopping wood and clearing up. He wouldn't look me in the eye. The house was so cold but inside, my heart burned and still burns today. You left a hole so big you could sink a world in it.

'I kept thinking I would find you here, playing under this bed, climbing over that chair, running into our house, running around, crying here, laughing there. I kept thinking you were just playing one of your hide and seek games, you were in a trunk somewhere and I'd locked it by mistake. That night, I didn't go to bed but just stared up at the stars, just to see a glimpse of your plane. I didn't see anything. I couldn't eat until your grandfather's telegram arrived saying you were safe.

'But I was a walking corpse by then, living only for those days when your letters arrived. At first you wrote once every long week, then once every few weeks, then once every few months. And then you stopped writing at all.

'I begged your father and grandfather to bring you back. But no one listened. I went to every shrine and prayed and begged for your return. Each day became a lifetime and my whole life felt like one long day. Once I walked across to where we'd go together to cut grass. I thought I saw you following me. Then I became frightened that you were trapped somewhere back in the house, kicking and calling, and I ran back calling for you, listening. I lost my will to live, Saleem. One day I went and laid down across that railway line near those trees you used to love watching Karachi trains from. I prayed and prayed for a train to come. I closed my eyes. Everything was spinning. I heard a train hurtling somewhere through the hills behind me. When I opened my eyes I was at home. Your father was there and there were others, crowds of others. I thought they were there to tell me you'd been found. I begged your father's forgiveness for losing you. I'd been a bad mother who'd lost her firstborn son. But they hadn't found you. Your father said you were in England, probably chasing after English girls and that you would come back home soon. Then I quickly got up and ran to get your clothes so you would have something to wear when you got back. Each year I used to have new clothes made for you. This way I knew how tall you were getting. I put the keys to the old trunk in the trouser pocket of each new pair. But one year I reached into the pocket of the last year's trousers and they'd gone. I looked everywhere, but couldn't find them. It seemed so funny for me to be looking for keys when I didn't have a son. I started laughing and all I could think and say was, "Keys." I wanted keys for the house, keys for your father's suitcase, keys to that day when I let you go. Keys to let you out, let you out, let you out. I laughed and laughed and laughed until I couldn't stop laughing.

'All Doctor Kassam could suggest was I take up smoking. He said they would help calm me down. At first I used to feel sick each time I tried one, and then I couldn't go to sleep till I had had one. I became an old woman although I was still young.

'I hope you never smoke, Saleem. But I suppose you will. All men in our family smoke. That is, apart from your father.

'And then, like Eid's moon, you came back to me. You probably don't even remember, but you brought me a pair of shoes.

I still have them. They are still in that box you brought them in where I keep our quilts.

'You stayed with me for five weeks and three days. You had grown so big and you were so handsome and just seeing you made me feel young again. When you went back to England you wrote to me every week again, but now you wrote to me in English. It didn't matter to me what language you wrote to me in, but you wrote to me and I knew you weren't angry with me. Then I don't know what happened but all of a sudden you stopped writing to me and you didn't write to me for five years.

'I didn't know where you were and no one would tell me anything about you. Whether you were alive or dead, my God only knew. Your grandfather stopped replying to my letters and your uncle said you had "become a hippy" and had "gone off with hippies."

'During those days your grandfather fell ill and he came back to Pakistan to die. He should have died out there in that cursed land where he belonged, then I would not have had to set eyes on him again. Before breathing his last, he cried and asked me to forgive him for taking you away.

'I used to sit by the GT Road looking for hippies. One day I saw what must have been some. They came in a great big bus and stopped near Domeli Morr. I thought you had come back. If those hippy men didn't have beards then they would have looked just like their women. They looked so dirty. I ran towards them. They were smoking charas and some of them were drinking sharab as well. I ran around their group and forced my way onto their bus. They had a Pakistani bus driver and he translated for me. I was crying and one of those hippies offered me a hundred rupees. I think he thought I was a beggar. I threw it back in his face and they all got scared of me and quickly got back on their bus and went away.

'Whenever I heard of white people passing through the area I would rush to find them. No one knew you, but I never stopped looking.

'I wanted to go to England. One day I went to Islamabad's

British Embassy. I went on my own because your father wouldn't take me. I begged a white officer. At first she wouldn't say anything to me. She just smiled and nodded and kept saying something to a Pakistani man who kept telling me to leave. I made so much noise that two tall white men came out with two Pakistani guards. They listened to me and then their guards pushed me out. I nearly didn't come back home and my God knows if I wasn't carrying your younger brother I may never have done so either.

'And one day you just came back. You just turned up. Silly boy. You didn't even let us know you were coming and I had no time to get myself ready for you. Do you remember that hot day when you just walked in? I would so much have liked to have met you at Islamabad airport, just like all those other mothers. But my son has to be different and just turn up!

'Do you remember once you came back from Jhelum and knocked all your food out of my hands. You asked me then why I had given you nothing when all parents give their children so much. Those words of yours, they tear at me and I have never stopped thinking about them. But son, I would have liked to have given you so much more, and not just life. If you can find it in your heart to forgive your old mother then I will rest happy after I leave this world. But son it wasn't that I didn't give you what I should have given you, it was England that stopped you from receiving what I had to give you, what I needed to give – more than all that money that your father thought we needed. That bastard of a white country robbed both of us from each other and now I can no more turn a clock back than I can save my life or put off that day when I will go and meet my maker. I know I have a lot to ask Him.

'What is it about that mother fucking country that makes you all forget us back here, eh?' her voice reproaches me with a new vigour. 'Is it the white women? Is it sharab? Is it the air? I don't know, but you forgot me again. You only ever wrote once since your last visit and I haven't heard a word since.

'Anyway, I beg my Lord to keep you safe. I have never once believed you have done anything wrong and even if you have,

I will always have been there for you. But what can I do now?

'I am going to stop now, my son. God has been more generous to me than perhaps I deserve. A few years back your father started selling hay. I don't know where this crazy man got his idea from, but one day he just got up and said he was off to sell hay. That night he came back with a sack of notes. I thought he had robbed someone. He tried to tell me what he did but to this day I don't understand what he does. He used to come back and give me a bundle of notes and I always told people it was you who was sending me money from England. You may still find a bundle stuffed in some pillow or other. That's what I used to do each time he gave me money. He has a lot of money now and there is even an account for you and you have a lot of money in it. If ever you come back, then there will always be money for you to spend on whatever you like.'

Her voice trails off and I can hear a struggle deep in her throat. After a moment she continues in a shaking voice: 'Anyway, son, you will always be my special precious child. And don't forget now, you have a lovely brother and a sister and don't be angry with them because of me. Your father is old now and don't be angry with him either. Forgive us for what we have done to you and don't cry too much when you come to my grave, for if you do, like that branch I too will cry.

'Make sure you stop smoking and don't forget your religion. May God look after you...'

Mother cries quietly as her hands seem to knock against the tape recorder.

VII

The letter I posted to Mother finally arrives.

'Here, elder brother,' Shabnam hisses resentfully, flicking a large white envelope towards me. 'Go read it to her grave.' The envelope knocks against the green leaves of the hibiscus plant, Mother's pride and joy. The branches tremble and a bright red flower falls to the ground. A crow cackles and takes off from the top a eucalyptus tree that Mother had planted against the outer wall, and which now provides privacy against the prying eyes of men who sit on top of passing busses.

I stand up in terror. My throat drying and my stomach in knots. The tips of my ears burn. The envelope hovers over a jasmine flower that has been planted in between a bed of broken bricks. I try to shut my eyes, hoping to escape the onslaught of the words in the letter, but they stubbornly remain open. Burning wood crackles in the tandoor behind me. A few stray sparks blow over me, brush my face before dying angrily. The letter continues on in its accusing journey towards me, slowly slicing through the air. My sister runs out of the house, crying. Her dupatta brushes over a pool of dirty water and follows her out.

The envelope slides to my feet, blocking the path of a long line of ants. By the time I stretch down to pick it up, the ants have established an alternative route.

The letter feels heavier than when I posted it in England.

I was in prison for just over a month when I started writing the first line: *Mother, I am now in jail, in this bitch of a country called England. I may never see you again...*

My daydreaming ended abruptly. Gower accompanied by the two plain clothes reentered the room. With Gower standing by the door, the other two moved the chairs towards me and sat themselves down. They each carried a large bag which they placed on the floor next to them. For a while the three of them stared at me in silence. Eventually Gower said, 'These officers want to talk to you.' He introduced the short scruffy one as Officer X and the other, a tall man with flaming hair as Officer Y.

'What's this bollocks?' I protested nodding towards Officers X and Y. 'Have these things got no proper names.'

'Our names are of no concern of yours,' Officer X said in a croaky voice.

'I need to know me accusers' names at least...'

'We are not your accusers,' Officer X interrupted. 'We are not interested in what you have done.'

'I've done fuck all.'

'We just want to have a chat, Saleem,' Officer Y said in a BBC voice.

'Shall we go down t'Jacobs Well for a pint, like?' I said.

Officer X opened his bag and took out a box file marked 'EVIDENCE'. He scribbled something into his notebook. Taking a few books out of the box file, he asked without looking at me, 'Have you read these?'

I recognised my books and blurted indignantly, 'You should. Perhaps you might learn something about the world you're defending.'

Officer X looked at me coldly.

'Am I on trial for reading?'

'You are not on trial,' Office Y replied.

'You have lots of Socialist Workers Party pamphlets in your flat,' Officer X said.

'Are you a member?' Officer Y asked.

'No. I am not a Trot.'

'Why then have you so much of their literature?' Officer X asked.

'For fuck's sake,' I protested, 'some of their ideas are barmy, but I didn't think reading their stuff would land me in here.'

'You have books about the Black Panthers,' Officer X said.

'I read them to learn from their experiences.'

'Do you think this country's like America?' Officer X asked.

'No, but you lot are up its arse though.'

'Why do you have pamphlets in your flat stating the Falklands don't belong to the UK?' Officer X asked.

'What's that got to do with anything?' I asked.

'We are about to go to war to get them back and you ask this question?' Officer Y demanded.

'How the fuck do the Malvinas Islands, out there near Argentina belong to you lot, eh?' I rise to the bait. 'Have they discovered oil out there or something?'

The officers flicked a stare at each other and continued.

'Why have you been involved in so much anti-police activity?' Officer X asked.

'I fight for what I believe is right.'

'What do you think the main job of the police is?' Officer Y asked.

'It is an instrument of oppression.'

'What should be done with this "instrument of oppression"? Officer Y asked.

Officer X added, 'Destroy it, join it or change it?'

I paused. I was beginning to enjoy the discussion. It was a challenge; I had almost forgotten where I was and who I was talking to. You are being interrogated by the political police, I thought, you daft git, get a hold of yourself. You ought to keep that trap of yours shut rather than sing like a bleedin' canary. I was slowly waking up to my own naïveté. The officers looked on in anticipation. 'Any of you boys got a fag?'

D S Gower leaned back and pulled a packet out of his trouser pocket and pushed it across the table towards me. I took one and was about to push the packet back towards him when he said, 'Keep it.'

'I want to see my solicitor,' I demanded.

'What for?' Gower asked offering me a light.

'It's my right.'

'If you've done nothing wrong then you don't need one,' Gower said, putting the lighter back in his pocket.

'I want to talk to my solicitor, now,' I insisted.

'Write the name and telephone number on this,' Gower said, pushing a pen and piece of paper towards me.

I wrote the name and number of my solicitor and pushed the paper back towards him. He looked at it for a moment and then raised his fluffy eyebrows saying, 'That communist bitch. I ought to have guessed.'

Turning towards X and Y, I hissed, 'Unless you give me your name and rank and which fucking department you're from you can both get stuffed.'

'There's no need for that, Saleem,' Officer X said. 'What has got into you?'

'Your talking to us is purely voluntary,' Officer Y added.

'Well fuck off then!'

Officers X and Y exchanged a smile and sat staring at me

for a while.

'Now tell me, Saleem,' Office X said looking through his folder, 'what should be done with "the instrument of oppression" as you put it.'

I sat silently trying not to reply. After a few moments Gower broke the silence, 'Saleem may be hungry, it's way past lunchtime.' Smiling broadly at me he asked, 'Feeling a bit peckish are you, kid?'

'I could eat a horse and chase the jockey.'

The three officers stood up to leave. DS Gower opened the door. When they got to it X and Y stopped and turned around. Officer X was holding a dark yellow 12inch of mine, the corner of the sleeve dog-eared over the record inside. The title read *Inglan Is a Bitch*. Officer X ran his finger over the cover saying, 'This sort of rubbish can really screw up your head.'

'True his voice could wake up the dead, but the magic is in the word,' I laughed falsely. 'D'you get what I mean?'

I was left alone for a long stretch. I lost track of time. Judging by my rumbling stomach I guessed it must be past mid-day. The more I thought about X and Y, the more apprehensive I became. Until these two came in I had been comfortable with the thought that I'd done nothing wrong or illegal, and that they had no evidence against me. I'd been in police stations before and had done everything experienced cons advise against. I'd broken all the basic rules: keep your mouth shut. It didn't matter what you said, it would only end up being used against you. There were no friends in here among the police. They all shared in one ambition – to have you locked up. They don't get promoted proving people's innocence. Keep your mouth shut. Do not make a statement. Do not sign a statement. Sooner or later, they will either have to kill you, and this is not normal, or let you go. It is always better to take a few days discomfort than spend a lifetime in jail. I was trying to strengthen my resolve not to co-operate with the police when DS Gower popped his head round the door and said with a paternal smile, 'Would you like a drink, Saleem?'

'Pint of Tetley's please. And can I talk to my solicitor now.'

'Still waiting on the boss to decide, mate,' Gower replied shutting the door after him.

'Waiting for the boss me arse,' I said out loud after he'd gone, 'you lying twat.'

Gower returned a short while later and placed a can of orange juice in front of me.

'Why is it open?'

'Rules,' Detective Sergeant Gower replied closing the door with his backside.

"What about my telephone call?" I asked, sipping.

'I asked the boss and he said he would let me know.'

'What's there to decide,' I said, finishing the drink in a few quick gulps. 'It's my right.'

'Your head is full of shit,' Gower said taking the can out of my hand. 'You watch too much TV.'

'At least let me tell one of my friends where I am.'

'In due time, sonny,' Gower said crushing the empty can in his hand.

DS Gower looked at me straight in the eye. His pink cheeks reddened. The pupils in his eyes contracted. He clenched his fist and said, 'You can make it as tough or as easy as you like.' He paused, took a deep breath unclenched his fist and added, 'Either way. You're going down.'

We sat opposite each other silently for a while. Gower pulled a tabloid paper out of his pocket, unfolded it and buried himself in it. I started to tap a Panjabi rhythm on the table.

'Cut it out,' Gower ordered.

I carried on tapping, deliberately varying the rhythms to cause maximum irritation. Gower unfolded the newspaper and flicked impatiently through it. Ever since drinking the can of orange juice I was buzzing with energy. It was as though I'd taken amphetamines. Officers X and Y had stirred something deep inside me. Why didn't they just ask the obvious question? What were they softening me up for? What had happened to poor Sajad? 'You'll remember to not run away from home next time, you poor sod,' I thought. I wondered about how many of my comrades had been busted. Was I right to do what I did, or was it just ultra-left adventurism that had brought everyone to jail? What would now happen to the organisation we had been trying to build?

A uniformed officer placed a tray of food in front of me, steam rising from the plastic mug of tea on it.

'Vegetarian,' Gower said, flicking a look at me before returning to his crossword.

I ate in silence and was halfway through the meal when Inspector Handley came in. He beckoned Gower outside where they whispered together.

Gower came back a few moments later with raging eyes. Slamming his fist on the table, he thundered, 'I know what you had in mind for us, you little bastard.'

Tea splashed out of the cup, landed on the table and dribbled down onto the floor.

'Oh, fuck off!' I groaned with a mouth full of food. I was beyond caring what they said or did.

'You arrogant tit of a two-bit terrorist you,' Gower hissed, his mouth frothing slightly. He was straining to stop himself hitting me.

'I have committed no crime,' I said holding my head up. Detective Sergeant Gower's rage chased all fear from me.

Gower smashed the tray off the table. Bits of food, the plastic plate and the mug of tea flew across to the other end. He pushed the table away and rushed towards me snorting.

I stood up, moved as far back as I could, clenched my fists

and shouted, 'Lay a finger on me and I'll give you one straight back.'

The door crashed open and four police officers charged me. They threw me on the floor. I managed to break the fall with my hands. One of them grabbed my arms and twisted them behind my back. They turned me over and threw a few punches into my stomach and then sat on my legs. DS Gower raised his foot to kick me. A pain ripped through my body. I don't know how long this continued.

'That's enough,' an authoritative voice ordered. 'What the fuck are you lot doing?'

I didn't see the face of the officer who'd stopped the attack. I was whisked off the floor and forced back into the chair.

'Either way we'll get what we want.' A few hours later Gower was back leaning over me again, hissing. 'You can play the hard cunt or you can co-operate. For what you tried to do, if it was up to me, I would deal with terrorists like you in one way.' Gower grabbed my groin, squeezed and said, 'I would hang, draw and quarter shite like you.'

I folded trying to kick my way out of the chair but the other officers held me and pushed me back down into it.

'I see you're getting acquainted with each other,' Inspector Handley said putting a file on to the table with a bang.

'No more fucking games,' DS Gower said releasing my testicles.

The other officers released me at the same time.

DI Handley sat down opposite me and started reading through the papers, every now and then he gave me an angry accusing stare. A nervous twitch ran across his leathery cheeks.

'I want my solicitor,' I croaked trying to swallow some spit which wouldn't go down.

'You are lucky to be sitting there in one piece,' D I Handley replied coldly.

'I have done nothing.'

'You tried to *kill* police officers!'

'Bollocks!' I said nursing my groin.

'And you tried to blow up large shops!'

'And may the pigs – that's you guys – fly,' I said.

'We have your co-conspirators inside. They have all made statements clearly implicating you as the main ring leader.'

'Do you know about Saif-Al-Maluk?' I asked, looking up at Gower.

Handley flicked back over his notes, casting a look across at DS Gower who said, 'Now that wasn't that difficult, was it?'

DI Handley wrote something down and asked, 'What was *his* role in this whole affair then?

'He only acted on what he wanted to achieve,' I replied.

'I respect men like that,' said DS Gower.

'But he didn't want riches,' I said.

'But he would've destroyed anything that stood in his way, though?' DI Handley addded.

'That's correct. That was him,' I smirked.

'You see in this country, Saleem, we have laws to protect other people's property,' Handley said after making more notes.

'But he cared not for this country of yours,' I said giving the D I time to finish the last note.

'So *he*'s where you get your fucking loony ideas from,' DS Gower hissed.

'Where does Saif live, Saleem?'

I didn't reply.

'Answer the Inspector,' DS Gower said clenching his fist at me, 'or do you need reminding.'

I laughed falsely. DI Handley nodded to DS Gower and both men left the room.

I leant back in the chair and considered the mythical figure of Saif-al-Maluk, prince of Egypt, son of King Asim, and the story of him falling in love with a painting of Badi-al-Jamal, a fairy whom he'd never met. Such was Maluk's love for the fairy, that he proclaimed he would give up all his worldly wealth in search of true love. His father, in the hope of saving his son from the path of love, had him locked up in a cell. But even here, the prince met his beloved in his dreams and she told him how to get to the land of the fairies and giants. Saif-al-Maluk set off into stormy oceans, accompanied by an army of soldiers and advisors. But the prince's ships were blown off course, and he was shipwrecked. He was lost and strayed through many lands inhabited by strange, magical creatures – one had giant crocodiles, so enormous they could split whole ships with their jaws; another had monstrous birds that snatched up human beings like insects; another had insects the size of dogs, another men with dogs' faces. Saif-al-Maluk wandered lonely among them all, still pursuing his quest for true love. Eventually he came upon a land only of women, where each grew desperate for the company of men. In their absence, and when desire became too strong, these women would bathe in a special pool of water, and only here found satisfaction. In time they became pregnant, but only ever gave birth to more girls. The island's women offered Saif all he desired in this world, but the prince turned away, cold. He only wanted his beloved.

I hummed a few verses of an anecdote from his story. It was the story of a hunter and a dove. The hunter had tired from the heat of the chase and entered a garden and sat down under a tree to rest. In the tree above him sat a dove and hovering hungrily above the dove was a hawk. The hunter looked up and saw the dove. If she stayed he would slay her, she realised, and if she flew she would be killed by the hawk. The hunter took aim with his arrow. The hawk dived at her. The dove prayed to her maker to save her. At that instant a snake came out of the long grass around where the hunter sat and stung him, just as he released the arrow. It struck the hawk, freeing the dove.

The cell door slammed open. DI Handley and DS Gower stomped into the room. Handley dropped a file of papers on the table and said, 'We know where the conspiracy took place; it was in the flat on Great Horton Road. We know it took place at 12.30pm and who was present and what was planned.'

I was stunned.

'What sort of a leader are you,' D I Handley continued after staring at me for a moment, 'leading us up the garden path, stalling, getting young lads into so much trouble? You should be man enough to take responsibility for your actions.'

'I don't know what you're on about.'

'Oh, I think you do, Saleem. I think you know that everything I'm saying is the truth.'

'Anything else I can help you with?' I asked, trying to stay composed.

DI Handley pushed a pen and paper towards me and said, 'A leader like you should write his own statement. Or would you like to dictate it and DS Gower will write it down for you?'

I'm in deep shit, I thought. But they might be bluffing. They can't possibly have anything on me. They could have four of the others, and Shak, the only one who could provide any evidence against me, had already seen our solicitor and knew not to make any kind of a statement.

'Should DS Gower write it for you?' DI Handley asked leaning over towards me.

'Is he literate?' I sniggered trying to buy some time.

'Please yourself,' DI Handley said, standing up. Screwing his eyes, he added, 'Up till now we've tried to be civil. But you obviously understand a different language.'

They are going to leave me with this fat bastard, I thought. I was right. Gower followed Handley to the door and shut it gently after him. He turned around, stiffened and stared menacingly at me. He pulled a pair of black gloves out of his trouser pocket and slowly pushed his fingers into place. Looking me in the eye he hissed, 'Don't want shite contaminating me.'

'Just fuck off,' I said pushing my chair back.

A wry smile flashed across Gower's fat, red face. With a quick shove of his thighs, he pushed the table away to one side. Walking slowly towards me he withdrew a truncheon. I stood up and tried to move towards the table. Gower blocked my path. I retreated into the furthest corner. Gower raised the truncheon in his right hand. Blood rushed through my body as I clenched my fists. Gower lowered it again and began tapping it in his left hand saying, 'Now this is not a truncheon. This is my beauty and I really don't know if I should let it have a feast today or not.' Putting the truncheon back into its holder he said, ' Perhaps I will save it for a better day.'

Just as I unclenched Gower rushed me, grabbing me by the back of the neck and bowling me effortlessly towards the door. My face crashed against it. He rammed his knee into my back and pulled my neck backwards. I gasped for breath. The door opened. A uniformed police officer exchanged a quick glance with Gower who then jerked me towards the door barking, 'You're going down and I hope they throw the fucking key away.'

Accompanied by a large, stony-faced officer, DS Gower frogmarched me through another labyrinth of corridors, took me down towards the lock-up and pushed me into a cell.

Mother, the streets here are not 'sonay nal sajain'. Where I grew up, they are mostly strewn with dog shit. And some goray care more for their dogs than their own families.

Mother, I want to tell you about the first home I made for myself here in England. I used to live in a little house made from cardboard next to the walls of Lido Swimming Baths, in Manningham Park. It was under a point where old trees had bent over and intertwined their branches. Thick, green leaves of ivy covered these branches leaving a sheltered area below. I used to hide here sometimes as a child. It was well hidden from the world. The sides of my house were made out of cardboard boxes which I took from supermarkets and shops. Some of these boxes, especially those from Haji's Halal Meat, were used to transport chickens and were full of their bithaan. I turned these upside down and rubbed the chicken droppings off on the grass. Some boxes were those used to transport delicate, expensive goods. These had layers of soft board. This was my carpet. My ceiling was made out of plastic bags and the other pieces of waterproof material. As well as I could I tied these together, or overlapped them, stretching them across the overhanging branches to make a tent. Whenever it rained, and it nearly always rains here, water would slide down the branches and collect in the plastic and eventually flow out ruining my carpet. Sometimes I could push up with my hands where I could see it collecting and aim the water away. But no matter how much plastic I spread across the branches of bushes, I never escaped those drops.

Someone laughs close to the front gate. Turning to the laughter I close the letter.

'Valaiti Saabjee, you are too used to the good life,' the laughter changes to words that echo a friendship buried deep in childhood. The tall, slim Barkat with his shining black hair walks into the creeping shadow of the veranda. He throws his arms in the air and says, coming towards me, 'Why are you sitting in a tandoor, come and enjoy the cool free wealth of nature.'

Tucking the letter into my pocket I leave the veranda. A cold wind slams against me, freeing my face of its mask of sweat.

'Jamil Jat has been buried and my goats are back,' Barkat says grabbing my hand tightly. He shakes it affectionately. Nodding towards the letter in my hand, he adds mischievously, 'A love letter, eh?'

'It's not a love letter,' I moan. 'I wrote it to my mother.'

'Letters to mothers are always full of love.'

'Not the one I wrote.'

'Mothers always understand their sons.'

'I cursed her.'

'Mothers forgive.'

'I said terrible things.'

Barkat lights a cigarette and sniggers.

'She deserved a better son than me.'

'Why?'

'I swore at her in my letter.'

'A son can't curse his mother.'

'I did.'

'Why?'

'I failed her.'

'How?'

'I brought nothing back – not even my self, in time. And while she was alive all I did was blame her for my problems.'

'She sent you to England. It was her who suffered. She tore out her heart and sent it to a place where at least you would be able to change your future.'

'I lost my past.'

'It won't let you do that.'

Barkat pulls a manji over and sits. I sit on a murrah opposite him and glance across at his deep, black eyes.

'But I couldn't change anything in my mother's life. I couldn't even send money.'

'Some of us are made to endure suffering, but you have all there is to have. And England is *England,* eh?'

'When I was not cursing Mother, I tried to tell her about my life in England and...'

Barkat looks eagerly towards me. I can find nothing to say as the words I wrote in that letter, that night return to me:

Mother, sometimes I got scared at night, especially when the winds came and the branches tried to tear themselves apart from each other. And then there was no escape from the rain eating into my carpet.

I roll on to the manji that Bakart has vacated. There is still no electricity. The house is empty. It is enveloped in a strange silence, devoid of human sounds. A large, brightly coloured beetle buzzes noisily close to the motionless ceiling fan. The sun has lost its edge. Westerly shadows stretch out across the yard. A hot wind rustles the leaves of the tired trees. The beetle crashes against the fan blades and circles away, out of the shade of the veranda, across the shadows of the house and into the light.

With the sound of the beetle fading behind the trees, I begin to doze. The hum of the fans spinning back into life, throwing waves of air over my body, wakes me some time later. It is early evening. The house is teeming with people. After drinking a few glasses of water, I set off to Mother's grave and leave the house without speaking to anyone, walk silently through the narrow gallis, avoiding eye contact with passers-by.

By the time I get out of the village, the sky is darkened with heavy clouds, cool wind whistles through the wild shrubs and sighs through the hills above. The wild tali trees, clinging to the sides of the hills, flicker their leaves. The clouds thicken. The brown hills begin to acquire a reddish glow.

'Don't go too far, son,' an old woman says clambering out of a crevice. She balances a large bundle of firewood on her head, holds a water pitcher under her left arm, and tugs on a rope tied to a goat with her right. A warm smile spreads across her toothless face before she flips her eyes skywards saying, 'Today, our Lord will bring rain.'

'It always rains where I come from, bayjee.'

'That is Valaiti rain,' the old woman laughs. Without turning around she adds, 'We look forward to ours.'

A pack of stray dogs heads playfully down one of the hills and begin to prance around among the leaves, twisting and turning in a dust storm. Holding on to the letter I quicken my pace.

Someone has spread rose petals across Mother's grave. Most of these have been blown about a little. A few stubbornly cling to some wild thorns that have sprouted around the mound. A circle of red bricks rings the base of the grave. The wind howls angrily through the hills, carrying with it a faint sound of a bus's pressurised horn. I squat close to Mother's feet, holding the letter tightly. The pages are no longer in sequence. I run my eyes over the first page. The words on the page rush into my head, pricking my eyes. I close them. I see myself sitting in Armly Jail, leaning over from the lower bunk towards a table.

Mother, I could try to hide from the raindrops, but here it is illegal to sleep in the park and one day the park authorities discovered my house.

My second home was my first real house. Let me tell you about that. I started doing odd jobs for a nice English man called Mr Chambers. He had many houses. He let me live on the top floor, in the attic of one of his houses. It was a long room with four windows that opened outwards onto the roof. I could hear the world outside but could not see unless I stood on a chair. The sides of the attic were low and I had to bend to move around. Even then I still kept bumping my head on the beams. But the centre of it was high and I could stand up straight. Wild pigeons had made their nests in the outer corner of the roof, and they made such a terrible racket. I got used to their cooing but even here I was chased by the rain. If you turned the light off in the daytime, you could see the sky peeking through holes in the ceiling. The attic leaked in 22 places. I used to collect water in cups, glasses, paint tins and even plastic bags. After heavy rainfall, I used to lie back listening to the drips dancing to the music of the raindrops plopping into the containers. I would set these around the room. I kept a large bucket by the side of the door and used to empty the cups and tins into it. At night the wood used to creak, as though someone was walking around. Sometimes, especially if it was windy outside, the attic door would slam shut.

Thunder rumbles further off, its echo fading in the hills. Lightning cracks. The wind suddenly stops. A startled bird jumps out of the bushes close by and flies off squawking.

Though he is far away in England, I feel the presence of my uncle. As the only literate man on our street in those early years he'd often sit me on his knee and write letters to my mother on my behalf, or read ones she'd sent. At first Mother had been real, something warm and protective, which had been snatched away from me. But slowly she became just words, and words written in Urdu at that, a language she had never once spoken to me. As I got older I started writing to her in English, a language that had to be translated to her at the other end. I began to think there never was language that anyone shared; that language was just a kind of dream or a hoax we'd all bought into.

I thought of my letter again.

Mother, when days were hot, the attic was like a tandoor and when they were cold, it was like a fridge.

VIII

A rumble of thunder pulls me away from the paper. Darkness has crept over the hills. Lightning flickers, now in the distance, now overhead as gusts of wind toy with the treetops, threatening an onslaught. I find myself in the village graveyard. A raindrop skims down my cheek. Another splashes the letter, spreading and magnifying the word 'murder'.

Mother I am in a new home now. I might be here long after you've left this world. Let me tell you about this home.

The white walls of the cell were etched generously in graffiti. A dirty toilet in the corner filled the room with a pungent odour. No light came in despite a series of thick, square, plate glass windows. I climbed up on the bench, under the window, and jumped up to see if I could make anything out. It was dark. Perhaps the cell window didn't back out onto natural light. It may be another softener, I thought. I couldn't tell anymore. My neck, back and groin still ached. Hunger pulled at my stomach.

Every now and then the spy hole would spin open and a white face would peep into my cell and disappear again. Pacing around the cell I read the graffiti: *Spud was ere, July 22 1980. Why am*

I in here? Steve – born in prison, life in jail. Paki scum. Suck it and See. There's always tomorrow.

Stretching out on the cold, wooden bench I closed my eyes and tried to block out the overhead fluorescent light, hiding my head under my left arm, using the other to cushion it. There was a bitter chill in there. Each time I dozed off the cold pricked me back to consciousness. I lost track of time. Eventually the cell door crashed open.

'You're not on fucking holiday,' Gower thundered. 'Get the fuck up.'

I obeyed silently. Gower made way and I instinctively walked out of the cell. Gower then pushed me around the lock-up area, past cells with lines of shoes outside them. I recognised a number of pairs. I was shoved into a room, the door slammed shut after me. It was much like the room I'd first been brought to, only this one was windowless and below ground. Letting out a tired yawn I slumped onto a cold, white metal chair that was bolted to the floor. A wooden table with white metal legs was also bolted to the floor. The white walls were free of graffiti. The doors were white. Even the doorknobs were white. Judging by the behaviour of DS Gower, things were clearly coming to a head. I was determined not to make a statement.

I didn't have to wait long before the door opened again and DI Handley and DS Gower marched in. DI Handley carried a bundle of papers under his arm.

'Now let's get this charade over with,' DI Handley said slamming the papers on the table. A uniformed police officer followed a few moments later carrying two chairs. DI Handley pulled one in front of me and slumped into it. DS Gower placed his chair at the end of the table and leaned over onto his elbows. Nodding to the folder DS Handley said, 'These are signed statements by your comrades. Each one admitting their role and taking full responsibility for their actions.' He pulled a handwritten statement out, pushed it towards me and asked, 'Do you recognise this handwriting?'

I nodded, reading the first line. A chill awoke in my back. My name was mentioned in the first few words. My heart started beating faster. Pulling the statement back he offered me a cigarette. I took it. He flicked a lighter and pushed the flame towards me. I lit the cigarette and inhaled. The nicotine rushed through my body. I felt dizzy. DI Handley said softly, 'Saleem, we are all very tired.' He tapped his fingers impatiently on the table and added, 'Look, son, at the end of the day nothing really happened. The courts will understand this. It all goes in your favour. We have a lot of kids locked up. They should be at home, not in a place like this. You are the last one who still hasn't signed a statement. You have to own up to your part in this silly little affair. You'll be doing yourself and your mates a favour. I'll put in a good word for you. It is no big issue for us. And it won't be for you. For God's sake, can't you see sense? Just admit your role and let's all go home.'

I sat in deep thought. It is true nothing really happened. There was nothing really they could charge me with. If I got out of there I could at least get back to work. I had only missed one day and probably wouldn't get sacked. Was all this hassle worth another day inside? DI Handley pushed the packet of cigarettes towards me. Without thinking I lit another one.

'I now fully understand what happened,' DI Handley said, looking over the notes. 'You are right to be worried about your community. I'm no lover of these fascists and skinheads myself. They're scum of the earth. Who knows better about fascists than us. Did we not fight Hitler? But I am not interested in your political views, Saleem. For me it is a simple matter of tying up the loose end of this story. You are a young man, an intelligent young lad, anyone can see that, and all I want is for you to accept your own role. I know what happened. Your comrades met in the flat, near the university. You were not present. Now how would we know this without someone telling us? You ordered the making of the petrol bombs, because you believed that that is what you had to do. I have no problem with this. Shall I read you out the statement of your comrade, Shak. He has given us each and every name of the persons in the meeting and all those who went with you to the city centre later that day. He was clever enough to help us. He even took us to houses when he didn't know the street names.' DI Handley paused, looked over at me and asked, 'Shall I read you the statement?'

'No. Let me see it.'

DI Handley pushed Shak's statement towards me. I read it in silence.

'What did you do to him to get him to write this?' I asked, reading.

'Nothing,' DI Handley said. 'He has written it in his own handwriting. Would we be able to force him to do this?'

'I don't believe you.' I shook my head, 'I want to see him.'

'That's not possible till you admit your own role.'

'I won't sign anything unless I see him.'

D I Handley tightened his lips and shook his head.

'Who else have you got in here?'

'You know that, Saleem. Please let us stop playing games. I am tired and running out of patience.'

I didn't reply.

After a short silence DI Handley said, 'OK, I will bring him to you. But on one condition.'

I remained silent.

'You don't speak to each other in your own language,' DI Handley said.

I nodded.

Whilst DI Handley and I sat silently opposite each other, DS Gower left the room and returned a short while later. Shak followed him. His eyes were bloodshot. His hair ruffled. His bearded faced twitched with shame.

'Sister fucker what have you done?' I swore in Punjabi staring Shak in the eyes.

Shak turned his face away from me and muttered under his breath in Punjabi, 'We can go home as soon as you sign.'

'Cut that jungle talk!' DS Gower thundered.

I stared into Shak's reddened eyes. In that moment, I lost a comrade. I wanted to scream at him: *How could you do this? It's you and I, and not the young lads who should be held to account. Not all those other lads. You betrayed all that we believed in. How can you live with yourself? You bastard.*

If we'd been left alone, there and then, I might have killed him.

'Please, yaar, ' Shak said in English, his head still lowered. 'Just sign the statement so we can all go home.'

The sound of Shak switching to English filled me with shame. I felt humiliated in front of the two policemen. It was now me who was keeping all my friends locked up. I had been putting on a show in front of the police and would have continued if I hadn't seen Shak. He was standing in front of me, with his head bowed in disgrace, he robbed me of all my strength. The two of us were the most senior members of the youth league. We had built it together. We had fought the fascists together. Ever since its inception, we had organised against police brutality and the criminalisation of black people. We were proud of never having lost a single case or a campaign. We dreamt of a Britain without skinheads or NFs, without Monday Clubs or racist police forces, a country united by comradeship, united by its differences, not torn into petty parts and partitions. But now where was that?

I continued glaring at Shak, who stole a few pleading glances at me, each time lowering his head again. His eyes left no room for doubt. He believed I was keeping all my comrades in jail. He bit his thick, black lip, placed a hand on his forehead and walked barefoot out of the room. DS Gower followed him.

DI Handley pushed a pen and paper towards me. I read over the first paragraph: *I, Saleem Raza, make this statement of my own free will. I have been told that I need not say anything unless I wish to do so and that whatever I say may be given in evidence.* I tried not to pick up the pen, but it rolled into my hand. I thought as clearly as I could. What had really happened? A few milk bottles had been filled with petrol, and these had foolishly been stored in an open field. They were meant to be destroyed, but I could not do this as I did not know where they were. Shak had taken the job on but for reasons I couldn't understand he hadn't done it. The police obviously knew of my role. But I couldn't see any law that had been broken. I cursed myself for talking to the police. I should just have kept silent. Why the hell did I get into political discussions with the bastards? They were the enemy. One doesn't have debates with the enemy, especially when they've imprisoned you. Whatever else happens, I will not make a statement.

'Well, shall I write it for you?' DI Handley asked.

'I'll do it myself.'

The paper stuck to my moist fingertips. I found it hard to hold the biro in my right hand. A voice inside me warned me against what I was trying to do. I hesitated.

'Just put down whatever you want to say in your own words,' DI Handley encouraged. 'Just get it off your chest.'

Blood rushed through my ears. I could hear it throbbing. A strange heat pulsed off the walls, imprisoning me. A wall clock behind DI Handley ticked loudly. It had been invisible and silent until then. The long hand seemed to catch against the small one as it moved relentlessly round and round.

'Your own words, son,' DI Handley repeated.

All strength had left me. I was ashamed and defeated. How could Shak have asked me to do this in front of the police? A stinging pain raced through my head.

'There is a long story behind why this happened,' DI Handley said, 'and I understand. It's just a formality, Saleem. I won't keep the young lads in here a moment longer than necessary. Just tell us your story...' Handley stopped abruptly.

I'd lost the battle. I pulled the official paper over to me and looked down it. At the top it said: WEST YORKSHIRE METROPOLITAN POLICE.

I wrote my name, age and address in the appropriate boxes and put 'worker' under 'Occupation'.

I signed the caution of the first paragraph without thinking about its meaning, and then taking a deep breath I wrote:

In view of what had recently happened in Southall, London and other areas where black families have been petrol-bombed and in some cases murdered, or in places like Deptford where black youths have been burnt to death, we took the news that coach loads of skinheads were coming to Bradford very seriously. Many people in Bradford, of all walks of life, were openly talking this.

On the morning of Saturday 11 July I went into the town centre, where I met several people who I've known for some time and all of whom were talking about the prospect of skinheads invading Bradford. It is my belief that when people are attacked it is their right to act in self-defence. The nature of that defence depends upon the nature of the attack and the attackers. Some of the people I discussed this with are among those who are here today. Having discussed the threat the previous day we had decided to go into the town centre to see what was materialising. Moving around the centre we saw and heard several small groups of skinheads gathering – each around three or four strong, and promising more on the way. Agreeing that the defence of our community was imperative – again in view of what had happened in other parts of the country – we chose to act upon our decision. At some juncture during the course of the day, I believe it was I who first brought it up, the means of our defence was discussed. In light of the Southall attacks, and the fact that in several cases these had involved petrol bombs, the suggestion of making petrol bombs of our own as a defensive measure arose.

I remained in town while various comrades went to see to the above task. Later that day I learnt that petrol bombs had indeed been prepared. The sole objective of the devices, as I've stated above, was to be a defensive reaction in response to any eventual attack. They were never intended to be used pre-emptively or in any other circumstance. As the events demonstrate, no petrol bombs were used as no further groups of skinheads of any significant number arrived in Bradford that evening.

The mentioning of 'skinheads' in my statement does not imply any person who wears the skinhead uniform, but only those who have been recruited into fascist organisations or have extreme right wing tendencies, and as a result are pursuing violent campaigns against our people.

In my view the defence of black people, or any people threatened by the menace of violent right wing activity necessitates the forming of defensive organisations. It was with this in mind that we did what we did.

After signing my statement, I was left alone in my cell and, nuzzling up against the cold wall, soon fell asleep. I was woken up some time later by the sight of Detective Inspector Handley and Detective Sergeant Gower flushed with happiness. They stood by the open door of my cell. Following them out I asked, 'Can I go home now that you've got my statement?'

'Just keep moving,' Gower replied in a drink-slurred voice.

I was lead to the charge room. DI Handley smiled and read my charges: 'On or about 11 July, together or with others, you did conspire to destroy property belonging to others, thereby endangering life of person or persons unknown. Furthermore, you did, together with others, possess explosive substances with intent to cause serious damage to property and injury to person or persons unknown.'

Someone's laughter came from a nearby room as I was led out again, the charge sheet sticking to the sweat of my hand.

In the graveyard, my letter flaps in the wind between my fingers. Crickets and frogs join the sleepless birds, cackling in gratitude for the cool air. Their songs mix with the sound of the gushing kas. It is dark, but I can just make out the words of the letter:

Mother I am in a new home now. I might be here long after you've left this world. Let me tell you about this home. It is a small cell, just big enough for a bed and a table. The red brick walls are damp. Paint is flaking off the ceiling next to an etching of by some previous occupant. It reads: MOM. Soon the cockroaches will start foraging on the floor. The cell door has been slammed shut for the night and the streetlights have been turned on. It is early evening here in Leeds. You must be fast asleep in Pakistan. I am again sitting awake on the top bunk, staring out of the bars of my cell. A prisoner is screaming somewhere in one of the cells to my right. Lights in our cells have long since been turned off. There are two other prisoners in here. Two of us sleep on a bunk bed and the other on another bed, which is set against the opposite wall. There is just enough room to stand in between the beds. The other prisoners are asleep. One of them is snoring. He does this every night, keeping the rest of us awake. We use a bucket for a toilet in the night and take turns cleaning it in the morning. The bucket in our cell leaks slightly. There is a strong, pungent smell of piss.

It has been raining for two days without a break. When it rains we are not let out of the cells. Before coming in here, I used to hate the rain. But now, I am holding my left hand out of the cell window and feeling it fall free. It cannot be imprisoned. And just a drop of it takes me out of this place.

Though I have been cruel to you at times, Mother, should we ever meet again – if I lose my case, then I will no doubt spend many years in here – but should we meet, then I will sit by you and tell you what happened to me here. Whatever happens, you must not think of me as a criminal. Do not let anyone tell you your first-born son is a criminal. I have robbed no one. I have not tried to gain from someone else's misfortune. Along with my comrades, I have merely considered my people, I have thought about us. I have remembered you. Should I lose – walk with your head high for being my mother and forgive me for all the pain I have caused you..

'No Mother,' I cry out aloud in Pothowari, tearing my eyes off my letter. 'This letter makes no sense today. We are together and this is but a piece of paper, with words in a language you do not understand. They stole your son and robbed me of a mother.'

I bend forward, kneel and kiss the moist grave. A strange

warmth runs over my body, embracing me. Sitting back, without thinking, I start to tear up the letter. The wind stops. But for the water in the kas, all living sounds leave the wild. I carry on ripping up the letter. A gentle wind starts again. The wild comes back to life. I spread the pieces over the grave and whisper, 'Here, Mother, this is your story. But tell me. Should I go back and face what I have to face, should I go back and fight, or just stay here and forget that place?'

The shreds of paper stick to the grave. A moment later a few of them are lifted up by the wind. They start spiralling skywards, glinting like tiny stars. Just as they disappear I remember her voice, it is somewhere deep inside me, singing lines from *Saif-al-Maluk*:

Lo-ay lo-ay phar lay kurryae
Jay tudh phandha pharna
Shaam Payee, bin shaam Mohammad,
Khar Jandhi nay darna.

Pothowari-Pahari English Glossary

Pothowari is the language of the region of north Punjab in Pakistan and Kashmir. It is distinct from from the Punjabi language as spoken in the lower Punjab region, but is often regarded as a mere dialect of the latter. It is spoken by an estimated 25 million people, and around 700,000 in the UK making it, some argue, the second most widely spoken language in Britain after English. It has no indigenous written form.

aam/ambh – mango (Pothowari/ Urdu)

Abbajee – Father dear

ahmin – amen

ak – a type of wild plant

alif sey aam – 'alaf' (first letter of Urdu alphabet) is for mango

alaf nal ambh – 'alif' (first letter of the Pothowari alphabet) is for mango

amma – mother

Ammajee – Mother dear

Angraiz – English people

Araby – Arabic

autr – childless

azaan – call to prayers

babajee, bavajee – respectable term for old man

babu – gentleman

badmashes hd haramis – hoodlums and bastards

baer – wild berry

baethak – living room

baint – form of folk singing

bakra phatak – goat jail

baang – call to prayers

bang – bangle

banglawallahs – bungalow wallahs

baqwas – claptrap

basaar – veranda

bava – respectable term for old man

bavays – old men

Bayjee – dear mother/grandmother

begar – forced labour

beedi – leaf–wrapped cigarette

biradari – extended family

bithaan – bird droppings

buddah – Buddha

bundh – arse

buzzrg – sage

caffan – burial sheet

chacha – paternal uncle

chackarbaaz – fraudster

chah – tea

chah–sha – tea, etc.

chall putter – let's go, son

charaels – witches

charas – cannibis

charpaee – bed

chatni pakaroy – snacks

chhalla – foolhardy

chhallayah – foolhardy one

chichi – little (finger)

cholay – chick peas

chour – thief

chourbazaari – fraud

chulla – earthen cooker

cukkar – cockerel

Dacoits – bandits

dada – paternal grandfather

dadi – paternal grandmother

demon–sheeman koi nee – there
    are no demons or the like

desi – of the (rural) homeland

Dogra – former ruling family
    of Kashmir, also a tribe

dupatta – woman's headscarf

fit-faat – fit and healthy

fauji – soldier

galli – street

gap-shap – chit–chat

gara – clay mixture

Gilgit – region of Northern
    Jumma Kashmir

gora – white man

gorays – white men

gorian – white women sing

gorayaan alla pul – white man's
    bridge

gurrutti – the first sweet taste for
    a new born

hajis – those who have performed
    pilgrimage to Mecca

Hajs – pilgrimages

hakims – herbalist

halva – semolina basedsweet dish

haram – impure

harrami – bastard

Heer – mythical heroine in
    Punjabi folklore

Inshahallah – god willing

jalebee – a type of sweet

Jamaat ghoondas – hoodlums of
    the right wing politico–
    religious party
    Jamaat–i–Islami

Janaab – sir

jandh – a type of berry tree

jat – the Punjab farmer cast

jath – mop of coarse hair

jee, saab – yes, sir

jull yaar – let's go, mate

josh but no hosh – courage but no
    comprehension/wisdom

jowan – youth, young

junglee – of the wild

kabaddi – a wrestling game

kacha – mud house

kafirs – nonbelievers

Kaido – uncle of Heer who
    betrayed and poisoned her

kakri pathri – gall stones

kalya – darkie

kalma – Islamic recitation

kameez – shirt

kas – seasonal stream

katti – baby female buffalo

khala – maternal aunt

khalajee – aunty dear

khotian – donkeys

kothian – bungalows

kikker – a type of acacia tree

kulfi – a type of sweet

korkillees – type of lizard

lachi – cardamom

lafangas – vagabonds

lakhs – hundreds of thousands

lalajee – dear elder brother
lathi – wooden staff
lullahs – pillocks
lulli – penis
lulls – dicks
ma sadqay – maternal blessing
maasi – maternal aunt
machoud – motherfucker
maim – madame
mamays – maternal uncles
manji – traditional bed
ma–raja – Maharaja
ma–jee – Mother, dear
maulvi – Islamic priest
Mirpuriay – of the city of Mirpur
Mohallah – an area of a city
momins – real believers
morr – peacock
mulke khudhadad – God's country
mullah – Islamic priest
murrah – cane stool
naani – maternal grandmother
naik saab – truck owners' overseer
nasha – intoxication
ohy – oi!
paak – pure
pah – dung
painchoud – sister fucker
pakhand – pretence
pakka house – brick- or stone-built
    house
pakkay harramis – real bastards
pallahi – a type of wild tree
parandahs – women's head bands
paratha – buttered chappatti
pardesi – foreigner
parna – scarf

peg-sheg – small drink measure
phook – to blow
phuray murray – bad boys
pir – holy man
pohai – the turn
poondhs – beetles
puhri – condolence space
purda – a viel / protected space
purri – small fried roti
putter – son
raat ni rani – princess of the night
rahmees – bastards
rani keth – Newcastle Disease
    (affecting fowl)
roala – noise
rotis – chappattis
saab – sir
saabjee – dear sir
safarshi – coming through
    patronage
sammi – pothowari folk dance
sandah – male buffalo
sapaee – soldier
sarkaari saan – official lout
saroot – a razor sharp grass
seel cukkar – type of cockerel used
    in fighting
shabraat – the night of Arch Angel
    Gabriel's annual journey to
    earth where fate is ordained
shaer–khwans – singers of folk
    poetry in the Pothowar
    region
sharab – booze
sipara – a section of the Quran
sirkari – of the state/official
sofa – living room
sowri – mother–in–law

stepney – spare wheel
takbir – call to greatness
tali – a type of a tree
tandoor – oven
tandoorchi – worker on tandor
    making rotis or naans
tangas – horsedrawn carriages
tarrapar – slipper or shoe
'tation – station
tava – hotplate/cooking pan
taveezes – amulets with
incantations
thallah – base for resting
thoo – arse
Tilla Jogian – a place in legend
    where Heer's lover took his
    sojourn, now a weapons
    testing base

toap – cannon
toba – repentence
tokras – baskets
tthol – drum
ttholki – small drum
union-shoonian – union type
things
vachara – poor sod
vail – hail
Valaiti – Britisher
Valaitis – Britishers
voozoo – ritualistic cleansing
before   prayers
yaar – mate
yaari – friendship
yarkaan – hepatitis
zabah – slaughter

from *Saif-Al-Maluk*

Lo-ay lo-ay phar lay kurryae
Jay tudh phandha pharna;
Shaam Payee, bin shaam Mohammad,
Khar Jandhi nay darna.

While there is light, child,
Fill your pitcher with water;
When darkness falls
Going home will be fearful

9

Also from available from Comma Press

Home Is Where
by Heather Beck
(£7.95 ISBN: 1 85754 730 6)

Hyphen
an anthology of short stories by poets
Edited by Ra Page
(£7.95 ISBN: 1 85754 731 4)

Comma
an anthology
Edited by Ra Page
(£9.95 ISBN: 1 85754 685 7)

Manchester Stories *parts 1-7*
(featuring six specially commissioned short stories each, by new and established novelists, poets and journalists, £2.50 each)

Leeds Stories *parts 1-2*
(featuring stories by Tony Harrison, David Peace, Martyn Bedford, Sophie Hannah and many others, £2.50 each)

Available to order from any bookshop, through Carcanet Press or Littlehampton Book Services.